FOR YOUR PAWS ONLY

BOOK TWO: SUPERNATURAL ENFORCERS AGENCY

ELIZABETH ANN PRICE

- Holiday Mates (short stories)
5. The Bear and the Unicorn
6. Scared to Death (novella)
7. A Bite Before Dying
8. Wolfman: The Lioness and the Wolf
    - Valentine's Mates (short stories)

Gargoyles

1. When a Gargoyle Awakens
2. When a Gargoyle Lives
3. When a Gargoyle Flies
4. When a Gargoyle Pretends to be Santa Claus (novella)
5. When a Gargoyle Dreams
6. When a Gargoyle Kidnaps (novella)
7. When a Gargoyle Falls (novella)
8. When a Gargoyle Investigates
9. When a Gargoyle Takes a Rose (novella)

Bride-napping Jaguars

1. Be Still my Cheetah Heart
2. Jaguar on my Mind
3. Beauty and the Jaguar

Reindeer Holidays

1. The Reindeer's Secret Santa Gift
2. The Reindeer's St. Patrick's Surprise
3. The Reindeer's Easter Family
4. The Reindeer's Mother's Day Mistake
5. The Reindeer's Halloween Claim
6. The Reindeer Gives Thanks

One Shot Shifter Romances

- Loving the Tiger
- Keeping the Wolf

Monsters

- Monster Love (short stories)

CONTENTS

Life was pretty straightforward for Cutter, a wolf shifter and an agent for the Supernatural Enforcers Agency – solve cases, attend anger management classes and avoid the attentions of a cute but tenacious hedgehog shifter. That is until his old partner is murdered, and a witness from a former case goes missing. Now, Cutter finds himself the prime suspect and with nowhere else to turn, but to the one person he knows won't betray him.

Curvy hedgehog shifter Lucie has spent a year chasing the commitment-phobic wolf, and is she downhearted that he still runs in the opposite direction when he sees her coming? You bet your sweet patootie she isn't! He may be playing hard to get, but she'll wear him down yet. But, before she can say nutty fudgkins, Lucie comes home to find her wolf, naked and bleeding all over her couch, and Lucie, in spite of his howling objections, is determined to help him solve his case.

While working shoulder to, uh, shoulder, can Lucie convince him that she's the right hedgehog for him? And will Cutter finally give in and admit to the feelings that have been dogging him ever since the adorable hedgehog bounced into his life?

PROLOGUE

He watched as the SEA agents poured out of the bar. He sneered as the brutish polar bear shifter fawned over the human woman. It was enough to make him sick. Mixed species matings should be illegal. The half-breed children those two will make should be drowned at birth.

But he was getting off track. He wasn't there for them. He was there for one reason – the wolf shifter currently skulking in the shadows like the coward he was.

Yes, the wolf would pay for what he had done, and when he was through, Cutter was going to wish he'd never been born.

He shook his head from side to side, trying to flick away the droplets of rain pattering onto his head. He shouldn't be there. He'd been told to stay away, but he couldn't help himself. He had to see him. He was a few years older and a few pounds lighter, but it was definitely him. *Traitor.*

He froze as Cutter cocked his head on one side and sniffed the air. Maybe he was too close to his quarry. He had doused himself in scent muffling deodorant, but the fucking wolf was like a damn bloodhound. His body tensed as Cutter looked in his direction. As much as he wanted the wolf dead, it wouldn't be tonight. He didn't want to go head to head with the wolf with all his friends milling around, determined to spoil the party.

A couple of raucous shifters tumbled out of the bar and distracted Cutter. He took the opportunity to slip away, ducking through the alleys.

A tramp – a hedgehog shifter - saw his approach and lifted a grubby hand. "Spare some change? Oof!"

He kicked the tramp in the stomach and continued on his way. He reached his car and was about to get in when he heard the painfully mumbled words of the tramp.

"Stupid fucking wolf."

He pulled off his jacket, threw it in the car, and slammed the door shut. He usually preferred his meals to be a little cleaner, and hedgehog shifters weren't his favorite, but he couldn't allow disrespect to go unpunished.

He cracked his neck and turned to see the hedgehog looking directly at him. The tramp must have seen something in his eyes because his little face was awash with fear, and he started limping in the opposite direction.

He smiled as the little man scurried away – his first genuine smile in years. He did love it when his food played hard to get. *Maybe this was going to be more fun than he thought.*

CHAPTER ONE

One week later - Monday

Cutter tried not to roll his eyes as the director ranted about something or other. After half an hour, he'd stopped paying attention.

Everyone always said how cool, calm and collected the director always was. And as a cold-blooded python shifter, that was probably usually true. The only exception seemed to be whenever Cutter was nearby. Yep, apparently the wolf shifter made the director's cold blood heat up to boiling point.

In Cutter's defense, he hadn't meant for the situation – that the director seemed to be still chewing him out for - to turn into a hostage negotiation. That young bobcat shifter was stealing a grape jelly filled donut, and it warranted a show of force on Cutter's end. How was Cutter to know that the young man would grab a nearby shopper and hold his claws to her throat?

"One week! One week Gunner has been gone, and already I have a dozen lawyers breathing down my neck about lawsuits. Not to mention what you did to the vending machine. Do you never learn from all the anger management courses we send you on?"

Cutter shifted in his seat and scowled at the loud fart-like noise the movement elicited. The director kept the chair just to disconcert anyone sitting in front of him! His wolf prowled, angrily demanding release.

Okay, so maybe ever since his team leader went on an extended honeymoon with his new bride, Erin, he had been overdoing things a little. But he was just trying to fill Gunner's big, polar bear-sized shoes. He didn't know how Gunner did it. The polar bear shifter could be equally as aggressive as Cutter and yet, for the most part, he seemed to avoid all the complaints and lawsuits that plagued Cutter. *It didn't seem fair.*

As for the vending machine... Well, a flamingo shifter from archives was bitching, whining and kicking the machine after it ate his money. By shooting out the glass in a fit of rage, Cutter actually did the guy a favor – he got his candy bar!

The director appeared to have stopped ranting and, instead, was staring at Cutter in exasperation. "Can you give me any good news about your cases?"

"Uhh..."

"The hedgehog shifter that was torn apart? Or how about the bride – that bird shifter – who was killed on her wedding day?"

He prickled defensively as his wolf snarled. "We're working on it."

They were working on it. It wasn't his fault there were no witnesses, evidence or motives to speak of, in either case.

The director clucked his tongue. *Jeez, apparently Cutter couldn't do anything right.*

"And just when are you going to have your physical done?" hissed the director.

Cutter tensed, and his wolf whined. Yes, he'd been putting that off for a couple of months now.

"It's way overdue," snapped the director. "I shouldn't have to remind you, you're not a child. And don't give me any bullshit about being scared, just get your ass down to the medical bay – pronto."

"Are we done?" ground out Cutter.

The director grunted. "Yes, and I don't want to hear your name again –
not even a whisper – unless it's good news. Understand?"

Cutter folded his arms, sulkily. "Yes."

"You're practically a ghost, get it?"

"Yes, yes, I get it!"

Cutter got up and stomped to the exit.

The director called after him, "Don't slam the…"

The rest of that sentence was cut off by the slamming door. Well, the
director was already mad – one slamming door couldn't make it any worse.

He made his way to the elevator and pushed the button. Nothing
happened. His wolf howled impatiently. He tried it again, and again and
again until finally he was slamming his fist into it.

Suddenly, to the annoyance of his beast, he held up his hands and took a
step back, breathing deeply. Anger wouldn't solve anything. Getting mad
and ripping out the control panel wouldn't make him feel better. His wolf
huffed, dubiously. Okay, momentarily, it would make him feel better, but,
in the long run, it would only make everything worse.

He thought back to his anger management classes. He'd taken the course
several times, always scraping a pass in the end, but he never seemed to be
able to apply anything he learned there into the real world. He had an angry
asshole for a wolf, and no amount of chanting 'calm blue ocean' and
numerous trips to his imaginary 'happy place' could change that. For the
most part, Cutter could deal with the raging animal within. But, some things
really ground his gears, and he couldn't hide how pissed he was.

He wasn't actually angry about the elevator, no, of course not, it was
everything that was currently going wrong with his life that caused him to
want to take it out on the elevator.

Although, the fucking elevator still hadn't arrived. *Piece of useless shit.* He
took a couple more deep breaths and decided to take the stairs.

Cutter had been a member of the Alpha team at the Los Lobos section of the Supernatural Enforcers Agency for a few years. Previously, he had worked at the Ursa branch in Georgia, but after some *unpleasantness*, he had thought it prudent to get out of town. When his colleague and friend, Gunner was given a promotion to come to Los Lobos and head the Alpha team, Cutter followed.

Each team dealt with different kinds of cases pertaining to supernatural beings. Such as the Zeta team that dealt with missing persons, or the Gamma team that handled robberies. The Alpha team was assigned the worst cases – murders and rapes.

Although, Cutter couldn't deny there were times when he lost his temper and acted just a little extreme, he had to admit that the job suited him. He got to hunt down monsters and drag them in by using force - if necessary. *What wasn't there to like?* Of course, in a perfect world, he'd prefer it if none of these monsters did any of the crazy things leading to their arrest – but, hey, the world was far from perfect.

At that moment, he just seemed to be having a small problem with dealing with the administrative side of the job. *Or rather, the bullshit.* Normally, Gunner dealt with the director and things like who they were getting sued by, and who was angry that there was a shoot-out in their living room. But now that it was Cutter's responsibility… he didn't like that one bit.

His wolf naturally had alpha tendencies, which is one reason why he chose to leave his pack at the age of eighteen and join the army. Otherwise, he might have felt compelled to try and fight his two cousins and four older brothers to get to the alpha spot. Currently, his uncle held the position, but there were plenty of other wolves keen to get their paws on it once he stepped down. Plus, his pack kind of insisted he leave and not come back until he learned a little more control. Sixteen years later, and he still hadn't returned.

However, Cutter's alpha traits certainly didn't extend toward diplomacy. He'd always thought that being in charge of the team, being the alpha to a small group of other shifters was something he wanted, and something that would suit him. But, now that he was, his contrary wolf still wasn't happy. Not that much made him happy these days, no, man and beast were still at war over one prickly, little issue.

He bit back his annoyance as another SEA agent fell into step beside him. Diaz was a jaguar shifter and led the Beta team. He was also slimy and shifty, and Cutter couldn't stand him.

Diaz smirked at him as he followed him into the stairwell. "Going down?"

"Obviously," muttered Cutter, as he trudged down the stairs, heavily.

His wolf snarled as Diaz kept pace with him. Couldn't the damn cat sense that he wanted to be alone? Wasn't he giving off a strong enough 'fuck off' vibe?

"How are Gunner and Erin?" asked Diaz conversationally.

Cutter pursed his lips. It was a well-known fact around the SEA office – even if Erin refused to believe it – that Diaz had been actively trying to get into Erin's panties, even after it became clear that she was dating Gunner. He wanted to punch the cat on Gunner's behalf.

"The fuck should I know? They're on their honeymoon."

Who in their right mind would want to discuss work when they were trying to enjoy time alone with their mate?

Diaz nodded, completely unperturbed by Cutter's murderous tone. "Sure, just looking forward to when Erin gets back, we all miss her."

Cutter held back his wolf who wanted to let out an almighty growl. Originally, Erin had been assigned to the Alpha team. But after she and Gunner became an item, Erin requested a transfer, and to the ire of Gunner, she landed on Diaz's team. Although it royally pissed off Gunner, and in a fit of solidarity Cutter was pissed off too, it wasn't a big deal. Erin was the sweetest, most loyal woman he'd ever met. Well, no, that wasn't true. His wolf simpered, and Cutter hushed him. Erin was only the second sweetest woman he ever met. *There was another who unequivocally held that title.*

He shook his head; no, he couldn't start thinking about *her* at that moment.

It took him a few seconds to realize that Diaz was still talking to him. He was blathering on about something or other, and Cutter would have zoned him out were it not for a couple of words that sent warning signals coursing through him. The words were nurse and hedgehog. His wolf bared his fangs, and he tuned back into the one-sided conversation.

"I think it's kind of a waste of time, I mean, what do we need physicals for? We're shifters; we heal ourselves," babbled Diaz, completely unaware of the mounting fury of his audience. "I say we should just make the human employees get physicals – they're the ones at risk of broken bones and disease."

"You should refuse to go out of protest," said Cutter, gruffly.

Diaz shrugged. "Yeah, I thought of that, and even hinted as much to the director. He practically bit my head off. Besides, I hear that the hedgehog has really warm hands."

Cutter felt his jaw crack with the effort of maintaining control. "I hear the bear shifter has hands like vises."

The SEA had two nurses at their Los Lobos offices. Ostensibly, they were there in case anyone got sick, but given that the majority of the workforce was made up of shifters, vampires, and witches – who brewed their own tonics, they rarely did. Instead, they were there to perform the yearly physicals – *that were pretty pointless* – and to assist the medical examiner. The polar bear shifter nurse, a six-foot-two, no-nonsense, middle-aged she-bear called Helga, also performed massages. She was pretty good if you liked being pummeled. The other nurse – the five-foot-three hedgehog – spent most of her time helping the medical examiner. Although, they didn't really have one at that time.

Their last medical examiner had gone a little crazy, and had been killing people and harvesting their organs. It was a messy affair that everyone was trying to pretend didn't happen. Currently, the previous medical examiner - a retired and extremely crotchety raccoon called Marvin – was filling in. He was, however, keen to get back to his fishing boat or golf game - or something else retired men do, so a full-time replacement needed to be found and fast.

Diaz snorted. "Trust me, I know all about Helga's healing hands. I once accidentally told her my shoulder ached after a tussle with a bull shifter. After half an hour with her, I was in agony for a week."

The wolf shifter tried to hide his smile at that. It was wrong to feel pleased about other people's pain. *Really it was.* Maybe he should tell Helga that Diaz had been complaining about leg pain, too.

"Besides, I'm sure I can persuade the hedgehog to do me."

Cutter gave him a sidelong glance and noticed the jaguar shifter's eyebrows were waggling up and down at an alarming rate.

"Whatever you say, man," murmured Cutter ignoring the rumblings of his beast.

Diaz frowned at his reaction and, thankfully, fell silent for a few moments. It was a welcome reprieve. Whatever reaction Diaz was hoping to get from him, he wasn't going to oblige.

The jaguar seemed to bounce back from his disappointment, with a resumed gleam in his eye. "Maybe I'll ask her out, after my physical. By then she'll already be impressed by my physique…"

"Or disappointed," interjected Cutter, trying not to choke with a mixture of laughter and indignation.

"And she won't be able to resist."

"Or stop laughing," sneered Cutter.

His wolf was yowling at the nerve of the cat to suppose anything about the hedgehog shifter. As if she would be swayed by such things as looks and muscles, she had far too much integrity. Besides, Cutter was even taller and more muscled than Diaz – there was no contest!

Diaz seemed completely unfazed. "She's single, right?"

The cat gave him an almost innocent, questioning look. Cutter wanted to rip his head off. His beast pushed him to say no, pushed him to force this idiot male to drop his pathetic pursuit of the hedgehog, but he didn't. Instead, he rolled his shoulders and said, "Nothing to fucking well do with

9

me."

"Yeah, she's kind of pretty, nothing special, and I usually prefer tall women. She's kind of small and dumpy."

Cutter could feel his eyes turning to amber. His claws pushed out of his fingertips, and he dug them into his palms, lest they find purchase in the irritating cat shifter.

"Then why the fuck are you bothering with her?"

Yes, go and find some other woman to torment with his sleazy charms and leave the hedgehog alone.

Diaz gave an exaggerated shrug. "I've never been with a hedgehog. I'm curious."

Curiosity killed the cat. Cutter wondered if he could trip Diaz up and let him fall down the stairs without anyone noticing.

"Well, here we are," announced Diaz, grinning.

Cutter blinked and looked around. While distracted, he had completely bypassed his own floor and walked all the way down to the basement with Diaz. Or rather, down to the medical bay.

Diaz opened the door, and the smell of bleach hit them, but it was soon drowned out by something much sweeter, and much more alluring. The mouthwatering scent of blueberries and cream not so much hit him as wafted through his body alighting every inch of him, and he knew then that he was in trouble.

He heard the soft patter of footsteps as the dangerous presence moved in their direction. While his wolf wanted to bask in the intoxicating scent, Cutter knew he had to get out of there before… *oh crap.*

"Cutter!" exclaimed a melodic voice.

He tensed and raised his stormy eyes to meet to baby blues of Lucie. The reason why he couldn't get his physical done.

No, he wasn't scared of the actual physical – he was a fine specimen, even if he did say so himself – more like he was scared of what lurked in the medical bay. Something more terrifying than he'd ever encountered in all the years combined at the SEA.

Lucie the nurse. Lucie the hedgehog shifter. Lucie the five-foot-three bundle of sweetness and tenacity that had been hounding him into going on a date with her for the past year.

If he went into that medical bay for a physical, she'd have him by the balls – *literally* – and then how was he supposed to say no to her none-too-subtle come-ons?

She had latched onto him the first day she started working there, and would not take no for an answer. She was determined that they should be together and he... wasn't.

It wasn't that he didn't like her. What wasn't there to like? She was a nice person. His wolf howled in objection. Okay, she was more than nice – she was wonderful. And like wasn't a strong enough word; he wanted her, desired her, needed her with a fierceness that would terrify her if she knew. She was... staring at him expectantly with a small smile curling those bee-stung pink lips. Lips that would look beautiful stretched around his... *oh crap.*

"I'm here for my physical," declared Diaz, effectively slicing through the rising sexual tension.

Cutter could have kissed him in thanks. The cat did it for his own selfish reasons, but it had given him a reprieve at least.

Her smile faltered a little, but she soon slapped it back into place. "Are you here for your physical?" she asked Cutter, hopefully.

"No," he grunted. "I'm busy."

She opened her mouth to speak, but he didn't give her chance to say anything. Rudely, he spun on his heel and mounted the stairs two at a time, ignoring the disappointment that streaked over her features, and the sneering chuckles of Diaz.

His wolf snarled, growled, and roared at him to stop, but he couldn't. He needed to get away from her. She wanted to be with him, but he didn't want to be with her. If he weren't careful, she could persuade him otherwise, so it was better for him just to stay away.

He didn't stop running up the stairs until he made it to his floor, pushed past several other agents who shouted at him to look where he was going, and was sitting, brooding at his desk.

It wasn't that he didn't find her attractive. *Fuck no.* His wolf agreed with him vociferously. Her curvy little self featured in more of his erotic fantasies than he cared to admit. It was her peachy ass that did it, no, her breasts. Her bountiful breasts that always strained against whatever top that happened to be striving to keep them under control. The pink shirt she was wearing today was particularly fetching.

Fuck.

Cutter scrubbed a hand down his face. He needed to stop thinking about her. Walking around the SEA offices with an erection that could pound nails was just inviting trouble.

He needed to concentrate on work. He pulled a couple of files open on his desk and tried to read through them again. They currently had two open cases that the director wanted them to close - and quickly.

The first was the murder of a hedgehog shifter. He'd been living on the streets, and a care worker who visited him regularly reported him missing from his usual spot. They found him – *or at least his remains* – about a mile away in a dumpster. He'd been ripped apart by some kind of wild animal, or most likely a shifter, given that they didn't have any lingering scents. Whoever it was had covered his tracks well enough to dispose of the body in a public dumpster. Due to the lack of physical evidence, and the fact that it seemed to be entirely random, they weren't getting very far with that.

The second case was of a toucan shifter who had been murdered on her wedding day. Even before she was murdered, it wasn't shaping up to be the happiest day of her life. The wedding had been arranged by her parents, and there were a lot of people opposed to the marriage, and a lot of fighting and backstabbing going on. They were having trouble narrowing down their suspects and picking out a solid motive amongst all the arguments. Plus, they didn't actually have a body – just blood, lots and lots of blood.

Cutter huffed and closed the files. He laced his fingers behind his head and leaned back in his chair. *What would Gunner do?* He probably wouldn't run away and hide from a hedgehog shifter. His wolf sneered at him. No, probably not, admitted Cutter. He just didn't know what to do about her.

Lucie was determined that they should be together, but Cutter wasn't. As much as he wanted her, she wasn't right for him, she was too sweet and innocent, she deserved a mate who would treat her like a princess, not one who was liable to wake up from a nightmare and try to strangle her. Cutter battled his own demons, and it wasn't a battle he wanted to share with her. She deserved more than that.

The problem was that she didn't seem to want to take no for an answer. He'd tried being nice and, lord knows, that hadn't been easy. The badgering he got from his wolf, and the guilt he felt every time he saw disappointment in her eyes, was threatening to drive him insane. But, she just wouldn't give up. The only option he had left was to be nasty.

If he were vicious and treated her badly – if he gave her a taste of what he was really capable of – she would soon back off. It's just that the thought of doing anything like that was less than palatable. He wanted her to move on and find someone else to bestow her attentions on, but did he really want her to hate him? He could live with his wolf hating him – the beast had made it abundantly clear how he felt about the matter ever since Lucie first waltzed into their lives and started terrorizing him into going on a date with her. But, could he really stand it if Lucie did despise him?

Cutter sighed and closed his eyes. *Life wasn't fucking fair.*

He opened an eye as he felt and scented the approach of his lion shifter teammate, Avery. She plopped a coffee on his desk, uncaring as it slopped over the side of the cup.

"Nice to see you're getting a bit of shut eye while we're working our butts off," she snapped.

Cutter groaned. Avery was usually even tempered, but he could guess at what was irritating her.

Their team usually comprised of him, Gunner, Avery, Wayne, a gator shifter, and Jessie, a squirrel shifter who was their tech advisor, or computer geek, which she was happy to be known by. The sixth member of their team used to be a bear shifter called Zane, but he was unceremoniously fired. His replacement was Erin, and after she left, they were assigned a hyena shifter called Primrose. *And prim she was.*

Cutter had known her, briefly, when they both worked in Ursa, but he'd never had much contact with her, or been hit with the full force of her personality. Technically, they couldn't find anything wrong with her behavior. She was a rising star at the SEA. She had all the rules memorized; she was quick witted and diligent and very keen to point out other people's mistakes. Yep, she was the perfect agent, and no one else on the team could stand her. The snide comments about their professionalism, the constant questioning of their methods, and her arrogant nature all amassed to one very unlikeable agent. It was hard to get along with someone who was convinced that she was never wrong and thought everyone else beneath her. Their bosses at the SEA thought she was great. *Just wait until she was gunning for one of their jobs.*

In particular, as the only other female field agent, Primrose seemed to go out of her way to antagonize Avery. And given that Avery was usually quite calm and collected, just how much Primrose bothered her was saying something.

Cutter ignored her angry crack about sleeping. "Where's her ladyship?" he asked warily.

They'd taken to calling Primrose that. It was nothing compared to some of the things she called them.

"Out trying to solve our cases single-handedly – apparently our bumbling just hampers her crime fighting abilities. Anyone would think she was bloody Batman!"

Avery flipped her long, blonde hair over her shoulder and took a few angry slurps of her own coffee.

Cutter blew out a breath in relief. "It's not all bad news then."

If Primrose was out trying to bring down bad guys on her own like some nutty vigilante, it meant she wasn't there. If she wasn't there, it meant that she wasn't lurking anywhere, spying on them, and trying to catch them doing something wrong. Wayne dipped out of the office for a few minutes to have one cigarette, and she felt it necessary to run to the director and tell him that the gator shifter was shirking his duties. Thankfully, the director wasn't going to crack the whip over something like that, although he had nearly hit the roof when Primrose informed him that Jessie had been looking at an online dating site during office hours. The snake shifter was fuming, and Jessie had almost been in tears over it. Another reason they hated the hyena shifter. Jessie worked harder than anyone and didn't deserve that.

"Wayne's still trying to get a hold of our hedgehog shifter's next of kin and Dale's…" She rolled her eyes. "I have no idea what Dale's up to."

Dale was a temporary replacement. Like Cutter, he was a wolf shifter and had been at the academy at the same time as Gunner and Cutter. They'd been good friends at the time, but working with your friends wasn't always such a good idea. Gunner and Cutter got along, mainly because, although Gunner was his boss, Cutter would still defer to him and do as he was told even if he didn't agree with what he had to do. He had a teeny tiny problem with authority figures, but he respected Gunner. Dale, on the other hand, had no respect for anyone and wasn't afraid to make that fact known.

He was passed from branch to branch, inciting fury and outrage wherever he went. Nobody dare try and get rid of him as his father was on the Council of Supernaturals. Firing Dale would be akin to career suicide. Even Primrose was smart enough not to make a complaint about him, and anyone could see that his actions infuriated the hell out of her. It would be funny if it weren't for the fact that they were essentially forced to do Dale's job for him and cover up his blunders.

Now, it was Los Lobos' turn to house the Agency's most unmanageable agent. The Director figured that Cutter would be the best option to control Dale. He figured wrong. Whatever warm and fuzzy feelings Dale might have had toward his old friend didn't extend to doing as he was told.

Cutter blamed himself. There was a time, back before he came to Los Lobos, when he was practically out of control. He'd spent a long time undercover back in Ursa, and the experience had left him a little worse for wear. It resulted in heavy drinking, heavy womanizing – after his wife left him - and dodging work responsibilities. At that time, he and Dale had virtually been inseparable. Cutter looked back on those days with a shudder. He almost lost everything that was important to him. Luckily, Cutter had a mom who refused to take any crap from him, and Gunner to yell at him to pull himself together. He got his life back on track, managed to salvage his relationships and started afresh in Los Lobos. Cutter had tried to do the same for Dale, but the wayward wolf really wasn't interested. Dale had a free pass to act like an irresponsible ass, and he was prepared to take full advantage of it for as long as he could.

The problem was that Dale didn't seem to think that Cutter had changed, while Cutter was adamant that he was a new man. Dale refused to take anything Cutter said seriously. Thankfully, he only had to put up with it for a few more weeks.

"Have you spoken to Dale yet?" demanded Avery, savagely as her eyes flashed yellow.

"I've tried," began Cutter in resignation.

His wolf grumbled. He'd like nothing more for the other wolf to fall in line, but he doubted it was ever going to happen.

Avery, for her part, took against Dale within thirty seconds of meeting him. Greeting her with a 's'up, babe?' and a slap to her ass was never going to end well. The slap she gave him in return could be heard on the next floor.

"Maybe you should report him to the director," grouched Avery.

"Can't see what good it would do."

If he did, the director, being the goody-two-shoes that he was, would feel the need to do something about Dale's behavior. Dale would act like an idiot, and the director would try to fire him. Then boom goes the director's career. It wasn't worth it for the sake of a few more weeks.

"I guess not," lamented Avery.

Cutter looked through the files again, just for the sake of something to do, and the hope that some kind of divine inspiration might strike. *Fat chance.*

"You checked in with Jessie today?"

Avery nodded. "Yeah, she's hit a brick wall in both cases. For the hedgehog, he had zero online presence, and there were no cameras in the area, so she really can't help with that. As for our toucan bride, nothing came up with financials or phone records, and she's still going through e-mails and her online social profiles – our victim was very prolific in that department."

"Funny," he remarked, stonily. "My gut says there's something seriously off about the whole murder of that bride."

She cracked a genuine smile, something that seemed to be in short supply at that moment. "That your spider sense again, TBB?"

His eyes narrowed at the name he'd been assigned, TBB – temporary bad bossman. It was in honor of Gunner whom they generally referred to as BBB – big bad bossman.

"Sure, call it whatever you want. But it bothers me that there isn't a body and that the bride was acting strange right up until she supposedly died."

Avery nodded in agreement. "So our official theory is she faked her death?"

Cutter sipped his own coffee and moaned at the bitter taste. He was probably the only agent in the building who actually enjoyed the god-awful break room coffee. It had been percolating since, *what felt like*, the dawn of time.

"Yep, and it really is just a theory. If she managed to disappear, she had help, but I don't know who."

"You want to take another crack at some of her friends?"

Cutter grimaced. Interviewing them had been frustrating, to say the least. When they weren't breaking down into tears, they were threatening to call on their exorbitantly expensive lawyers.

His wolf suddenly perked up as the scent of blueberries and cream invaded his senses. The animal was practically doing the Macarena while Cutter started panicking.

"Yes," he snapped, startling Avery. "Let's go, right now."

"Now?"

He caught sight of a certain curvy little form out of the corner of his eye. *Time was running out.* "Yes, now, now, now!"

Cutter grabbed his jacket and made a dash for the exit, with a complaining Avery trailing behind him. Well, she could bitch and whine all she wanted, but there was no way that he was going to get trapped in the office by Lucie.

His beast yowled in dismay at his cowardice, but Cutter could give a crap. When he met Lucie, and she batted those big, round, baby blues at him for the very first time, he made a vow that he was going to leave her alone. He didn't want a mate, and she deserved better than him, and nothing that had happened in the last year had done anything to change his mind.

Nope, despite his wailing wolf, nothing was going to happen with Lucie. Definitely not. He was one hundred percent certain. One hundred percent. *That's what he kept telling himself.*

CHAPTER TWO

Thirty minutes ago

Lucie sighed inwardly and smiled as Diaz threw her another pickup line. Something about it hurting when she fell to earth because she was an angel. *She wasn't really listening.*

It wasn't that she wasn't flattered. *No, wait - it was that.* If she wanted corny attempts to get into her panties, she'd go to a nightclub. Now, she was at work, and she demanded professionalism. Okay, maybe that was a bit much. She was more than happy to stalk Cutter around the building, and constantly barrage him with *her* flirtations. She could just do without them from Diaz. Okay, yes he was a handsome jaguar shifter, but he just paled in comparison to Cutter. All men paled in comparison to Cutter, she thought, sadly.

Her hedgehog snuffled at her, and she felt a little better. Automatically, she started testing Diaz's blood pressure. She'd done this so many times that she could practically do it in her sleep. Which was lucky because her mind was definitely not on the job. No, her thoughts wandered aimlessly until they came to rest on the object of her affections. He still had the power to make her swoon and send her nether regions into an aroused frenzy.

When he came down to the basement, she hoped against hope that he'd been there to see her. *No such luck.* He had looked cute when he was all flustered, but she couldn't get over the stab of disappointment when he fled from her. Never mind, there'd be plenty of more opportunities to corner him later. *Plenty*.

Diaz let out a squawk as the blood pressure cuff tightened around his arm to an insane degree. Lucie quickly shut it off and gave him a disarming smile, completely convincing him that she meant to do that. Well, if nothing else it stopped his cheesy chat-up lines.

He gave her a watchful look as she set up the treadmill for him. She told him to run for ten minutes while she monitored his heart. He started going but was careful to make sure that he kept her in his sights. Lord knows what he thought she was going to do to him.

Cutter still hadn't had his physical. She'd made sure the director was aware of it so he would remind the stubborn wolf shifter yet again. Personally, she couldn't wait to get her hands on his big, hot body. She fanned herself as heat pooled between her thighs. Just the thought of him sent her crazy.

Lucie had felt the attraction since the first moment she saw him. She joined the SEA a year ago, having previously worked as a personal nurse to an elderly elephant shifter. After her charge had died – *from natural causes* – she decided on a change of scenery and, on a whim, filled out an application. She was both amazed and delighted when she got the job.

She was on a tour of the building when she first saw him. Everyone else faded into a blur of faces and names, but, from the second she saw him, James Cutter was ingrained in her memory.

He stood a foot taller than her at six-foot-three; his body was long, muscled and gorgeous. He wore jeans that molded perfectly to his thick, ropy thighs, and a tight, white t-shirt that stretched across his wide shoulders. His eyes were an incredible shade of green that were startling against his dark brown skin. And if that wasn't spectacular enough, his voice was velvety smooth, and deep, and seemed to have a hotline directly to her sex. So, in one word, he was *perfect*.

Her usually docile, little beastie was virtually dancing around at meeting him, and even better she scented his arousal from the moment he clapped eyes on her. Yep, he wanted her too. Which made his continued rejection of her advances baffling.

It started with him running in the opposite direction whenever he saw her, and now it meant that he actually rejected her when she asked him to go out with her. Some women would have been put off by this, but not Lucie.

She may be small, her favorite color may be pink, and she enjoyed knitting as a hobby, but she was scrappy. From a young age, she realized that people would look down on her because of her size, species and somewhat largely proportioned hips and breasts, and with that realization came a tenacity of spirit. One that meant she would never back down, and she would never give in to the feelings of despair – even when they tried to creep up on her after she was orphaned at the age of ten. Be it a schoolyard bully or a wolf shifter who can't admit to his own feelings – she was always up for a challenge. Of course, in later years, she also realized that big breasts were hardly a hindrance. As an adult, they came in extremely handy, in fact. Cutter himself couldn't help looking at them, and salivating, whenever they ran into each other – which wasn't as often as she would like. Ha, he should see them *sans clothes* – his head would probably explode.

But, she had to admit that after a year, nothing seemed to have changed. She still flirted like crazy, and he still retreated. She knew that there had to be a reason as to why he was so determined to stay away from her – *not necessarily a good reason* – but she had no clue as to what it was.

At first, she'd assumed he was married, but a quick inquiry around the gossipy office had soon confirmed that he was single. A state of being that happily dogged him to that day. Lucie had been very alert as to whether he had been with another woman, and she was almost one hundred percent certain that – *like her* - he had remained celibate since the day they met. Which only increased her zeal for the two of them to be together. By all accounts he used to be a bit of a womanizer, so surely this self-imposed abstinence was for her benefit. She couldn't imagine herself being with another man, so, clearly, he couldn't imagine himself being with another woman. Yet, he still kept her at arm's length. Yeah, like she said – *baffling*.

Hmmm, maybe she needed to make some kind of gesture – something to knock him off his feet and grab his attention. She just didn't have a clue what that would be. The only things he seemed to be interested in were working and drinking. So, short of murdering someone in the hopes that he'd investigate the case, or buying a brewery, she had no idea what to do.

Her hedgehog wrinkled her nose. Her little beast had been nothing but supportive and encouraging, but even she was starting to get a little impatient with the gruff wolf shifter.

Maybe she just needed to shower him with attention. She could tell she had an affect on him, so maybe if she were around him more, he would be so filled with lust that he would be powerless to resist her.

Lucie bit her lip. Well, in the absence of a better plan – *her only other current plan involved a Stephen King Misery type scenario* – it was worth a shot. As soon as she was done with Diaz, she would get upstairs and start her plan of smothering him with attention until he finally gave in and agreed to be her boyfriend.

Her small animal mewled in agreement. *Yep, look out Cutter - she was coming for him.*

*

It was a bitter disappointment to note that Cutter was leaving in the opposite direction as soon as she made it up to the office floor.

Lucie deflated a little and made her way back to the elevator. She'd give him the benefit of the doubt. He was kind of busy trying to fill in for his polar bear shifter boss; she could understand why he needed to leave in a hurry. She just hoped he wasn't running away on her account. Her hedgehog chuffed at her. *Yep, they'd get him tomorrow.*

"Oh, Lucie, I'm glad I caught you," called her very harried-looking boss, Cecile.

Cecile was a director at the SEA, in charge of medical and maintenance staff. She was a swan shifter and usually tackled life with zen-like calm. Unlike the other directors, she was on a first name basis with all her staff – *often acting more like a mother hen than a boss* - and was captain of the office softball team. Today, however, she appeared to be having a bad day.

Lucie shook off her own discontent at missing Cutter and plastered a bright smile on her face. Like Aunt Mae always said, 'when life gives you lemons, just quit your whining and eat your darn lemons.' Aunt Mae said the oddest things, but she combined a smiley outlook on life with a steely resolve that would make a rhino shifter pause before going up against her.

"Hi, Cecile, what can I do for you?"

Cecile waved the piece of paper she held in her hand. "I have good news; we've found a new medical examiner, and he starts tomorrow. We can finally get rid of that Doctor freaking Frankenstein."

Lucie's eyes widened in surprise; it was the first time she'd ever heard her boss badmouth anyone. The crotchety, retired, raccoon, Marvin didn't get on with anyone, but usually Cecile always found some good in everyone.

The swan shifter shook her head. "I'm sorry; that was unprofessional. I'm just having a bad day."

"Do you want to talk about it?" offered Lucie.

"No, it's nothing an hour in the batting cages won't fix. Let's just say I'll be glad when the newest member of the Alpha team gets reassigned. Damn wolf shifter seems to have eight hands."

Yes, there were a lot of female agents who had also already come to that same conclusion about Dale. Lucie, for her part, hoped to stay off his radar. His type seemed to be tall blondes, so most likely she was safe from his dubious charms. Another reason she was more than content with being short and having tawny brown hair - even if she did need help to reach the top shelf at her local grocery shop. However, Dale had taken to showing up in the medical bay at odd times. She'd come back from the bathroom and he'd suddenly be there. Maybe he was into Helga. Well, she was tall and blonde, but also happily married with seven children. Her husband was a mole shifter and half a foot shorter than her – he was in awe of his Valkyrie-like wife, and darn they did look cute together.

"So, his name is Doctor Rick Powers…"

"Great name," commented Lucie.

"Agreed, and he's a lion shifter. He's been with the SEA for five years, and previously he was at the SEA offices in Serpens City, Illinois. Would you mind showing him around and getting him settled in tomorrow?"

"Of course not."

Cecile seemed to lose a little of her tenseness. "Thank you. I can't wait to give Marvin the good news. He can go back to butchering rounds of golf instead of our corpses."

Lucie raised an eyebrow and Cecile chuckled ruefully.

"Sorry, I know – completely unprofessional. I'm just glad that I won't be getting any more complaints from irate family members about the stitch jobs Marvin does after he finishes their autopsies."

Lucie winced. She had to admit that Doctor Frankenstein wasn't a bad fit for Marvin. Families want to send their loved ones into the next life with dignity, not having them look like a prop from a horror film. Marvin wasn't exactly what anyone would call considerate.

"I'm sure the new guy will do a good job."

Cecile smiled. "Yes, me too. We're lucky to get him. He's moving here to be near his family. As frustrating as the last six months have been, I'm glad we didn't find a replacement sooner. I wonder if he plays softball."

She tapped her chin thoughtfully, and Lucie giggled softly.

"Are you okay?" asked Cecile, solicitously. "You look a little pale."

Oh, the man I'm absolutely obsessed with virtually refuses to even acknowledge I'm alive. But other than that… "Peachy, thanks."

Cecile nodded but still looked a little concerned. "Well, my door's always open if you want to talk about anything."

"Thanks, Cecile. Don't worry about the new doctor, I'll see that he settles in, and I'll see you on Saturday for the game."

The swan shifter grinned widely. "Those firemen won't know what hit them."

The softball team was competing against the LLFD on Saturday. If there was one thing Cecile loved it was a friendly game of softball. And when Cecile was in charge, it was always friendly. She was as gracious at winning as she was at losing. Apparently things had been a little different a couple of years ago when a certain wolf shifter, *who definitely wasn't a gracious loser*, was captain of the team.

Lucie groaned. Son of a monkey, everything seemed to come back to Cutter.

She watched as Cecile glided down the corridor. *Swan shifters were so graceful.* She thought about airing her woes to her boss, but decided against it. Lucie would have been more than happy to complain until the cows came home – *she had no idea where they were coming home from, it was just something Aunt Mae used to say* – but that just wasn't her style. Rather than sitting around bellyaching about her problems, she preferred to take action and try and fix them, and being lovesick was hardly a major catastrophe.

It's just that all the actions she took didn't seem to get her any closer to actually fixing it. Maybe it was time she got some outside help.

CHAPTER THREE

"Screw him!"

Lucie blinked at Avery, and the blonde lioness flicked her hair back garnering more than a few admiring glances from patrons at the busy bar.

They were perched on high stools around a table at the Red Moon Bar. It was a watering hole, frequented by numerous SEA agents, that cultivated a sexually charged atmosphere. In particular, Lucie had spent the better part of the evening watching, *longingly*, as a crocodile shifter and a rabbit shifter virtually dry-humped each other in a booth.

Feeling despondent, she had called on her gaggle of friends for advice about Cutter. Currently, they weren't saying anything she wanted to hear.

Jessie, the squirrel shifter, stirred her appletini. "I think you need to move on."

Lucie snapped to attention, and her beast, true to form, prickled. "Move on?"

The squirrel nodded her long, mahogany red locks. For once, her hair was its natural color. Usually, it was dyed alternately in neon shades of yellow, pink, blue and green.

"It's been a year, Luce. He's not interested. You need to forget about him and find someone else. There's nothing worse than sitting at home every night pining over a guy who barely knows you exist."

A look of knowing sadness flitted over Jessie's face, but before Lucie could probe her, she was interrupted by Isis in all her obnoxious glory.

"No, sleep with his best friend," declared the tigress, as her eyes roved the bar looking for willing men – *or perhaps willing victims.*

Lucie rolled her eyes. "I'm not doing that, and even if I wanted to, his best friend is already mated to our friend, Erin."

Isis nodded thoughtfully. "Good point. Sleep with his second best friend."

"That's terrible advice, Tigger," snapped Avery, who seemed a little angrier than usual.

The tigress bared her fangs at the nickname. "What got your *considerable* panties in a bunch?"

Lucie almost choked on her own appletini. Implying Avery was anything other than slender or toned was a crime against nature. But then the two cats fought over just about anything.

"A morning spent trying to deal with a bitch of a hyena, and then an afternoon with the world's surliest wolf shifter – that's what happened!"

Isis, in an unusual fit of sympathy, actually softened. "You're right; spending the day with Primrose and Cutter sounds hellish to me. No offense," she commented to Lucie.

Avery relaxed a little. "Look, Cutter's an okay guy," she paused as Isis snorted, "but it's clear that he isn't into you. So my advice is to find someone new. Not the love of your life, just some rebound guy for a bit of casual sex."

"Or, does he have a brother?" inquired Isis.

Jeez Louise! Lucie bit her lip. "Guys, it's not that I don't, uh, appreciate all this advice, but I was kind of hoping for something a bit more practical. Like ways I could win him over."

Jessie gave her a pitying look that she chose to ignore. Her hedgehog pushed at her to do something. She wasn't quite ready to give up yet. She wasn't sure she ever could.

"Please, guys?"

The squirrel huffed half-heartedly. "Well, what does he like?"

"Swearing," volunteered Avery.

"Drinking," suggested Isis.

"Hitting things," laughed Avery.

Jessie gave them a scolding look. "No, I meant more along the lines of what does he like to eat or drink or does he have a hobby? Like you could pack a picnic of his favorite foods and take it to watch a football game or something like that. Try appealing to what he likes; try doing something romantic, and if that doesn't sway him, give it up as a lost cause."

Lucie nodded in agreement, liking everything she said until that last part. No, giving up wasn't an option.

Avery snapped her fingers. "Yes, that's it. Give him a big romantic gesture and if that doesn't work – fuck him. Go big or go home."

Isis shook her head. "No, this is easy, just turn up at his apartment wearing nothing but a trench coat. When he opens the door, drop the coat and, voilà, he's putty in your hands."

She was alarmed at how excited her little beast got over that idea. The plan certainly had its merits. Cutter wasn't made of stone – *even if parts of him certainly seemed to be rock hard.* When faced with a naked hedgehog shifter in possession of, *even if she did say so herself,* a very impressive bust, she highly doubted his resolve wouldn't crumble like old cheese.

"That's not bad," she admitted to a preening Isis.

"Just let me know if you need to borrow my trench coat – I have several." Isis clapped her hands together. "Alright, I am going to get us another round of drinks."

28

The lithe tigress sauntered away, swinging her hips, pushing her boobs out and eye-fondling just about every male in the bar. The good thing about Isis is that she always procured free drinks for everyone. Her record from leaving the table to getting a guy to offer her a drink was sixteen seconds.

Lucie couldn't help the giggle that escaped her as Isis blew air kisses at a very surprised looking panda shifter. He almost inhaled his bottle of beer in surprise.

Ah, to be a five-foot-ten tiger shifter.

*

Cutter snarled at a fellow wolf shifter who pushed past him as he was entering the bar. The wolf returned the snarl, and they kept going back and forth in a snarling contest until, finally, Wayne thumped him on the back and told him he was thirsty.

It had not been a good day.

His wolf had been sulky and irritable all day, even more than usual, and they hadn't made any headway with either of their cases. Plus, somehow, Primrose got wind of the fact that he had been within a hairsbreadth of Lucie getting her delectable fingers on him for his physical, and that he'd bolted. Primrose, naturally, reported that to the director and Cutter barely made it out of the office without having to pry the snake shifter's fingers from around his neck.

He sniffed as he entered the bar and almost howled in frustration. His treacherous animal was thrilled, but Cutter just wanted to run in the other direction. There, amongst all the sweat, perfume and arousal, was the sweetest scent of all – blueberries and cream.

Yep, Lucie was on the loose.

Dale noticed his discomfort and smirked. By now he had also scented Lucie and was looking forward to what was about to transpire. It had taken Dale all of five minutes to see how Lucie felt, and to see that Cutter was fervently trying to prevent anything from happening between them. Dale couldn't understand why Cutter didn't just take her to bed and be done with it. No, he wouldn't understand. He'd never turn down the offer of sex with a woman, whether she was his brother's girlfriend, whether she was married… To Dale, it was downright unmanly not to try and hump every woman he found attractive.

Cutter just thanked whichever gods were on his side that Dale wasn't after Lucie. He felt confident that Lucie would resist him – *she had way too much class for that randy loser* – but even the thought of Dale trying to touch her sent him wild. Wild enough that he shifted and burst out of his best shirt the first time the disgusting thought crossed his mind. The idea of that male's paws touching her creamy skin… Cutter felt his gut twist, and his wolf bared his fangs.

Easy, he soothed his animal. Lucie was safe from Dale – he'd make sure of it. Just like he made sure that she wouldn't be bothered by that reindeer shifter from tactical - who had wanted to take her out for coffee abut eight months ago. Not to mention the wombat shifter analyst who was trying to lure her into joining his RPG game, *The Wolves of Olde*. Cutter made damn sure she was safe from both those creeps – even if both times had resulted in another round of anger management classes. He scowled at the thought of those males. Coffee and RPG games – the sweet, little hedgehog deserved so much more than that.

Fuck, there she was.

Her hair, brown with natural blonde highlights, framed her flawless face. She smiled shyly in between sips of some god-awful looking green liquid. Her eyes, those big, erotically torturous, pools of blue were riveted on Isis, who appeared to be air-making-out with a red-faced panda shifter. His heart stuttered as he saw her curvy frame was draped in a figure hugging blue dress. Damnit, why did she have to wear something so fucking revealing? Okay, so it had a high neckline, long sleeves, and the hem fell below her knee – but people could still see her ankles!

He ducked out of sight before she could see him. Maybe she had scented him, but he doubted it. Her nose wasn't the greatest, and the bar was a sweaty throng of overheated horny bodies. His wolf whined a little; why was he disappointed that she couldn't pick him out of a crowd? It didn't matter one bit. Of course he could pick out her scent anywhere, he was a fantastic tracker, and it had nothing to do with the fact that her scent was the most glorious thing he had ever smelled in his life. *No siree.*

Cutter sat down heavily on a bar stool next to Dale and nodded at his fellow SEA agents, Wes and Lake. Wes was a liger shifter and led the Gamma team while Lake was an arctic wolf shifter and worked in tactical. Lake was a little shorter than him, but wider, and was known for being quiet and thoughtful in private, and a living battering ram out in the field.

Wayne had already abandoned them to flirt with a shifter groupie – a human who came to the shifter-oriented bar for the purpose of hooking up with shifters. He was treating her to a very toothy grin as he winked at Cutter.

He huffed and downed the beer Dale had set in front of him in one go. Dale gave him a knowing smirk and ordered him another.

Wes regarded him with interest. "So, I heard you're afraid to go and get your physical done because you don't want to be naked in front of Lucie, that true?"

"No," Cutter hissed, glaring at Dale, who wasn't even bothering to try and hide his chuckles.

The liger gave him a mock look of concern. "Look if it's a size issue..."

"I have no issues!" snarled Cutter as his wolf roared at the nerve of the cat. Fucking feline.

"You only have to be naked for a few minutes. Maybe you could turn the thermostat up before you go in. If it's warm, there'll be less shrinkage."

"What?!"

Wes rolled his shoulders. "Besides, Lucie's quite a small woman, I suppose anything next to her looks big. Even something like, I don't know, a pencil."

Dale, who had somehow already managed to down four beers, and was now moving on to hard liquor, was almost sobbing with laughter. Even Lake had to hide his smile.

"Although," said Wes, thoughtfully, "Lucie has seen all of us naked. I guess it would be a bit of a let down to see you…"

Cutter slammed his empty beer bottle down and spat each word in a thick, growly voice. "Thin. Fucking. Ice. Cat."

That just brought on more bouts of laughter. Cutter called them all assholes and left them to go to the bathroom. Annoyed by Wes' completely untrue ridicules, he made the mistake of letting his guard down and…

"Cutter!" cooed a very happy voice.

His wolf pranced around like a puppy as Cutter froze, and mentally tried to assess whether it would be easier to run to the exit, or throw himself through the window. Clearly, he spent too much time deciding, as the next thing he knew, a small, warm hand was tugging on his arm.

The touch of her skin burned him, sending hot desire scorching through him. His beast whimpered in ecstasy as he scented and wallowed in the aroma of her delicious arousal. He bet she tasted unbelievable. He bet that if he wanted to, he could fall to his knees, lift up her skirt and plunge his tongue right into her hot, beautiful sex. Even in this busy bar, he was sure she'd let him. Her cheeks turned a dusky shade of pink as if she could hear his lewd thoughts.

Cutter shook his head, trying to gain some control even as his mind turned to jelly. *Aroused, happy jelly, but jelly nonetheless.*

She flashed him an enchanting smile. "I didn't know you were here."

His first instinct was to apologize and beg her forgiveness. Well, no actually his first instinct was to grab hold of her and kiss her silly, while his second was the whole dropping to his knees and tasting her thing. But the apology was still up there in the top ten.

But, he remembered his miserable resolve. Lucie wasn't taking no for an answer, so he had to start showing her that he meant what he said.

"Yeah, well, I knew you were here."

It wasn't quite as mean as it could have been, but Cutter still wanted to beat himself up, not to mention what his wolf wanted to do to him.

Her megawatt smile dimmed a couple of notches, but she was undeterred. *Yep, it just couldn't be that easy, could it?*

"I was wondering if you wanted to come around to my house one night this week, and I'd cook you dinner. I remember how you said you hadn't had a home cooked meal in years."

Cutter frowned. He had mentioned that about eight months ago when Wayne was extolling the virtues of his momma's fish head stew. He was surprised Lucie remembered.

"I'm free any night this week," she blurted.

She must have realized that it made her sound a little desperate, and perhaps a little pathetic, as she immediately blushed, right from her ankles up to her hairline. He didn't think it sounded desperate; hearing that she wasn't lining up dates with random guys was, quite frankly, a huge relief. Although, he knew deep down he shouldn't be thinking like that, given that he was actually trying to drive her away and all.

"So? What day's good for you?"

The tip of her pink tongue darted out of her mouth and wet her plump lips. Cutter inwardly groaned. She wasn't making it easy.

"Never," he replied shortly. "I'm not interested."

"But…"

"But, nothing! I've told you before; nothing is going to happen between the two of us."

It took all of his strength – *which he had to wrestle from his inflamed wolf* – but there, he said it.

Lucie frowned. "You can't pretend that I don't affect you."

Cutter scrubbed a hand down his face. "What do you want from me,

33

Lucie? Fine, yeah, you're attractive, but that's just a physical reaction I don't have any control over."

She jutted her chin stubbornly. "It's not just physical."

"I'm not your mate, okay? I don't want a mate."

"But…"

"I mean it, Lucie," he told her warningly. "You need to forget about me and move on."

Cutter clenched his fists to stop them from trembling. No, no, he didn't want her moving on to another man, not deep down, but what could he do? He wasn't right for her, and she deserved to settle down with a successful husband in a big house with lots of kids… From experience, he knew he wasn't much of a father. He didn't deserve to be a dad again, either.

"But, what if you're my mate?" she asked quietly.

His beast howled, but Cutter remained stony. "I'm no one's mate."

Lucie scowled at him, defiantly but cutely, of course. "I'll wait for you as long as it takes."

He turned his back on her and started walking away. "You'll be waiting forever."

"We'll see," she muttered obstinately.

He made his way back to his friends – or at least those assholes he happened to be out drinking with. Dale was looking a little worse for wear. It took a lot for wolf shifters to get drunk, but Dale seemed determined to do so. Lake and Wes had abandoned the wolf to talk to other colleagues.

Cutter sank onto the stool next to him and signaled for a bottle of beer.

Dale leered in Lucie's direction. "Saw you talking to snuffles. Whatsamatter?" he slurred. "She knock you back?"

"No," said Cutter, tightly.

"She's not your type?"

No, he wouldn't have said a cute, chirpy, little hedgehog, whose favorite color was pink, collected stuffed toys, enjoyed carnival rides, and cotton candy really was his type. *Not before he met her, anyway.*

"Just leave it."

Dale started swaying ever so slightly. "You should just fuck her. That's what she wants."

His sullen wolf perked up at the suggestion, but Cutter wasn't moved. "I can't."

Dale pursed his lips together. "Well, maybe I will."

Fury lanced through Cutter, and as Dale moved to stand up, he kicked the stool out from under the inebriated wolf, sending him sprawling to the ground. Dale dissolved into laughter, shared by many other shifters in the bar.

Cutter grabbed Dale off the ground and half-carried him out the bar, pretending that he didn't see the wistful look on Lucie's face as he did.

In spite of his wolf's protests, he knew he was doing the right thing. She should have more than he could offer her. Despite how much he wanted her, he had to stay away. He just needed to make her see that before he gave in to temptation.

Ugh, life really wasn't fucking fair.

CHAPTER FOUR

Tuesday

Go big or go home. *Easy to say, not so easy to do.* Not that she had any inclination to 'going home' if her plan didn't work.

Lucie pondered what kind of gesture she could make as she rearranged the medical bay. Over the past year, she had rearranged everything thirty times. It irritated the heck out of her fellow nurse, Helga, but Lucie found it therapeutic, and it helped to pass the time. There wasn't a lot for her to do really. Other than the physicals, she was supposed to help out the medical examiner, but the last two certainly hadn't wanted her assistance. Hopefully, the new one would have his head planted firmly on his shoulders, rather than buried up his own patootie.

She heard a yelp followed by a moan. Helga was currently massaging a stressed-out otter shifter. Helga's massages were a strange mixture of pain and pleasure. She could just imagine the large she-bear working as a dominatrix. Lucie had once submitted for a massage, but never again. *She felt like Stretch Armstrong at the end of it.*

The problem with working at a place where the majority of workers were shifters was that they rarely got sick, and when they did get injured, more often than not their own healing abilities cured them. If they needed a doctor or a nurse, it usually meant they weren't likely to recover.

Okay, back to her problem. Go big or go home. Hmmm, the problem with Cutter was that he didn't seem to like anything. He complained about the things he didn't like – *and there were a lot of them*, but he didn't seem to mention if he actually liked anything.

She'd seen him drink beer. Maybe she could sneak into his apartment, fill his bathtub with beer and get into it *naked*. Her hedgehog fluttered in delight at that idea.

Lucie decided against it. While it had its merits, she doubted she'd be able to get into his apartment – she was hardly stealthy, and she didn't really want to walk around smelling like a brewery.

She had seen him eating cake. Well, once, when it was another agent's birthday. He hadn't admitted to anything as extravagant as liking it, but he didn't spit it out on the ground. Ooh, she could bake an enormous cake, have it delivered to his apartment, and then jump out of it – *naked*.

Again, she got encouragement from her little animal for this plan, but again, she decided to reject it. Her oven really wasn't big enough, and the thought of being trapped inside a cake wasn't enticing.

The right plan was out there somewhere; she just needed to latch onto it.

"Hi there," rumbled a deep voice behind her.

Lucie and her hedgehog yelped in surprise and threw a dozen bandages into the air, scattering them all over the floor. She spun to find herself staring at a tall, handsome lion shifter.

He leaned against the doorframe, nonchalantly and gave her a bemused smile. "My apologies, I didn't mean to startle you. I'm Rick."

Snickerdoodles! She'd totally forgotten that their new medical examiner was arriving. She was such a scatterbrain.

She rushed forward and gave his hand a thorough shake. "No, I'm sorry, Doctor Powers, I knew you were coming, I should have welcomed you up at reception."

The big lion shifter waved his hand. "Nonsense, I don't want you to go out of your way for me. And, please, call me Rick."

Lucie's cheeks warmed. "I'm Lucie; I'm one of the nurses."

Rick raised an eyebrow as the otter let out a cry before an almost orgasmic groan.

"And that's the handiwork of Helga, our other nurse," explained Lucie.

He cocked his head on one side and sniffed. "Polar bear shifter?"

Lucie nodded.

"Strong hands," he murmured, thoughtfully. He gave Lucie an appreciative glance that, to her surprise, made her blush. "Hedgehog?"

"Yep."

He gave her a wide grin that, if she hadn't been so hung up on Cutter, would have made her melt like an ice cream. Her hedgehog didn't like it, but Lucie had to admit the doctor sure was good looking. He was tall – maybe even an inch or so taller than Cutter – and he was built like a solid wall of muscle. His blonde hair was thick and wavy, framing his chiseled face. He was definitely going to turn a few heads in the office – *male and female heads.*

"I look forward to us working together," he purred as his eyes roved over her generous curves.

Lucie gulped. There was definitely some innuendo breathed into those words. She tried to hide her astonishment.

"Well, I, uh, how about I give you a tour of the building, introduce you around, and I'll get you a pass key sorted out."

Rick gave her a crooked smile that brought out a dimple in his left cheek. "That sounds wonderful. Lead the way."

She did, self-consciously aware that he was following behind and ogling her butt. *Her big, round butt.* Not that there was anything wrong with it, it just wasn't her favorite feature, and she'd never actually met a man who showed it quite the same appreciation Rick was doing. He'd only met her ten minutes ago – he certainly wasn't wasting any time!

Her little beast huffed. The prickly little being did not like this lion shifter one bit. Lucie, on the other hand, couldn't make up her mind. He certainly seemed charming and open, but his flirtiness was a little unnerving. Sure, plenty of men had flirted with her, but they'd never come on quite so strong, nor did they emit such powerful vibes as Rick. He was definitely a strong shifter, maybe even an alpha personality.

As they got in the elevator, Lucie suddenly became all too aware of just how tiny the metal box was. But, then again, she'd never been inside one with such a huge lion shifter, who seemed more than a little determined to brush up against her.

"So, umm, are you married? Or do you have a significant other?" she asked trying to sound casual. She may have just missed it, and instead sounded breathier than Jessica Rabbit.

Rick chuckled. "I'm single. I moved back here to be near my sister, she just had twins, and I want to spend time with my family. I'm looking to settle down and start my own family."

Oh! She and her hedgehog quivered. Those were such wonderful words to hear. She just wished they were coming out of the mouth of a stubborn wolf shifter. She wondered if she could introduce him to Cutter, maybe he would be a good influence.

"Umm, why don't we start with the gym?"

"Perfect, I like to work out every day if possible. If I don't, then I like to go sailing on my yacht."

Of course he did. He couldn't just be handsome, charming and a doctor, apparently he had to be rich, too. This guy was Mr. Perfect. *Or rather, Doctor Perfect.*

Oh, he was definitely going to be popular with the female denizens of the building.

*

Cutter kicked a stone with his scuffed boot and huffed as it ricocheted off a dumpster. He was trying to replay how their hedgehog victim had been murdered, while trying to forget his own hedgehog shifter problems.

His wolf had, uncharacteristically, opted to give him the silent treatment over what happened last night. Cutter didn't like to admit it, but it was a welcome change from dealing with an almost unmanageably loud wolf. But he certainly didn't want it to become a regular occurrence. He'd met shifters who had lost touch with their animals, and were forced to live as humans. The haunted looks on their faces said it all – *it was like losing your soul.*

A very hungover Dale, and an extremely unimpressed Primrose, had been dispatched to re-interview the toucan bride's family. The more he thought about the case, the more he was certain that their victim had faked her own death. There was too much that didn't fit, and he didn't like the fact that they didn't have a body. Who could just walk around a wedding carrying a corpse? Although, the bride seemed to have disappeared in the middle of it, so maybe it wasn't that hard for something odd to go unnoticed.

His hope was that the obnoxious agents would somehow irritate a confession out of one of the bride's nearest and dearest. Hell, twenty minutes alone with those two might even tempt one of them to confess to being Jack the Ripper.

Avery stared at him, hands on hips. The sun glinted off her aviator shades. "Are we ready yet?"

"Settle down, Topgun," grumbled Cutter. "We want to get this right if it ever gets to court."

Wayne smirked and crossed his sinewy arms over his chest. "Since when do you care about that? You usually terrify suspects into volunteering themselves onto death row."

"Since I became the boss," he snapped.

Avery grimaced. "Remind me again, when's Gunner coming back?"

"Not fucking soon enough," muttered Cutter.

He kneeled on the ground and traced his fingers over the spot where a few drops of blood had been found. The body of their victim had been discovered elsewhere, but they guessed that the attack had started in the alley where Reginald, their hedgehog, kept his makeshift home, which was a kind of shelter made out of old mattresses and magazines, and held together by used extension cords. The care worker told them that Reginald never strayed far from home for fear that someone else would take it over. He was very proud and territorial over his shack. They did wonder if the murder had occurred from a fight over that – *a heat of the moment deal* – but they weren't sure.

They guessed that the killer had hurt Reginald, perhaps hitting him hard enough to draw a little blood outside the shack, and then Reginald had tried to run, with the killer in pursuit. Small drips of blood, and also fibers from Reginald's worn clothes had been found until they reached the alley where he was killed. His body, what was left of it, had been tossed into a dumpster, but the killer hadn't tried to clean up the copious amount of blood.

Cutter let out a long breath. "Okay, Wayne, you be the victim. Avery, you're the killer."

"Why am I always the victim?" griped Wayne as he gingerly sat in front of the shack.

Avery gave him a playful pout. "You're so much better at it than me."

Cutter hushed them with a scowl. "Okay let's try it a few different ways. Avery, you're walking down the alley."

She started walking. "Strange that I'm out here in the middle of the night."

Wayne pointed to the other end of the alley. "There's free parking down there at night."

"So maybe I'm walking to my car, but it's still kind of dangerous to be out at night."

Cutter nodded. "Marvin couldn't really tell us anything other than a big predator with sharp teeth attacked our victim."

"Wolf, cat or bear?"

"Yeah, those would be my first guesses. I'd lean to wolf or cat, though. Hedgehog shifters can actually be quite fast." He almost smiled as he thought of the light-footed Lucie chasing him around the office.

Avery stopped when she arrived at Wayne. "So then what?"

"Maybe Reginald asked for some spare change or something and he got a punch for his troubles," suggested Wayne.

The parts of his body they found had enough bruises for that to be true.

"Okay, show me," said Cutter.

Wayne and Avery play-acted that, with Wayne flailing around on the ground, over-acting in a manner that would make the hammiest actor proud.

Avery rolled her eyes. "Settle down, Brando. Now, what?"

The gator shifter rolled to his knees. "Maybe they got in an argument and our killer just lost his temper." He gave Cutter a sly grin. "Wouldn't be the first time a wolf shifter went nuts for no reason."

"We're still not sure a wolf did this," he muttered.

Avery tapped a finger against her lip. "At that time of night and in this part of town, they could have been drunk and not exactly thinking clearly."

Cutter rubbed his forehead. "I don't think this is helping. All we're doing is guessing, and even if we're right, we're still no closer to finding out who did this." He stared at Reginald's makeshift home. "Did the crime scene techs look over all his stuff?"

"They did," replied Wayne. "They took a few things back to the lab to look at, but given that the murder happened elsewhere, they didn't really bother with this place."

Cutter dug out the crime scene photo. The alley had been cordoned off for a couple of nights before being released. Since it wasn't actually the scene of the murder, it wasn't deemed important. It was odd that no one else had tried to take over the hedgehog's area. His wolf stirred uneasily.

"Didn't that care worker say that Reginald never liked to leave his home because he was afraid that someone else would try to move in on his turf?"

Avery nodded. "Yeah, he was apparently really obsessive about it."

"But it's been a week, and Reginald is definitely not coming back, yet no one else has tried to, why not?"

Wayne shrugged. "Maybe they're too scared."

The lioness pulled off her sunglasses. "You think there's something to that?"

He wasn't the best at solving puzzles and working things out, so he relied on the instincts of his wolf to steer him in the right direction. And his wolf seemed to think it was odd.

"It just seems weird, I mean, Reginald has blankets and even canned food in there – why wouldn't another homeless person want them? It's not like Reginald is coming back for them."

"Something's scaring them away," she agreed.

"Do you think you guys can find out what?"

Wayne nodded. "We'll grab that care worker and see about finding some people who knew Reginald."

"Good, I guess I'm going to look through the stuff the techs actually did take from this place." Cutter sifted through the paperwork he had on the case. "I can't find a report on it."

Avery snorted. "There isn't one. Hale didn't do anything with it."

His wolf rumbled at the mention the chief crime scene technician. Hale was a crocodile shifter who suffered from a superiority complex – namely that he believed every single person on the planet was beneath him.

"Fucking crocodile," grumbled Wayne.

Hale wasn't exactly liked throughout the SEA, but, in particular, he didn't get along with the gator shifter. It wasn't a matter of personality; it was a matter of *species*. Wayne had tried to explain it once. Apparently there was this big rivalry between alligators and crocodile shifters. Crocodiles tended to be richer, snootier and had serious chips on their shoulders, and considered gators to be the lesser hicks of the shifter world.

As far as Cutter was concerned, they were all just lizards and almost the same. Although, he didn't say that out loud, not after the first time when Wayne went berserk. Hale treated Wayne with as much respect as gum he'd stepped in, and was having trouble scraping off the bottom of his shoe.

"Why hasn't Hale done anything with it?"

"Well, when I asked him about it, he told me it was low priority," said Avery. "He explained that the items weren't from the actual crime scene, and because the murder was of a homeless man, he considered the case to be less important than his other cases."

His beast growled as he snapped the file shut. "He actually said that?"

"Almost word for word," confirmed Avery.

"Fucking crocodile," reiterated Wayne.

Cutter rubbed his head, running his hand over his short, bristly hair. "I'll go talk to him."

Avery pouted. "Aww, I'm sorry I'm going to miss it. Usually, when you talk to someone, it ends with punching. After the crap he gave me over the case, I'd have loved to have seen Hale getting punched."

"Wouldn't we all," muttered Wayne.

"I'm not punching anyone."

The lioness threw back her head and barked with laughter. "Gets funnier every time you say that. C'mon, Leatherhead, let's go."

Wayne stood up and stretched his lithe form. "Leatherhead?" he inquired in amusement.

Avery gave him a look of mock exasperation. "Apparently you're not as well versed in eighties cartoons as I am."

The alligator gave her a cheery, crooked smile. "Nah, growing up, we never had a TV. My momma said it rotted your brain."

Cutter bit his tongue. He could have argued that fish head stew, and all the other putrid sounding dishes he raved over, might do that. But, like crocodiles, he'd learned that his momma's kitchen prowess was a sore subject. Seriously, though, his family seemed to eat all the parts of animals that everyone else threw away.

The lioness looked at Wayne agape. "You poor thing, how on earth did you survive your childhood?"

Wayne put his hand on his heart. "It was rough."

"Well, let me educate you," she said, purposefully. "Leatherhead was a mutated alligator in Teenage Mutant Ninja Turtles."

"Right, didn't a film come out about them recently?"

Avery grimaced. "The cartoon is better; you should watch it - it's awesome. And if you like that, you'll love Thundercats."

Wayne waved a hand at Cutter as they walked away, trying to hide his smirk as Avery started explaining about Lion-O and Mumm-Ra.

Cutter shook his head. When he first met Avery, he'd thought her to be so prim and proper. She looked like she belonged on a catwalk – *pardon the pun* - instead of hunting down murderers. But, no, he'd soon come to realize that she was a kickboxing, cartoon-loving, sports-addicted tomboy at heart. She was the star pitcher of the office softball team.

He scowled at that thought. It still irked him that he'd been overthrown as captain in a hostile takeover. Alright, so he probably shouldn't have lost his temper and chased the umpire around the field, but that umpire was completely biased to the other team! At least they still let him play. He needed all the physical release he could get.

Cutter made his way back to his car. He needed to tackle Hale. The fucking crocodile had no right to decide which victims were worthier than others. Yes, he needed to slam his thin, arrogant face into a wall...

No, no violence. He would talk to him like a rational creature, one shifter to another.

His wolf huffed in irritation. The beast wanted nothing more than to pound away the tension permeating his body. He had a year's worth of sexual frustration built up, and his only outlets were fighting and exercise. He wouldn't admit it to anyone, but he hadn't had sex in over a year. He made up for it by exercising more, boxing, and taking the office softball matches far more seriously than necessary, but even those things didn't seem to help much anymore.

The fact that his self-imposed celibacy seemed to have started at about the time a certain hedgehog shifter arrived at the SEA was completely coincidental. *Yep, totally.* The only reason why he hadn't been with another woman was because he just couldn't find one that interested him. Yep, that was all there was to it. Nothing else; nothing whatsoever.

Ugh.

The strains of the Imperial March from Star Wars started echoing out of his back pocket. With a sigh, he grabbed his phone. He wasn't much of a sci-fi fan, but Darth Vader's theme suited the director.

"Yeah?"

"There's been a murder," snapped the director agitatedly.

Cutter frowned. Usually, Jessie called to let them know this kind of thing. If the director was calling, it meant it was really bad news.

"What's wrong?"

"The victim was a former SEA agent. It was your old partner, Clayton Reeves."

"In Ursa?"

"No, he was here, in Los Lobos."

"Give me the address," Cutter growled hoarsely.

The director rattled off the details, and Cutter hung up as he ran to his car. His wolf howled mournfully. Clayton, a sly eagle shifter, had been his mentor and partner, right up until Clayton retired, and Cutter moved to Los Lobos.

The son of a bitch was a tough old bird and a former army sergeant. Cutter couldn't imagine anyone being able to get the drop on him.

Fuck, things just kept getting worse and worse.

CHAPTER FIVE

Cutter hauled a couple of agents who were chatting and sipping coffee out of his way. They glared at him but were soon cowed by the ferocious snarl he let loose. He could barely control his wolf.

One of the agency's greatest agents had just been murdered, and they were gossiping about the janitor getting it on with the head of human resources!

He pushed by a crime scene tech and made his way into the crowded motel room. It was a surprise to find that Clayton had been in town, never mind that he was crashing at a fleapit like the Shifty Bear Motel. The place was known for renting rooms by the hour, and for keeping pest control companies in business.

A number of other crime scene techs moved around the room, and a large, blonde, somewhat familiar lion was leaning over Clayton's body. His wolf whined, and his gut twisted at the sight of his former mentor prostrate on the bed. A look of surprise was etched into his face, and his body was riddled with gunshot holes.

Cutter sniffed, taking in the familiar Old Spice mixed with cigars and bourbon that always adorned the old eagle shifter. But it was mixed with blood and silver. Someone had shot him with silver bullets, making sure he died quickly and painfully. Shifters weren't quite as un-killable as say Highlander was, but they were allergic to silver, and attacking them with silver weapons was a sure way to stop them from breathing again.

He stilled, and his wolf whimpered as the familiar scent of blueberries and cream invaded his senses. *Oh, no…*

Lucie entered the room behind him, followed by the director.

"You're here," remarked the cold snake shifter.

He didn't even bother with a sarcastic comeback. He was too upset over the death of his friend, and too interested in what the hedgehog shifter was doing there to be his usual, snarky self.

His eyes caught Lucie's, and she threw him a look of sympathy that eased the sharp pain of loss welling within. His beast was caught between wanting her there to ease his suffering and needing her to leave. It was a need based on protectiveness. He didn't want her there with that dead body; he didn't want her to be exposed to the evils of the world. He wanted the sweet, little hedgehog untainted and innocent to the vicious acts of others. It was insane to think that he could protect her from all that, but, nevertheless, the desire to do so was there.

He watched Lucie as she walked over to the lion shifter and passed him what looked like a thermometer.

"Here you go, Doctor," she murmured.

The lion lifted his blonde head and flashed her a quick smile. "Thank you, Lucie."

A twinge of trepidation blossomed inside him at those three words, and his beast was not a happy little wolf. He didn't like the way the male lion had said them; he didn't like the way her name almost came out as a caress on his tongue. *No, he didn't like that one bit.*

"What happened?" he asked the director, refusing to take his eyes off the lion doctor.

Lucie melted into the background, but Cutter was painfully aware of her presence, and more than ready to step between her and the doctor – should the lion make a move to her. God help him if he tried to shake her hand or something.

"He's been shot," said the doctor.

"I can see that!" roared Cutter, barely managing to control his animal.

"Control yourself or step outside," hissed the director.

The lion raised an eyebrow at him, completely unfazed by his outburst. "I'd say he died about eight to nine hours ago, so some time between two and three this morning."

"Housekeeping found him about an hour ago," said Diaz as he made his way into the room. He nodded at Cutter, who jutted his chin in return. "I just spoke to the maid. I've got agents talking to other guests and the night porter, but no one appears to have heard anything out of the ordinary. But then, for this place, ordinary is noisy sex and arguing."

The jaguar eyed the doctor speculatively but didn't say anything.

"I wouldn't say gunshots are ordinary," murmured Lucie as she rubbed her hands up and down her arms.

Diaz turned to look at her and, surprisingly, softened a little. "No, my guess is a silencer was used. But, so far, no one heard any loud noises coming from this room."

"What was he doing here?" demanded the director, roughly.

"I don't know," admitted Cutter.

"You mean he wasn't in contact with you?"

"No, I had no idea he wasn't in Ursa." Enjoying a retirement plan that included getting drunk every day, hiring women to entertain him, and obsessing over his unsolved cases.

The director gave Diaz a meaningful glance, and he looked a little uneasy.

His wolf growled. "What?"

"Other than his personal items – clothes and a razor - and a bottle of bourbon, the only thing we found in the room was a note with your home address and phone numbers on," explained Diaz.

"Maybe he intended to contact Cutter," suggested Lucie, "but he just… uh…"

Her cheeks flushed, and her voice trailed away under the cool stare of the director.

Cutter's jaw ticked. As kind as it was for Lucie to try and stick up for him, he didn't want her in the firing line. Even if it did give him a warm, enjoyable buzz that he wasn't altogether comfortable with.

"Maybe he was going to call after he got settled," Cutter said, calmly.

The director pursed his lips. "He's been here almost a week."

Oh, not good.

"What was he doing here?"

Cutter threw up his hands in exasperation. "I have no idea. I swear I thought he was back in Ursa. I don't know why he came here."

"Whatever the reason, Diaz is going to lead the investigation into his death, and I expect your co-operation."

His wolf snarled. "Usually the Alpha team handles the deaths of agents."

The director narrowed his eyes. "First of all, he's a former agent. Second of all, he was your friend, you wouldn't be objective, and finally, this is my decision. I don't expect any further argument."

Cutter's nostrils flared as he breathed in and out quickly. His wolf wanted to challenge Diaz and prove he was the better male, but he doubted a primal show of force would really sway the director in this instance. If anything, it would just confirm that he had made the right decision.

Instinctively, he sought out Lucie. He looked into the calming blue of her eyes, and his beast was instantly mollified. Her presence always did that to him. She pacified and soothed his naturally fractious soul. It was why he couldn't be around her. If he became too calm, too enraptured with her hypnotic presence, he might just end up doing something he couldn't take back – like bonding her to him.

"Fine," said Cutter through gritted teeth.

"I expect Diaz will want to interview you later." The director looked to the jaguar for confirmation and he nodded. "Good, keep me informed." He angled his head toward the lion shifter. "Good to meet you, Rick."

The lion smiled easily. "You too, Gerry." His eyes flickered over to Lucie, and he winked. She smiled softly in return.

The director swept out of the room and Cutter snorted. *Gerry, huh?* He didn't know many underlings who could get away with that. Gunner did it on occasion, but only when he was really pissed off. Who did this damn lion think he was, swanking in there, calling the director by his first name, and eye-fucking Lucie? He could see that the two of them were not going to get on.

Diaz clapped a hand on his shoulder but quickly removed it when Cutter flashed his fangs. "Alright, settle down. Your interview, let's say three o'clock in my office?"

"Whatever," he muttered eyeing Clayton's body unhappily.

"I'd say let's wait until you're in a better mood, but we need the case to be solved sometime this decade."

Diaz chuckled at his own joke, but actually paled and quieted when it became clear the motor boat-like rumbling was emanating from Cutter.

He allowed his eyes to sweep over the room one last time before stomping out; the crime scene techs scattered out of his way. He stopped at his car, breathing deeply, trying to clear the scent of his dead mentor out of his nose.

Poor Clayton. The old bird could be a mean bastard, but he deserved more than this. Cutter should have been a better friend. Neither of them did Christmas or birthday cards, so their only communication boiled down to a couple of near-silent phone calls a year. They weren't big on talking, and if the mention of feelings had ever entered one of their conversations, Clayton had shot it down right away and called him a pussy.

Yep, Clayton was just like an older version of him, which is why they got on so well. Problems with rage, difficulty in maintaining relationships with women, gruff personality that didn't play well with others... His heart clenched and his wolf was stonily silent. Is this what the future held for him, too? Murdered in a dingy motel room and discovered by the maid? He doubted Clayton even had any next of kin. He'd fallen out with the few family members he had, and he certainly didn't have a mate or offspring. Cutter was probably the closest thing he had to family. *God that was depressing.*

He couldn't believe he was dead. He couldn't believe he had been in town and hadn't mentioned it. Cutter had a bad feeling that the reason why he hadn't, was that Clayton was doing something he shouldn't have been. *Or something no one else could know about.* It wouldn't have surprised him. Clayton was a good guy – deep, deep down – but he saw rules more as loose guidelines.

His wolf mewled as tingles went through his body. He felt a soothing presence approach him.

"I'm really sorry about your friend," murmured Lucie.

She placed a hand on his arm, and he closed his eyes, reveling in the pleasurable sensations shooting through his body.

"Thank you," he mumbled.

"Let me know if there's anything I can do."

She removed her hand, and he almost snarled at the loss. His wolf grumbled as the heavenly vibes she elicited disappeared, only to be replaced by dull emptiness. An inordinate amount of anger swept through him for allowing her to do that to him. *Anger that he unfortunately decided to direct at her.*

Cutter turned on her with flashing amber eyes. "What are you doing here?" he barked.

Lucie looked at him with patient, compassionate eyes. "I just drove the doctor here; he's new in town. He didn't know the way."

"The doctor? That lion?" he sneered. "The one that wants to fuck you."

She blanched ever so slightly at the harshness of his tone, but his words didn't seem to bother her. "I can't say whether Rick wants that…"

"Rick, is it?" he jeered. "Fucking cat."

"But, it wouldn't matter if he did. You know how I feel about you. I don't want anyone but you."

The sincerity and love in her beautiful face almost destroyed him. Those were the words he wanted to hear, and he hated himself for it. He hated himself because he'd been telling Lucie to leave him alone for a year, but as soon as he needed some warmth and love, he treated her like shit and expected her to declare how she felt. *She did, too.* His wolf howled mournfully. He was furious at himself. Furious that he wasn't good enough for her, and furious that he didn't treat her the way she deserved.

Rashly, he cupped her cheek and leaned his forehead against hers. "I'm sorry," he mumbled. "You don't deserve… fuck."

He let go of her and fumbled for the door of his car, ignoring the shock on her face. That was probably the most intimate gesture he had ever made toward her. He got in the car and drove away as fast as he could.

His wolf pawed at him to turn around, to go back to her. It had been a slip of the tongue. He'd said sorry when what he actually meant to say was, I love you.

Cutter shook his head. No, he couldn't say those words to her. He was just messed up because of Clayton. That was all there was to it. He wasn't in a position to be her mate and offer her the life she wanted. No matter how much he wanted her to be his, for his own selfish reasons, he wouldn't tether her to him for the rest of her life.

He was determined to be unselfish about this. No matter how much his wolf railed against him, he still believed that this was for the best. *Yes, definitely.* He was ninety percent sure of it. Well, maybe eighty percent.

For now, he had bigger concerns. Maybe he could figure out just what

Clayton was up to that ended with his murder. Yes, that should take his mind off the curvy, little hedgehog. At least for a few days.

*

Cutter stared at the screen of his computer. He was trying to read a report from the Hale, the chief crime scene tech, but he couldn't focus on the words. Something about finding a toothpick that had trace DNA on it.

After leaving Clayton's crime scene, he dropped in on Hale and harangued him over not processing all the evidence he collected for the hedgehog's murder. Hale tried to argue, in his usual obnoxious way, but Cutter's fury knew no bounds, and before long he had the crocodile shifter completely browbeaten and prepared to do whatever he was told.

Not that Cutter thought he'd actually find something, but it had felt good to vent at someone who kind of deserved it. Avery and Wayne were still out interviewing people, so hopefully they might uncover something of use.

As much as he wanted to run out and try to solve Clayton's murder, he had to remember that he had other obligations. Their other victims deserved the same respect as Clayton. Although, he would dearly love to get his paws on Clayton's crime scene.

"Ahem."

Cutter narrowed his eyes but didn't take them off the screen in front of him. There was no mistaking who that pissy sounding 'ahem' had come from.

"What?" he hissed trying not to sneeze at her artificial lily of the valley perfume.

Primrose clucked her tongue. "I solved the toucan case," she announced smugly.

Okay, that got his attention. His wolf huffed as Cutter turned his attention to her. "So, what happened?"

The hyena shifter gave him a superior smile. "According to the crime scene technicians, the blood wasn't all fresh, meaning that some of it had been drawn from her body before the day she was supposedly killed."

Cutter was right; she had been planning to fake her own death.

"So, I surmised that it must have been her cousin, the nurse, who had drawn the blood from her, and I got him to lead us to her."

He folded his arms. "How'd you do that?"

"I told him the truth, that we suspected she was still alive, and he ran to her. We tailed him and found her. They've both been arrested for wasting our time; I expect they'll get some community service. Their family is livid." Her eyes gleamed at that; apparently she enjoyed this kind of thing.

"Did they say why they did it?"

Primrose waved her hand dismissively. "They were in love and wanted to marry, but she said her father would kill her if she didn't marry who she was told. The usual soap opera exaggerations."

His wolf snarled at her lack of concern. "Did you think there might be something to that?"

She rolled her eyes. "If she wants to make a complaint against her father for making threats against her, she can. Otherwise, this isn't any of our business."

Cutter groaned inwardly. And people called him a stone cold bastard. "The director..."

"Already knows that I've solved the case. I made sure to tell him in person."

Yeah, he bet she did. She was nothing if not thorough in trying to crawl up the promotional ladder. He thought about yelling at her, telling her to make sure the toucan was safe, and that she shouldn't go over his head to the director, but what was the point? He honestly didn't care about who got the plaudits for solving the case. He'd never done the job so he could get a slap on the back and a hearty well done. He'd speak to the director himself about the toucan's safety. Or maybe just send him an e-mail; no need to piss him off in person.

"Good work, where's Dale?"

She seemed a little put out by his reaction – like she was expecting an argument from him and was disappointed when it didn't happen. But that feeling passed quickly.

"I have no idea," she said snippily. "I heard Clayton Reeves was murdered."

He jutted his chin defensively as his wolf prowled. "Yes."

It might have been his imagination, but she looked a little worried. "Do they know why yet?"

"I wouldn't know; the case is being handled by Diaz. Did you know him when you worked in Ursa?"

Primrose scoffed. "Everyone knew Clayton Reeves. The guy was an asshole."

"Who's now dead," he spat through gritted teeth.

"Doesn't change the fact that he was an asshole. There was some speculation that he was here investigating something."

She gave him a searching look as he stared at her blankly.

"News to me if he was."

"I have to finish up my report," Primrose muttered.

She turned on her heel and stalked over to her desk. She furiously bashed at her keyboard. *Jeez, what did the computer ever do to her?*

Speculation? He'd considered the same thing, which would explain why Clayton came into town without telling him. But, he was curious as to who else thought that too, and whether it was something that would have actually led to Clayton's murder.

Clayton wasn't someone who could let things go, and he didn't do well with downtime. Getting drunk and playing with prostitutes could only take up so much of his time. Cutter wondered if Clayton had held onto his unsolved case files from the past thirty years, and had been trying to solve them during his retirement. Admittedly, it was something that Cutter would do, too. Whenever he had been forced into taking vacation days, he spent them hassling witnesses from unsolved cases. And when asked, Clayton had been pretty darn cagey about just what he was getting up to in his free time.

But, he didn't know what had caused him to come to Los Lobos. Unlike most agents, Clayton had spent his entire career in Ursa.

With a grunt, he realized that it was time for his interview with Diaz. Great, now he had to play nice with the jaguar asshole who delighted in leering at his hedgehog.

He wondered what the director would do if he accidentally punched Diaz in the face.

*

"I'm sorry about your friend," said Avery.

Cutter grunted as other agents murmured the same sentiment. "Thanks, I don't want to talk about it."

They were at the Red Moon Bar. They already raised a toast to Clayton, and now, Cutter was trying to forget all about his day.

He looked around the bar; he didn't want to admit it, but he was disappointed that Lucie wasn't there. She didn't come to the bar as often as he did, but he had been kind of hoping to see her friendly face. He just didn't realize how much he wanted to see her until that moment.

He also noted, with some trepidation, that the new doctor wasn't there. He had a bad feeling about that.

Dale passed him another beer as soon as he finished his last one. "Drink up, the night is young."

Cutter took a sip of his beer and, casually, tried to start a conversation. "Has anyone met the new doctor?"

Isis smirked. "You mean, Doctor Hotness? Sure have."

"Not that hot," grumbled Cutter.

Avery shook her head. "No, he is, he's extremely hot."

Cutter scowled at her; Avery was usually the voice of reason when compared the Isis, who was a man-eater.

"I heard he's single, too," offered Jessie.

His wolf growled. *Terrific.*

Wes gave them a reproving look. "Is that all men are to you women – pieces of meat?"

Isis snickered. "No, he's a piece of meat – like prime rib. You guys," she looked in turn between Cutter, Dale, Wes and Wayne, "you guys are more like hamburger patties."

Wayne affected a wounded look. "I'll have you know I'm more like beef jerky."

Avery eyed him dubiously "What, chewy and leathery?"

"No, tough and I last a long time."

He winked at the women, and they burst into fits of giggles. His wolf grumbled at their antics.

"What's the doctor like? Why isn't he here tonight?" asked Cutter trying to steer the conversation back to his original point.

Jessie shrugged. "He seems great, funny, charming…"

"Has a tight, tight ass," offered Isis.

"But, he said he's still settling in, and needs to unpack all his boxes after the move. He said he'd love to come out with us another night. And Cecile already asked him to be on the softball team."

Cutter slapped down his beer. "But she hasn't even seen him play!"

Isis snorted. "Doesn't matter, you should have seen the way Cecile was simpering all over him when Lucie was giving him a tour of the building. I swear I thought the swan shifter was going to faint like a southern belle."

His wolf stirred at the mention of Lucie. He figured she was only giving him a tour because she was being nice, and they were going to be working together. *She was too nice for her own good.*

He tried to sound nonchalant. "So, he's at home, right? Not, anywhere else?"

Not out on a date with a hedgehog shifter? Lucie had said specifically that she was only interested in him, but what if the lion shifter tricked her into a date. She was so sweet and innocent; he could have bamboozled her into having dinner with him. Lord, they could be eating pasta in a romantic, Italian restaurant at that very moment!

Dale gave him a sideways look. "What do you care? You don't want the doctor for yourself, do you?"

"Of course, not," he muttered. "I'm just curious; he seems kind of familiar."

"A few years ago, he worked at the Ursa SEA. But, still, you seem really interested in him."

Cutter rolled his eyes, told Dale to fuck off, and sucked on his beer. His wolf was a little mollified. He guessed that if Lucie had gone on a date with the lion, Jessie would know. She had her tiny finger on the pulse of all the gossip in the building.

As the evening wore on, people drifted away to talk to other friends, and hook up with new friends, until Cutter was left drinking with Dale.

"Shame about Clayton," observed Dale dispassionately.

There had been no love lost between Dale and Clayton. In fact, the older eagle shifter had been suspended a couple of times for punching Dale.

"Yeah," murmured Cutter.

"You should do something to take your mind off it."

Cutter nodded. He'd been thinking about doing just that. He was thinking about leaving, shifting, and going for a run. Letting his wolf free might be just what he needed. He excused himself to go to the bathroom and intended to leave altogether when he got back.

When he did return to the table, it was to find that another beer had been lined up for him, Dale was grinning namely, and they had been joined by twin peacock shifters.

He sat down and glared at the twin girls – *and yes, they were little more than girls.* He considered asking them for ID to make sure they were allowed to be in the bar. They both flipped their black hair over the shoulders in unison and stared at him disinterestedly.

"Cutter, this is Taryn and Sharon."

He nodded in their direction and leaned over to Dale. "What the fuck are you doing?" he whispered, furiously.

Dale chuckled. "No need to thank me. You're tense; you need to get laid. These girls are horny. Pretty copacetic, right?"

"When did you learn such a big word?" he taunted as his wolf yapped miserably.

There was no way he was going home with one of those girls, so Dale would just have to entertain them both. In fact, he'd probably enjoy that.

"I'm not interested, okay?"

Dale frowned. "Just have your drink and enjoy their company. If you're not interested after you've finished, then all you have to do is leave, and I'll take care of them."

All his instincts said no – his wolf howled at him to get up and get the hell out of there – but Cutter gave in. *What could one beer hurt?*

"Fine."

Dale grinned and started chatting to the girls. They were in college, majoring in English Literature, and played lacrosse, but they didn't let that get in the way of their true passion of partying.

Cutter grabbed his beer. Fuck, he'd need alcohol just to listen to these vacuous girls. He'd rather listen to Lucie explain the difference between knitting and crocheting. *Damn, he could have listened to her talk about that all day long.*

He took a long swig and frowned at the slightly bitter taste. The twins were gushing about how they won a wet t-shirt contest on their last spring break. Cutter gulped down his drink; he didn't care about the taste, he just needed alcohol – stat. This was going to be a very boring conversation.

*

He watched as Cutter lurched and shambled to the open door of the cab. The peacock shifter trying to shepherd him into the vehicle swore and slapped at him. The intoxicated wolf shifter laughed uproariously at a joke no one else seemed to get.

He snorted. What a fucking joke. He smiled as he considered that taking that peacock home would rupture any chance he would have with the hedgehog shifter Cutter was lusting after.

Huh, maybe he'd kill the hedgehog, too. Before he killed Cutter, just to make the fucker suffer. In the years he'd spent dreaming of the things he'd like to do to Cutter, he hadn't factored in hurting his female. Might make it even more fun.

"You coming, baby?" slurred his own female for the night.

He turned back to watch her rubbing up and down against his car. He gave her an indulgent smile, mixed with contempt. He gave one last look at Cutter, who was trying to get out of the other side of the cab, and the peacock who was trying to grab onto his arm.

"Yes, I am."

CHAPTER SIX

Wednesday

Lucie felt butterflies fluttering in her stomach. *Ten-pound, mutant butterflies by the feel of them.* She was just a teeny bit nervous.

Go big or go home. Well, maybe more like *biggish*.

This probably wasn't what Avery had in mind, but this was a gesture that was very her. She didn't want to do something that was out of character; she wanted Cutter to love her just as she came. A somewhat cute, stubborn as nails, curvaceous hedgehog shifter.

She had considered Isis' suggestion of turning up in her birthday suit and giving him a sensual mauling. But she was ever so slightly concerned about a huge gust of wind blowing up her coat and giving everyone a free peep show. Perhaps, it was something they could try later – like for a one-year anniversary or something.

For now, she needed to do this her way. So, she spent the previous evening baking his favorite treat - blueberry muffins. She assumed they were his favorite because every time he went to the coffee shop they were his choice du jour of sweet treats. *Yeah, her stalking had finally paid off.*

She had arranged them all pretty-like in a basket, and had specifically chosen a blue sundress that highlighted her eyes and accentuated her best assets. She giggled as she had a brief feeling of being Little Red Riding

Hood, and Cutter playing the part of the Big Bad Wolf. Or maybe she'd be Little Blue Riding Hood. *Either way.*

Her hedgehog snuffled and wrinkled her nose in excitement. Yep, this was it. She would lay her soul bare, tell him she loved him, and she would ask him once and for all if he could ever be with her. In about ten minutes, she was going to be very happy or very sad – but at least she will have tried. Then, she'd give it a week, come up with a new plan, and try again!

Lucie rapped on Cutter's apartment door. The door swung open and… the smile froze on her face as a half-naked, young peacock shifter stood framed in the doorway. In Cutter's doorway! The girl's expression was one of boredom, and Lucie couldn't fail to notice that she was wearing one of Cutter's shirts.

She felt sharp prickles at her heart as her hedgehog whined unhappily. Nope, this didn't mean anything. Not, yet. There could be a perfectly reasonable explanation.

"Uhh, hi, I thought this was Cutter's place."

The girl shrugged. "It is."

Well, so much for hoping she just had the wrong door.

"Are you his sister?"

Maybe his parents had adopted her… yeah, that or she was grasping at straws.

The peacock snorted. "No, sweetie, we just hooked up last night, he's still in bed. Can I help you with something? Hey, are those muffins that I smell?"

The girl grasped at the basket and Lucie, too stunned for action, let her take them away.

"Yes," Lucie murmured faintly, "I just came to drop off his… ah, order of muffins, enjoy."

"Mmmm, yummy, thank you."

The girl disappeared inside the apartment and slammed the door shut with her foot.

Lucie was standing, staring at the door for a couple of minutes before she closed her mouth and dejectedly dragged her feet all the way back to her car. Her beast was whimpering sadly, but Lucie was too stunned to commiserate.

In the year she'd been stalking him, she'd never even seen him flirt with another woman, never mind dating or sleeping with one. That had given her hope. She knew he was attracted to her, but a real sign that a shifter had already chosen their mate was that they wouldn't be able to have sex with another woman. She couldn't bear the thought of another male touching her; she had hoped it was the same for him with women.

Clearly, that hope had been misplaced. Who was to say how many other women he had been with? She hadn't watched him every second of every day; he could have been with dozens of other women. All the while laughing at the silly hedgehog for chasing after him.

It was like her heart was ripping apart, but she had to face the truth - he really didn't feel the way she felt. The truth was... *crushing*. It shouldn't be, but it was. He hadn't made any promises to her; she had no right to expect him to be faithful to her, and yet, she had. The fact that he hadn't been devastated her, and she couldn't even be angry with him. Technically, he hadn't even done anything wrong!

Her lip trembled. No, she would not cry. This incident wasn't worth her tears - it really wasn't.

Now, all she had to do was keep telling herself that over and over and maybe, eventually, she and her hedgehog would believe it.

*

Cutter growled awake, furious at himself for getting drunk. He hadn't been blind, stinking drunk in over three years.

Ugh, his head. It felt like a fucking elephant was bouncing up and down on him.

His nose tickled at the unfamiliar scent of sandalwood. Yuck, the smell made him want to vomit. He tried to bury his head in his pillow but froze as he heard movement in the room, and the scent intensified.

Who the fuck was that?

"Finally, you're awake," sniffed a bored voice.

His eyes snapped open, and he sat up in bed far too quickly. Pain lanced through his head, but he ignored it, choosing to focus on the peacock shifter sitting cross-legged on his bed and licking her fingers.

He squinted at her as dribs and drabs of the previous night filtered through.

He had a fifty-fifty shot. "Sharon?"

She rolled her eyes. "Taryn."

He nodded but finding out just which twin she was didn't explain how she had made it to his apartment, and why she was wearing his favorite Johnny Cash, Folsom Prison t-shirt. He looked over his own body and was relieved to find that he was still wearing all his clothes from the previous night.

Cutter rubbed his forehead, ignoring the annoyed grunts of his wolf. "What are you doing here?" he asked trying to sound as neutral as possible, and not show the fury that was bubbling inside him.

Even in the days when he did have casual sex, he didn't invite women back to his place. This was his den; he liked his privacy. He wanted to tell her to get the fuck out of his apartment, but he wasn't an ogre. Well... he wasn't a *total* ogre.

"Don't you remember?" she asked, mockingly.

"Obviously not," he ground out, fisting the covers. He needed to busy his hands, or they might find their way around her neck to throttle the smug look off her face.

Taryn started munching on a muffin; in between bites, she said, "You were drunk off your ass, so I brought you home."

Try as he might, he couldn't recall being dragged home by Taryn at all. Lord, what else didn't he remember?! He was almost as agitated as his braying wolf.

"We didn't fuck, did we?" he choked out.

Taryn gave him a look of disbelief. "No, and if we had, you would have remembered me." She preened for a second and Cutter fought the urge to vomit. "You were practically in a coma by the time we got here, and you kept moaning the name Lacey or something – that was definitely not a turn on."

Cutter exhaled a long breath and lay back on the bed. "Thank fucking hell."

"Thanks a bunch," she grumbled, sarcastically.

His wolf yipped in relieved joy. He didn't think he could have gotten it up for the young peacock shifter, but he had to be sure. If he was finally being honest, his desire for other women had died the day he met Lucie. Other women left him limp, but just the thought of Lucie doing anything mundane like scratching her nose sent blood rushing to his groin with the ferocity of a tidal wave. At that, his manhood stirred, and Cutter silently groaned. *Not now, you insatiable fucker, he thought.* His dick really did have a mind of its own.

"It's not you; it's me," he muttered half-heartedly. "Why are you wearing my shirt? I don't see why you needed to get undressed," he griped, eyeing her half-naked form with irritation.

"That's all thanks to your buddy, Dale. He decided we should reenact the wet t-shirt contest and threw beer all over Sharon and me. Anyway, I'm gonna use your shower, and then you're gonna give me money to reimburse me for the cab last night, and the cab I'm gonna take to get home this morning, and given that your friend ruined my clothes, I'm taking some of yours."

"Fine, yes, whatever."

She could have his fricking TV at that moment, and he wouldn't give a shit.

He just wanted her gone.

"Why didn't you just leave last night?" *And save him the hassle of dealing with her.*

"I ran out of money and there wasn't any in your wallet; I tried searching your apartment, but I couldn't find any. I found some really out of date condoms, though. Guess it's been a while, huh, champ?" She smirked at him. "But, if you did want to do anything, I can promise you I'm not fertile right now."

Her hand snaked over to him but froze mid-reach at the cold, stony look on his face. "Not interested."

Taryn huffed and went back to eating her muffin. "You might have told me at the bar that you were impotent."

His wolf snorted more in amusement than anything. In any other context, he probably would have been frothing at the mouth at what she said, but getting her the heck away from him was far more important that any slights to his ability to satisfy women.

She gobbled the rest of her muffin and moaned at the taste. Cutter couldn't help licking his lips. Whatever it was had smelled delicious. His wolf rumbled in satisfaction as the smell permeated the air. It was the sweetest smell in the whole world – *blueberries.* Other than meat, he rarely salivated over food – it was just something he needed to consume to survive. But damn if those things didn't smell like a mixture of heaven, home and arousal. Fuck, he was getting horny from a darn pastry!

"What were you eating?" he asked curiously.

"Blueberry muffins," she replied with a genuine smile. "Want one?"

"Fuck, yes."

She bounced off the bed and disappeared into his living room. They must be good; based on his time with Taryn, he'd swear she was only capable of scowling and smirking. And even better, they were *blueberry* muffins.

He'd never really liked them until a year ago, until he met a certain hedgehog shifter who smelled just like them. Now, he couldn't stop eating them. They were rich, sweet, succulent, and delicious.

Taryn brought in a basket of them and settled it on the bed. He frowned as he looked inside at the moreish treats; they all had blue hearts iced on top. He sniffed the basket and felt a pulse of desire shoot through him. *Oh, no.*

"Where did you get these?" he demanded, hoarsely.

She shrugged and picked up another muffin. "Some woman dropped them off for you."

He leaped out of bed and his head protested vociferously at the sudden movements. "What woman?"

"She didn't leave her name; she was a hedgehog, though."

His heart almost stopped beating as panic and fear twisted within, making his wolf whimper. "Did you see her? Did she see you?"

Taryn eyed him like he was a lunatic. "No, I got her throw them through the window, of course she saw me."

"Fuck!" he yelled.

Thankfully, he was already dressed, but he realized his car must still be parked outside the bar. *Fuckity, fuck!* He grabbed his stash of cash and threw some bills at her.

"See yourself out," he barked as he ran for the door.

"You might want to bathe first," she called after him. "You don't smell all that good."

No, he imagined he didn't, but by that point, he didn't care. His wolf hounded him to move faster, and he did. His couldn't stand to wait for the elevator and, instead, hurled himself down the stairs a flight at a time. He ignored the outraged shouts of his neighbor Mr. Wozniak and pushed past him. He couldn't feel too bad about almost knocking him over; the old bastard had trained his cocker spaniel to try and take a bite out of Cutter every time he saw him. *They had an ongoing feud about parking spaces.*

None of that mattered, though. He had to get to Lucie and tell her that nothing happened with Taryn. He had to make sure that she didn't think he had slept with the peacock shifter. It was imperative that he do so as soon as possible.

A small, sly part of him wondered why he was in such a rush. After all, didn't he want Lucie to leave him alone? Wouldn't seeing him with another woman reach that objective?

His wolf roared. Yes, he wanted Lucie to move on, but not like this. The thought that she could be hurt by seeing Taryn at his apartment ate at him, and he needed to do something about it. *He felt like his life depended on it.*

*

Cutter skidded to a stop at the medical bay. He looked around the room, wildly. Where was she? Where the fuck was she?

He heard the unmistakable groans from Helga's latest victim, but other than that, the area was quiet. He ran his hands over his head. She had to be here somewhere. All he had to do was wait patiently, and she'd show up. How hard could that be? Twenty seconds later, he realized it was nigh on impossible in his agitated state.

The door opened and Cutter spun to find himself glaring at the new doctor. Both men looked at each other in surprise and then disappointment.

The doctor recovered first and flashed him a genial smile. "We haven't formally met; I'm Doctor Rick Powers. Please, call me Rick."

He swaggered over to Cutter and held out his hand. The wolf shifter sniffed, stared at the hand for a few beats, and then shook it, reluctantly. "Cutter," he mumbled.

Rick stepped back and cocked his head to one side. "Yes, I remember from yesterday. I'm afraid I can't give you any details on your deceased friend."

"I wasn't here for that," he said hotly, and feeling a little guilty for momentarily forgetting about Clayton's untimely demise.

The lion raised an eyebrow. "Oh, then can I help you with something?"

His wolf huffed at the other male. The lion came across as easygoing and charming, but Cutter could sense the tension beneath the surface. He didn't like Cutter being there.

"I was looking for Lucie," replied Cutter slowly, watching his reaction.

The lion's smile tightened almost imperceptibly. "As was I. I'm sure she'll be around here somewhere. I'm sure I can help you in her absence."

Cutter cracked his jaw. "I need to speak to Lucie."

"What about? If it's personal, I'm sure it can wait until after the working day has ended."

His beast yowled in fury. He hadn't been wrong about the damn lion - he was after Lucie! He was trying to put a claim on her.

An idea sparked within him. If Lucie was actually avoiding him, then there was one surefire way to get her attention. He'd have her as a captive audience. His wolf wagged his tail at the idea. Yep, he'd genuinely had a good idea.

"I need to arrange for my physical."

Rick relaxed a little and chuckled. "Well, why don't I ask Lucie to call you when she has a chance to book an appointment for you?"

Cutter clenched and unclenched his fists. "That sounds fine."

"Good, I think you can just run along then, don't you?"

He grunted at the lion's smarmy tone and turned on his heel to leave; every muscle in his body tensed as he fought the urge to shift.

"Oh, and a bit of advice, friend," called Rick to his retreating back, "take a shower – you reek of alcohol."

"I'm not your friend," rasped Cutter.

*

An hour later, freshly showered and wearing a change of clothes he had begged, or rather threatened, off Wayne, Cutter marched into the medical bay.

He'd received an e-mail from Lucie informing him that his physical was due to take place at 10am, and he was determined to set her straight about what she thought she saw at his apartment.

Hopes of that died when the no-nonsense Helga barreled through the door. She gave him a chilly smile. The phrase 'tender, loving care' was not in her vocabulary. *She treated patients with the same gentleness that POWs received.*

"Ready for your physical?" she barked.

"Uh, where's Lucie?"

"Assisting Doctor Powers. Now, don't just stand there; strip!"

Even his wolf felt terrified. Maybe if he ran really fast, he could make it to the exit. She must have sensed his fear; the large she-bear planted her body in front of the door and pursed her lips.

Oh, lord, there was no escape.

CHAPTER SEVEN

Lucie sighed as her hedgehog sulked. Okay, maybe she felt just a teeny bit guilty for asking Helga to do Cutter's physical, and maybe she was hiding from him, but only because she was confused and didn't want to make an ass out of herself.

Cutter had told her repeatedly that he wasn't interested in her and that she should move on. Due to her mulishness, she had refused to listen to him. So wasn't her inevitable heartbreak all her own fault? He'd never promised to be faithful, and just because she had been sitting at home every Friday night in a bid to save herself for him, it was ridiculous for her to expect him to do the same.

Bull spit! She was hurt and angry and had no one to blame but herself. She wasn't avoiding him because she was afraid of what he would say, but rather, she was afraid that she would behave like a loon and accuse him of cheating on her.

Lucie tried to slap on a happy smile as Rick glided into the room. "So, how is your second day at work going?"

He grinned showing a large amount of straight, white teeth. "Almost as wonderful as the first. I was thinking about trying out the staff canteen, would you care to join me?"

Her face took on a moue of distaste.

"That bad, huh?" he chuckled.

"They only serve food-based meals. Legally, that's what they have to call them. I believe astronauts eat better than we do."

He sat down on the edge of her desk, and she became very aware of his large, warm body and the sweet cinnamon smell he emitted. Her hedgehog huffed and puffed, but Lucie couldn't help the involuntary flush his nearness caused.

"Then let me take you out for lunch," he winked at her, "my treat."

"Ummm…" She tried to think of a good reason why she shouldn't. But, after the morning she'd had, a little friendly company and some nice food might do her the world of good. Her little beast squeaked at her to think of Cutter.

"It's just a meal," he purred, "no pressure."

He was right; it was just a meal. It didn't mean anything.

Lucie nodded. "Okay."

Rick beamed. "Terrific."

Yes, terrific.

*

Cutter rolled his shoulder back and forth. *Helga was a menace.* It would take him years to get over the physical and mental torture she just put him through.

He could have ignored all that if Lucie would just answer her damn phone! But no, according to Helga the Horrific, she had gone out to lunch. When pressed if she had gone alone, Helga had clammed up. Apparently she didn't approve of gossips - or any kind of physical weakness. She ought to enter the Ms. Universe competition.

Given that the doctor was also unavailable, Cutter had his suspicions, though.

He scrubbed his hands over his face. Fuck, what had he done? His wolf seconded that. He couldn't even remember getting that drunk last night. He remembered meeting the gruesome twosome twins, thinking that he'd just have one last beer, and then... ugh, nothing.

Had he ever been that drunk before? It took a hell of a lot of alcohol actually to knock out a shifter. Surely, he hadn't gone on and drunk that much more?

What was he supposed to do about Lucie? She was now walking around town thinking that he was sleeping with other women. His chest tightened. She must think that she now had carte blanche to sleep with other men, too.

No, no he didn't want that. *Did he?* Wasn't this really all for the best? Lucie might actually get the message that he didn't want her – no, not that he didn't want her, just that he didn't feel like he could be with her. It wasn't the same thing.

He wasn't right for her, so why was he all worked up at the actual thought of her finding someone who was right for her? He had tried to encourage her to do just that numerous times over the past year. Maybe it's just that until now, he didn't actually think she would. She had never been motivated to before.

But, if she couldn't be with him, then surely, she would have to find happiness with someone else. His wolf howled. No, he didn't want that. He didn't want anyone to touch her – ever. She was his, and only his.

What were his reasons for not being with her? Well, he, uh... He was too gruff and violent for her. He suffered from night terrors that, on occasion, had him reaching for his gun and shooting the wall – *another reason Mr. Wozniak hated him.*

If he had just claimed Lucie straight away, there wouldn't be any issues. The thought arose, unbidden, and – *not so much gnawed* – as munched on him.

That... ugh, the worrying direction of his thoughts was interrupted by the twangs of the Imperial March. Hey, maybe the director was calling to say well done for actually getting his physical done. Nah, that didn't seem likely.

He really should be focusing on work. Both Jessie and Primrose had been drafted onto Diaz's team temporarily to help solve Clayton's murder. It pissed him off to lose two members of the team, but at least he might actually get an update on the case from Jessie. He should be putting all his energy into helping Wayne and Avery with their hunt to find someone who knew their victim. Instead, he was moping around like a teenage girl who had been stood up for the prom.

With a grunt, he answered.

"Does the name Sadie Beauchamp mean anything to you?" demanded the director.

Cutter snapped to attention, and even his wolf went silent in uneasy recognition. "Yes, why?"

"How do you know that name?"

The director was dodging the question. He had a bad feeling about what that meant. "From an old case of mine. Why?"

"When was the last time you saw her?"

His wolf snarled in frustration. "Not since I moved to Los Lobos. For fuck's sake, why?!"

"Her sister has been murdered and it appears that she has disappeared. And, apparently, she met up with Clayton Reeves before he died, *and* she had a note with all your details written on it."

Well, that shut him up.

"Come up to my office; we need to talk."

The director hung up, and Cutter stared at his phone. *This was not good.*

CHAPTER EIGHT

Lucie pretended to rearrange her store of bandages as Diaz chattered to her, *inanely*. He was waiting for the preliminary results of the autopsy Rick was performing and seemed determined to stay and bother her.

"You know, I could call you as soon as he has finished," she offered.

Diaz waved his hand and smiled. "Nah, it's no problem."

She turned away from him and frowned. No, it was no bother for *him*. He didn't find her company irritating beyond belief. On a good day, she didn't particularly like Diaz, and this was not a good day.

It started off badly and just seemed to be getting progressively more irritating. Her lunch with the doctor had not gone well – in her opinion, at least. The doctor's opinion may differ. His non-stop flirting was unnerving, and the fact that he was laying out his numerous plans for the life he, and his future mate, would lead was worrying. Maybe she was reading it completely wrong, but it seemed to be he was trying to shoehorn her into that role.

She could not have gotten out of that restaurant fast enough, and was thanking whatever gods were actually looking out for her when Rick was called away to a crime scene. Oh, that sounded awful. Of course, she wasn't pleased that the poor woman had died, but the timing had been on her side.

Diaz was babbling away about his car, or maybe his cousin. A jaguar could easily be a car or a person. She just interjected an 'aha' now and then, and he seemed satisfied.

Rick strode through the door and started stripping off his plastic apron. "I've given the bullets to one of our techs for confirmation, but they appear to have been shot from the same gun used to murder the late Agent Reeves. Like Agent Reeves, I'd say she died in the early hours of the morning."

Diaz nodded thoughtfully. "Things aren't looking good for Cutter."

Lucie's eyes whipped up, and she caught Rick's gaze before she looked down again, pretending to concentrate on her bandages, and ignoring the fact that her cheeks were heating.

"Oh?" asked Rick with interest.

Diaz chuckled dryly. "Yeah, apparently, Cutter's connected to this victim, too, and she had his contact details. Her sister met up with Clayton the day before he died."

"You don't think Cutter had something to do with these murders, do you?"

"That's ridiculous!" blurted Lucie, as her hedgehog mewled in agreement. "Cutter would never do anything like that!"

She bit her lip as Diaz gave her a look of pity, and Rick raised an eyebrow in her direction. She muttered a quick 'excuse me' and fled the room.

It didn't stop her from hearing Diaz saying, "I'm not sure he's responsible for them, but I definitely think he is involved in all this somehow."

Son of a biscuit, she didn't like this at all. No matter how awkward her relationship may be with Cutter, the need to protect him still flowed through her. Maybe she should warn him about what was happening. The worst he could do was just laugh and tell her she was overreacting, but at least she'd feel a little better about the situation. Yes, as soon as she could, she would pull him to one side and warn him.

Yes, she still had feelings for her wolf. Her heart may have stuttered for a moment, but this made her realize her feelings weren't changed. *She still wanted him.* Her hedgehog snuffled in agreement. Yes, she had to make sure her wolf was okay. After all, if he was wrongly imprisoned or something, it would really put a strain on their future marriage and the dozen or so little hedgehogs they were bound to have. She should probably leave out that part when she spoke to him – she didn't want him to make a break for Mexico.

*

Cutter was not okay. He seethed as the wolf shifter gave him an evil look and then suggested that he be suspended. What the fuck? His own wolf howled in irritation.

When the director summoned Cutter to his office, he failed to mention the fact that a member of Internal Investigations would be there. No, the fact that a particularly cut-throat, asshole of an agent called Harvey Blue was sitting in, and interjecting with his less-than-helpful insights, was a nasty surprise.

Cutter had more dealings with Harvey than he cared to mention, back when they were both in Ursa, and now also in the few weeks that Harvey had been in Los Lobos. Internal Investigations dealt with complaints or cases of misconduct of SEA agents. Cutter tended to get a lot of complaints regarding his heavy-handed approach to crime, and Harvey relished taking him to task over it.

"Does he really need to be here?" hissed Cutter through gritted teeth.

"I have every right to be here," said Harvey, smoothly and smugly while completely ignoring the death glare being leveled at him by Cutter.

The director remained stonily impassive; the only giveaway that he was repressing an urge to throttle them both was the slight twitch to his eyebrow. "Harvey is just here to ensure that procedures are followed and that there aren't any conflicts of interest regarding you and Sadie Beauchamp."

Cutter threw up his hands in disgust. "What conflict could there be? Yes I met her a few times, she was a potential witness on a case me and Clayton worked on back in Ursa, but she didn't know anything, and nothing ever happened."

Harvey's eyes gleamed with interest as amber seeped into them. His wolf was pushing to the fore, and Cutter's did, too, ready to fight if necessary. The two wolves had never come to blows before, but it had been a close call once or twice. Harvey seemed determined to get Cutter kicked out of the SEA for some reason, or perhaps arrested. Okay, maybe there were one or two reasons he could use – Cutter's anger management issues, the fact that he was prone to violence, his lack of respect for authority – but it seemed to be more than that. There were agents in the SEA who were much worse than Cutter, mostly they worked in tactical where they could work out their anger issues on doors and random shifters who totally deserved it, but Harvey seemed to have a grudge against Cutter. There didn't seem to be a reason for it. Hey, maybe Cutter pushed in line one time and got the last cupcake that Harvey wanted. *Who knows?!* Not that Cutter really cared; he could live with being hated. Being hated was a normal fact of life for him – he was okay with it.

"This would be the Maroni case?" asked Harvey, keenly.

Cutter kept his face as blank as possible, for once trying to hide the thundering emotions that resided inside him. From experience, he had learned to be wary when talking about that particular case. "Yes," he stated plainly.

"When was the last time you saw Sadie?"

He tried to hold back his frustration. "Three years ago; back when I was investigating that case."

"Why would Clayton want to talk to her?"

"I have no idea," Cutter ground out. "As I have said before, dozens of times now, I didn't even know Clayton was in town."

"Do you think someone killed Clayton, and then tried to kill Sadie over the Maroni case? Do you think Clayton uncovered something about that case and he needed to talk to Sadie about it?"

The questions slapped him in the face and even halted his prowling wolf, but, in honesty, he was starting to think that was the case. But why now, after three years, he had no idea. He could only think that maybe Clayton had managed to dig something up, something that apparently he wanted to investigate further in Ursa, and something that involved the now-missing Sadie Beauchamp.

"I have no idea," answered Cutter honestly. His eyes flicked away from the obvious disbelief of Harvey to the poker-faced director. In this instance, the snake shifter wasn't giving anything away. Apart from the brief rage that Cutter's more extreme actions elicited, he tended to be quite restrained, and never showed much emotion, and this time was no different.

Cutter looked back at Harvey, and the all-too familiar look of loathing was blaring in his direction. Harvey would never tell Cutter he hated him, but he certainly seemed to be thinking it loudly, perhaps hoping to blow his head up through thoughts alone.

Harvey looked at the director. "Gerry, you need to put Cutter on suspension – now."

"What?!" roared Cutter, leaping out of his chair. His gaze roved between the sneering Harvey and the now pronounced eye twitching of the director.

The director didn't like the way Harvey familiarly used his first name, or gave him an order. Internal Investigations was considered outside of normal jurisdiction within the SEA, and they reported directly to the director's boss, but most agents in II were smart enough to show their director – the Investigative Team Director and the SEA's other directors some respect. Harvey was prone to act as if everyone in the SEA was beneath him, and showed them the same contempt that he would a smelly, out of date filet of fish.

The director leaned back in his chair and looked between the smug expression of Harvey and the murderous one of Cutter. "Look, Harv," the wolf sucked in an annoyed breath – he *hated* being called Harv, "I just think that it might be a bit of an overreaction. Cutter hasn't, in this instance, done anything wrong."

Harvey snorted. "He knew both victims."

"No," said the director in a deceptively soft voice, "he didn't."

Harvey looked at him, perplexed and on seeing the director's eyes narrow, Cutter soothed his beast a little and sat down. The director's ire, for a change, wasn't aimed at him, and Cutter felt a momentary warmth for his superior, and a little pleased that Harvey wasn't getting his own way.

"Cutter," continued the director, "knew Clayton. As did numerous other agents and directors working here. I had the pleasure of working with Clayton when I started my career in Ursa."

He paused momentarily as sadness briefly flashed in his eyes, and Cutter felt camaraderie with the snake shifter that had never been present in any of their previous dealings.

The director scooted forward in his chair and leaned on his desk, tenting his fingers. "Even you worked with Clayton back when you were in Ursa."

"I'd hardly say we worked together," scoffed Harvey.

The director held up a hand for silence, and Cutter was impressed that the now red-faced Harvey actually shushed.

"And as far as I'm aware, Cutter doesn't actually know our second victim."

Harvey furrowed his brow. "But Sadie…"

"Is not our second victim," the director told him sternly. "Our second victim is her sister, Marie. Did you know her sister, Cutter?"

"I barely knew Sadie," he grumbled.

"There, you see."

"But…" protested Harvey, heatedly.

"No, Harv," snapped the director. "Enough for now. I agreed to this meeting with mixed feelings, and I don't believe the situation warrants Cutter's suspension. We suspect the two murders may be linked, and we suspect someone attempted to murder Sadie, but we don't know that for sure, yet. For all we know, they are unrelated."

Harvey looked like he had been slapped in the face and Cutter thoroughly enjoyed it. The only thing that would have improved it would be if someone actually did slap him in the face.

For a second, Harvey looked pensive until his eyes lit up triumphantly. "We found notes with Cutter's contact details on at both crime scenes."

The director gave him a well-rehearsed look of boredom. "So?"

"So?!" spluttered Harvey.

"I'm sure that anyone could find Cutter's details if they wanted. I would guess that Clayton would want to visit his ex-partner, and as for Marie and Sadie Beauchamp… I'm sure Diaz will figure that out in the course of his investigation. Which we should leave him to get on with."

"But…"

"No buts!" the director told him firmly. "Cutter has already told us that neither victim contacted him recently. There is no evidence to suggest that he is lying about this."

"No, I damn well am not lying," snarled Cutter as his wolf roared.

The director's eyes flashed, warning him to be quiet. "Diaz is looking into the connection between these two murders, and he is also coordinating a search for Sadie Beauchamp, in case she is in danger. And while I insist that Cutter is not right to lead the investigation into either of these murders, Diaz may wish to consult with him over it. Given that Cutter still has his own active case, I believe suspending him would be a waste of time."

Harvey's jaw ticked as he mulled over the director's words, and his tone was more subdued than before. "Perhaps in my capacity as an II agent I should look over the evidence Diaz has compiled and make that decision for myself."

The director gave him a chilly smile. "No, you do not have jurisdiction to do so. According to SEA regulations, you are not permitted to peruse active evidence unless there are substantiated suspicions of wrongdoing by a SEA agent."

Harvey gave the director a look of pure hot loathing; a look that could melt a glacier and one that was usually reserved for Cutter. "I could take this directly to my boss," he threatened, mildly.

The snake shifter let out a put-on sigh. "Then why don't you do so, Harv, instead of wasting my time?"

Harvey looked at him hesitantly but ultimately backed down under the snake shifter's unrelenting stare. "But if evidence were found of wrongdoing on Cutter's part…"

"There won't be!" spat Cutter. The fucker was accusing him of being involved with two murders! *How dare he!*

"Then naturally he would be suspended and Internal Investigations would be privy to the case," replied the director evenly.

Harvey looked like he wanted to argue the point further, but the director started making noises about being busy and threw in a couple of pointed comments that Harvey also had work to do.

The wolf shifter huffed and puffed until eventually he threw out the word 'fine' with all the grace of a three-year-old who had been told that they couldn't have ice-cream until they ate all their broccoli. He stomped out of the door, only stopping to throw Cutter a contemptuous look.

After he was gone, the director trained a cold, searching look at Cutter. "Do you have any idea what brought Clayton to Los Lobos? Or whether his murder is linked to the death of Marie Beauchamp?"

Cutter's wolf started to growl. *Hadn't they already been through this already?* But Cutter quelled him. The director, at least, was giving him the benefit of the doubt, not something he would get from many other agents.

"I have no idea what Clayton was doing," he admitted, sadly thinking of his late friend. "We didn't talk much. But, if I had to guess, I would say he was investigating his old unsolved cases. He didn't let things go very easily, and given that he had so much free time…"

"I thought the Maroni case was solved. Nicolas Maroni is in prison."

"He is, but we never caught Maroni's mole. He had someone within the SEA on the take and we never found out who."

Someone who had caused the deaths of over a dozen SEA agents. Someone who thought that their lives were worth less than a few kickbacks from Maroni. The thought of it made Cutter sick and madder than holy hell at the same time. Three years hadn't dimmed his rage over the matter. Cutter had come out the other side of the case battered and beaten, but his pain was nothing compared to witnessing the suffering the mole's actions had caused over a dozen families. He pushed his claws into the palms of his hands to try and maintain a modicum of control.

"Yes, I heard about that," said the snake shifter, almost apologetically. "I also heard a rumor that II thought it was you."

Cutter barked out a mirthless laugh as his wolf snapped his jaws. "Not II, it was my best friend, Harv – *and him alone* - who thought I was the mole. I'll bet he still does in spite of what happened to me on that case."

The director cocked his head on one side and almost gave him a look of amusement. "Is that why Harv dislikes you so much?"

He pursed his lips. "No, he didn't like me before that."

"Your winning personality strikes again," murmured the snake before rolling his eyes. "For now, I'll keep our pal Harv at bay, just watch your back with him. I don't like to speak ill of other agents, but he has a malicious streak and you need to be careful."

"Can't I…"

"No!"

"You don't know what I was going to say," grouched Cutter.

"You were going to ask to help with the case." The director paused, waiting to see if Cutter would deny it, but he didn't. "Just continue with your case, and help Diaz out when he needs it."

The retort that Diaz needed all the help he could get nearly rolled off his tongue, but he stopped himself. His wolf huffed at him, but, being diplomatic – *for once in his life* – wasn't going to hurt him. Well, not by much anyway. Maybe he could run up to the rooftop and yell all the bad things he wanted to say into the sky. It might make him feel better, not as better as punching Harvey and telling Diaz he was a complete tool to his face would, but still, better.

"Okay," acquiesced Cutter, in a very grudging manner.

"You're not the only one who liked Clayton, you know?" The snake shifter took on an almost wistful expression. "Like you, in spite of his personality *quirks*, he was a good agent and he deserved better than to be murdered in some flea-ridden motel. I hope this can all be resolved quickly so he can be given a decent burial. By the way, do you have any idea about what funeral arrangements he wanted? Apparently his will just donated everything he had to the local animal shelter."

Cutter smirked. "He once told me he didn't care where he was buried, but he wanted to be buried face down."

"Why?"

"So everyone could continue kissing his ass even in death."

The director blinked for a few seconds before letting out an uncharacteristic guffaw of laughter. "Yeah, that sounds like Clayton."

CHAPTER NINE

Lucie watched Cutter like a hawk. Or at least like a stalker who was trying to act nonchalant, and not let on like she was actually stalking someone. *So, yeah, like a hawk.* She tracked his every move around the busy bar while keeping one ear out for the conversation her friends were having. Isis was telling them about her date with the panda she picked up the other night. Isis' stories were never boring; the tigress tended to have some strange ideas about what made dates fun. But as much fun as the stories were, she was more concerned about Cutter, so, every now and then, Lucie interjected an 'oh, that is unbelievable' or a 'crimeny' and she was golden.

She was a little put out that Cutter hadn't been trying to contact her to explain what happened that morning – with the peacock shifter. Her hedgehog huffed at her, and Lucie sighed. Okay, so he had tried, and Lucie had run away from him like a lily-livered little hedgehog, but did he really have to give up so easily? Not that he had anything to apologize for; he was technically single, footloose and fancy-free, *blah, blah, blah*. Yeah, she'd been having the same arguments with herself throughout the day.

That wasn't important at that moment, anyway. No, at that moment she was purely acting as one professional to another and affording him the same courtesy she would expect from him. She was warning him that his so-called friends were out to get him. Ooh, she should have made Diaz's physical more punishing; if she had known that he would turn around and do this to her sort-of – *in her wild dreams* - honey bunny, then she would have let Helga do his physical, too.

She perked up as she saw Cutter disengaging from his friends and moving away on his own. She felt like a predator after her prey. She mumbled that she was going to the bathroom and dashed after him. *The predatory hedgehog sights her prey; he has moved away from his herd and is making his way to the bathroom. The hedgehog moves in for the kill.*

Cutter turned around abruptly before she could tap him on the shoulder, sending a deep flush from her nose right down to her toes.

"Lucie," he breathed, almost sensually as his green eyes clouded stormy amber.

Nut bunnies! His deep voice was like the most decadent chocolate. She wanted to eat him up…

"I need to talk to you," they both said at the same time.

"Me first," he demanded.

She let out a squeak of annoyance that made his lips curl upwards. "Ladies first," she corrected him.

He harrumphed. "What I have to say is important, it's about this morning…"

Lucie felt a pang of worry and held up her hand to stop him. What if he was confessing to being in love with the peacock? What if they were getting married? What if she was pregnant with his pup?! Lucie was far too sober to deal with any revelations about his interlude with the peacock. No, she was all for ignoring what she stumbled on that morning, but how could she do that if he didn't stop yapping about it?

"It's fine, you don't have to explain," she told him dismissively, ignoring her prickly inner animal who definitely begged to differ.

His forehead creased, and he folded his big, muscled arms over his impressive chest. Lucie told herself over and over not to swoon. She placed one of her small hands on his arm; the paleness of her creamy pink skin contrasted beautifully to the dark brown of his own.

"I'm worried about you," she admitted, making her eyes look as big as possible. Her ex-husband had once said she had freakishly big eyes, and he couldn't deny her anything when she gave him that pleading, innocent look. They were still good friends and his inability to deny her anything hounded him to that day.

Cutter sucked in a breath, and she scented the increase in his arousal. Her eyes flicked down and yep, the evidence of his arousal was there for all to see. Inch, after inch, after inch... *and so on.* She blushed at her thoughts. Maybe she should have done his physical, after all - at the very least she might have got a glimpse of what Cutter was only just managing to hide in his pants.

Lucie quickly shook her head as she caught Cutter's smirk before his gaze landed on her heaving bosom. He must have guessed at what she was thinking, and, undoubtedly, he could scent her overwhelming arousal. Well, it had been a long year where the only sexual company she had ran on batteries, it was getting to the point where just a look from Cutter set her on fire. But that was no excuse - she had to focus.

"You need to be careful," she said in a high, strangled voice.

Perhaps trying to dim his own arousal, Cutter cleared his throat, and he looked away from her breasts. "Look, that girl," he started.

"Holy mackerel, I mean at work," she snapped impatiently. Did the idiot think she was trying to give him dating advice or something? Yes, her advice would be: don't run around with jailbait, trampy peacocks, and date her instead! A sentiment her hedgehog would love to have voiced.

Lucie darted her eyes around the darkened corridor to make sure no one they knew was around. She leaned toward him, and he did the same. "Diaz is really suspicious of you."

Cutter threw back his head and let out a guttural laugh.

"It's not funny," she said, grumpily.

He calmed and leaned toward her again, faintly sniffing her hair. "Diaz couldn't find chocolate at Willy Wonka's Chocolate Factory."

Lucie giggled at the unexpected reference. She couldn't imagine Cutter ever reading the book or watching the film of Charlie and the Chocolate Factory. She had always assumed he was born a badass and grew up worshiping at the altar of Die Hard. "Willy Wonka?"

His lip curled up. "I was going to say something else, but didn't think you'd appreciate it. I heard Erin say that Willy Wonka thing once and I had her explain it to me."

"What were you going to say?" she asked curiously.

Cutter leered at her. "I was going to say he couldn't find a whore's clit if she laid back and gave him directions."

Lucie pouted her lips in distaste. "Sorry I asked. But we're getting away from the point – you need to watch your back."

"I haven't done anything wrong," he said firmly.

He was trying to hide it, but she caught the frustration in his eyes.

"I know," she said soothingly and rubbed her fingers over his arm. She felt gratified when he smiled slightly. "But I don't want your reputation ruined by their untrue accusations."

"I reckon my reputation, such as it is, will be fine. Diaz couldn't… ah… work his way through a crossword puzzle. Was that better?"

Lucie tried not to laugh, but she couldn't help it. "Better than the, uh, other one, that's for sure."

Cutter's good mood seemed to evaporate as quickly as it came, and he returned to his usual, grumpy state. "What are you doing here tonight, anyway? Why are you encouraging that creep?"

Lucie stared at him, puzzled by the sudden venom in his tone. *Was that jealousy he was throwing her way?* "Do you mean Rick?" she asked, hesitantly.

The tightening of his jaw told her that Rick was indeed the *creep* he was referring to. He seemed to be ignoring the fact that before pursuing him on his way to the bathroom, she was actually surrounded by Isis, Jessie, Avery,

Rick and a turtle shifter from tech who was mooning over Jessie - Lucie couldn't remember his name. It's not like she was out on a date with Rick; he just happened to have shown up and joined them. She was a little miffed by his attitude, and even more so by her hedgehog who welcomed it.

She put on her haughtiest pout. "Like you, I'm out for a drink with work colleagues."

"My work colleagues don't want to fuck me," he told her brutally.

Lucie prickled. "You don't know that for certain."

Cutter snorted and glowered at her. "Yeah, I'm sure Wayne is just waiting for his chance to get into my panties."

"You don't wear panties," she murmured. She knew for a fact that he went commando. It was something that she had thought about over and over ever since she found out.

He raised his eyebrows in surprise and Lucie quickly continued. She didn't really want to explain how she knew *that*. "Rick is just being nice." Although, she didn't say it with much conviction.

"Men aren't nice," he grunted.

"You're not nice," she countered petulantly. *No, he was a big, bad, sexy wolf.* Lucie gave herself a mental slap.

"You're not serious about dating him, are you?" he demanded, angrily.

A part of her – the insipid hedgehog part – wanted to jump up and down, allaying his fears and shouting no, no, no! While the part that had a backbone was irritated that he thought it was okay to run around with a young – *very young* – bird shifter, and then chastise her for even considering dating a very appropriate doctor.

In the end, the two extreme reactions met in the middle, and Lucie replied on an even keel, "Nothing has happened with Rick."

Cutter gave her a pained and vulnerable look. "You once said you'd wait for me forever."

She gasped. "You told me not to." Why would he bring that up?

His lips twitched as he fought a smile. "Since when do you listen to what I say?"

"Since when do you care?" she replied sassily, snatching her hand away from his arm.

"So you are planning on dating him?" His body was riddled with tension, and his eyes had turned completely amber.

"I'm not planning anything. Maybe I just realized you weren't worth mooning over." *Lies, all lies, her hedgehog screamed.*

"I'm not," he said, tersely.

Lucie almost waved a white flag in defeat. It was a battle just trying to figure him out. "So then I'll just leave you be. I've told you my worries; my conscience is clear – I can go."

She turned to leave. "I'm sorry you had to see that this morning," he called after her.

Her heart raced, and her hedgehog mewled as she dashed back into the bar, not daring to respond. Did he really care if he hurt her? And why was he suddenly all jealous about another guy showing interest in her? A few other guys had asked her out over the last year – there was the reindeer from tactical, the wombat from tech – but she had given them their marching orders, and for some reason they actively avoided her now. In fact, they looked scared and ran in the other direction whenever they saw her. Their reactions seemed a little strange, but she didn't dwell on them. But the point was, Cutter never seemed to care about them so why was he getting all bent out of shape about Rick?

She slipped back into her seat and grimaced as she took a sip of her sex on the beach cocktail. *She was not letting Isis choose her drink ever again.* Rick smiled at her, but no one else seemed to notice her absence, or her sweaty palms and undoubtedly flushed countenance.

To her shock, Cutter strode toward their table and actually joined them.

Isis scowled at him as he nudged her out of the way to make room for himself, but that didn't stop her complaining diatribe. No one else seemed to take any notice of him, or thought it was odd that he was there.

Cutter gave her a searching look, and she looked away, biting her lip and wishing to become invisible. What wouldn't she have given for this attention yesterday?

She was surprised to see that Rick was eyeing Cutter with distaste. She knew that Cutter didn't like Rick – because of his asinine jealousy, which was completely at odds with his previous actions – but she didn't know the feeling was mutual. She knew they'd met, she just didn't realize they had managed to dislike each other so quickly.

Cutter wrenched his gaze away from her and focused a belligerent expression on the lion shifter. "So, Doc, why'd you want to become a medical examiner?"

Rick raised an eyebrow in amusement, which definitely didn't help Cutter's mood improve any. "I've always been interested in diagnostic medicine and…"

"Isn't that for the living," jeered Cutter.

The lion shifter narrowed his eyes ever so slightly, and the smile on his face was obviously false. The others around the table sensed the heightened tension between the two males and immediately dropped their own conversations to listen.

"Well, yes, that is correct, but as I was going to say, I enjoy the puzzle of finding out how people died. It's not something everyone can do."

Cutter pretended to ponder that. "So it doesn't bother you how creepy it is hanging around dead bodies all day?"

"Creepy?" repeated Rick, softly. "No creepier than going to a crime scene and looking at the dead body before trawling through victims' personal belongings."

The wolf shifter huffed. "Our last medical examiner started cutting people up and selling their organs."

"Yeah, he was creepy," agreed Avery, shuddering. "He kept asking me out on dates to go and look at his silent film archives – to this day I have no idea whether that was some kind of weird euphemism."

"Yeah, me too," said Isis. "He invited me to the museum of medical oddities – barf to that."

"And me," piped up Jessie, "he wanted me to go the aquarium with him. Which I guess was kind of normal in comparison."

Lucie frowned. "He never asked me out; he looked down on me because I was a nurse – he thought he could do better than me."

"Ridiculous," soothed Rick. "Lots of doctors marry their nurses."

He gave a pointed look at Cutter, whose eyes bulged worryingly, and Lucie just wished the damn ground would swallow her up. It was going to be a *long* night.

*

Cutter watched as Lucie left the bar, thankfully, with Jessie and not the jumped-up, arrogant, asshole, lion shifter doctor. Not that he had a problem with the lion shifter or anything. Nope, he was totally indifferent to the fucker.

Jessie's admirer, the turtle shifter, soon left, deflated, given that the object of his affections had completely ignored him all night and left with another woman. Isis and Avery soon drifted away, leaving Cutter and Rick.

Cutter downed his beer as quickly as possible. He was desperate to get away, but he wasn't about to waste beer.

Rick sipped his whiskey, watching Cutter through narrowed eyes. "Do you really think it's fair letting Lucie hang around you when you're not interested in her?"

He almost choked on his beer as his indignant wolf snarled. "What?" he spluttered.

The lion shifter let out a derisive humph. "I see the way she looks at you; it's not a secret that she has feelings for you, or that you don't reciprocate them. The SEA is ripe with gossip; I know she has been chasing after you for a year. It's just seems strange that all of a sudden you're hanging around her like a bad smell. I wonder if it's because of me."

"Don't flatter yourself," growled Cutter.

Who the fuck did this lion think he was? He wasn't acting any different to Lucie than he ever had. Just because this sleazebag had designs on her, it hadn't changed a fucking thing. Maybe he had warned Lucie away from him, but that was only because he knew the way lions operated. Male lions were big on having harems of wives, and if Lucie – *sweet, innocent, naïve Lucie* – weren't careful, she could end up sharing the man with six other women and given the nickname 'Saturday.'

The lion shifter gave him a patient, almost pitying look. "Don't you think you should leave her alone? Other people might have an interest in her."

His wolf was trying to push out and take a bite out of this asshole; the damn beast was virtually salivating at the thought. "Other people like you?"

Rick jutted his chin out and pushed his shoulders back, raising himself to his six-foot-four height. Yeah, he might have been a little taller and even a little broader than Cutter, but the wolf was confident he could take him in a fight. Ha, confidence nothing, he was already planning a victory dance in his head. Sadly, it probably wouldn't come to a fight.

"Yes, like me," replied the lion shifter simply. "I just worry that Lucie won't commit while you're still clinging to her. It seems to me that you've had more than enough chances to be with her, and now that she has a chance to be happy with someone else…"

Cutter slammed his bottle of beer down on the table, smashing it instantly. It made a few other patrons jump and incited some sarcastic clapping from more than one of his fellow SEA agents.

He ignored the wails of his animal and told the other male, "Lucie's a grown woman; if she wants to be with you, that's up to her."

Rick was actually a little taken back by his response. "So you'll back off?"

Cutter bared his fangs and a rumbling chuckle trickled out of his mouth. "You need me to?" he taunted.

"For her sake, yes. For mine, no," he said condescendingly, as he looked Cutter up and down. "It makes no odds to me whether a mangy mutt is hanging around, I'll still be the one she goes home with, but I just didn't think there was any reason for her to get hurt unnecessarily. Still, what will be will be. Take care, Cutter."

The lion shifter started whistling – *yes, he was actually whistling a jaunty tune* – as he strode out of the bar. Cutter ignored every instinct in his body to chase after the feline and rip him to shreds.

He couldn't do that; he couldn't give in to those instincts. Not because he would feel any kind of remorse about it, but because of the reaction it would elicit from Lucie. Would she be angry with him? Or worse, disappointed? Would that look of sweet longing she always threw in his direction disappear? It pained him to admit it, but he didn't want that.

But that still didn't lessen his fury. It had been too long since he had shifted. He could feel the fur pushing through his skin; his bones started cracking as the change came upon him.

Abruptly, he tore out of the bar, only just making it to the alley before his clothes ripped apart and he fell to the ground on all fours. He howled into the sky as his honed senses took in all the sights, sounds, and smells of the busy city. He caught the scent of a wild fox and took off after the beast. Yes, a little hunting was just what he needed.

CHAPTER TEN

Thursday

Cutter glared at the agents sitting in front of him. Diaz had the grace to look a little sheepish, but Primrose was remorselessly cold and dispassionate. Not that he expected anything less from her. Ice sculptures gave more away than her.

The two of them were asking him further questions about Clayton and Sadie Beauchamp. Apparently, they hadn't been able to locate Sadie; she wasn't on vacation – she had simply disappeared.

Her sister, Marie, had been murdered in Sadie's home. Sadie had moved to Los Lobos a couple of weeks ago; she was renting an apartment and working at a club as a waitress. Marie had come into town a few days ago. The two women were both bobcat shifters. While Sadie seemed to lead a normal life, apart from having previously worked at a mob-owned club back in Ursa, Marie had numerous drug related charges to her name, and was apparently a heavy user as well as an alleged dealer. She and her long-term loser boyfriend had been in many scrapes over the years. If it weren't for the fact that ballistics proved that the same gun killed both Marie and Clayton, they might have suspected Marie was actually the target. But, as it was, they suspected that both Sadie and Clayton knew something about the Maroni case, and someone had tried to shut them up. Drops of Sadie's blood were discovered at the crime scene, so it looked like she had been at least injured. Cutter guessed that they were checking all hospitals for her.

All of this just resulted in Cutter being asked the same questions over and over. He actually learned more about Sadie Beauchamp than he ever knew before that day. She worked at one of Maroni's BDSM clubs. He remembered interviewing her. She was a pretty woman, a little skittish, but she seemed too scared to lie to them. Clayton had pushed her hard, but she had remained adamant that she knew nothing of the inner workings of Maroni's mob, and they believed her. She knew Maroni – *somewhat intimately* – but she didn't know anything about his business.

At the time, Cutter hadn't known anything about Sadie's sister or that she dealt drugs. He couldn't fathom why Clayton would come all the way out to Los Lobos to see her, though. Cutter had managed to corner Jessie before his interview with Diaz the dummy and the ice bitch. The squirrel shifter had been a little reticent at first, but he soon needled her into giving him some details. Diaz and his team interviewed some of the people Sadie worked with, and a number reported seeing Clayton on several nights trying to talk to Sadie, and the last night he was there, they got into a huge fight and Clayton had to be ejected by the bouncers. Sadly, no one could hear what the fight was about.

Although Diaz didn't want to ask the questions over and over, he still did. Cutter's paper-thin patience was wearing out. If it weren't for a very satisfying night of chasing various wildlife throughout the city, and then a couple of hours spent guarding Lucie's house – *just to make sure no errant lions turned up* – his wolf would have been going nuts at that moment. As it was, the beast was kind of mellow, and Cutter wanted him to stay that way.

Primrose clucked her tongue. "Based on the Maroni case, do you think we'll have another victim?"

"Unless you two get off your butts and find Sadie, I predict she'll be killed next."

Diaz looked a little affronted, but Primrose wasn't moved.

"What? Not good enough for you?" sneered Cutter. "You want me to look in my fucking crystal ball again for you? How about you get out there and investigate instead of wasting my time asking me the same fucking stupid questions over and over again?"

He tipped his chair back and stared at the wall, growling lowly and incessantly. Okay, calling himself mellow may have been a *slight* exaggeration.

"You know, if you just give us something to work with…" started Diaz before trailing off as steam almost shot out of Cutter's ears.

His wolf was starting to stir, no longer satiated by the relaxation of hunting and ensuring that Lucie remained untouched. "I don't know how many fucking times I can tell you this. I don't fucking well know why Clayton was in town. I don't know why the fuck Clayton wanted to talk to Sadie, and I sure as fuck don't fucking know why someone would want to fucking kill her. All I fucking know is that you are wasting my fucking time!"

By this point, Cutter had unknowingly stood up and was leaning over the table, amber eyes flashing at the agents in front of him. Primrose arched a perfect eyebrow, completely unimpressed by his behavior. "Eight fucks in one outburst, is that a personal best?"

"Nah, his best so far is eighteen," chimed in Diaz, "and it was a lot shorter than that."

"Sit down, Cutter, we're not even remotely done here," ordered Primrose, imperiously.

"You may not be, but I am," he growled as he stomped to the exit.

Diaz sucked in a breath and stood up. "Cutter, you can't leave yet."

"Watch me," he muttered as his hand reached for the door handle. He was done answering inane questions. Anymore and he might just let his wolf out – *then they'd be sorry.*

"Not before you explain why two hundred thousand dollars was recently wired into your account," called Primrose.

Confusion stopped him cold; his hand hovered over the handle and even his beast stopped yowling long enough for Cutter to process what the hyena shifter had just told him. Slowly, he turned back to the two agents and regarded them warily. Primrose hadn't moved an inch and looked just as detached as ever, but the strain on Diaz's face was evident.

"Is that a joke?" asked Cutter, slowly. Were they actually playing some kind of dumb trick on him to get his attention?

Primrose pulled some papers out of her file and spread them over the table. She waved a hand over them. "See for yourself."

Cutter edged his way back into the room, almost expecting one of them to leap out of him and shout boo at any moment. *That's how ridiculous it was.*

He scanned the pieces of paper laid out in front of him. "This is a mistake," he said definitely. He didn't have that kind of money, and he didn't know anyone who did. It must have been sent to his account by accident; surely, it was meant for someone else.

Diaz relaxed a little on seeing that Cutter wasn't about to leave and sank back into his seat. "One hundred grand was put in your account the night before Clayton died and another hundred the night before Sadie, ah, disappeared."

Cutter snapped his head up to look at the jaguar shifter, who had the decency to squirm in his seat. "You better not be suggesting what I think you are."

Primrose gave him a hard look. "We're merely stating facts. What do you think we're suggesting?"

They might not want to admit it, but in their *oh-so-subtle* way, they were hinting that he had been paid off for murdering Clayton and Sadie. Or at least, attempting to murder Sadie.

Cutter stood up straight and rolled his shoulders. He affected an unconcerned and unflappable demeanor completely at odds with his fiery, grouchy nature. Damn, he was a good actor.

"Clearly, it's just a banking error. I'll call my bank today and get it straightened out. Thank you for pointing it out. Gee, aren't I lucky that you just happened to come across this."

Yes, why exactly had they been pawing their way through his personal life?

He didn't like that one bit. Not that he had anything to hide – his personal life was pretty mundane. Other than child support, all he did was pay his rent, bills, gym membership, and his tab at the bar. Maybe the gym membership seemed a little decadent, given that the SEA offices had its own gym, but sometimes he just liked to get away from his work mates. Plus going to two gyms afforded a wider range of shifters with which to spar with, *and therefore beat the hell out of.*

Diaz and Primrose gave each other matching, inscrutable looks. Diaz caved first. "The timing of it seems very… ah…"

Cutter gave him a hard stare. "I don't know why the bank made this mistake when they did. Fucking morons. How dare they give me money I don't want?"

"This isn't a laughing matter," said Primrose snippily. "I heard the rumors about you back in Ursa. A lot of people said you were in Nicolas Maroni's back pocket."

He felt his muscles twitch and his body heat. His wolf wanted out and in about fifty seconds, if he didn't calm down, there would be nothing he could do to stop him. The wolf wanted out, and heaven help anyone who was in his way.

"They were just rumors. I never did anything wrong. A lot of people suffered because of that man – me included. We're done here."

He strode to the exit, willing his body to stay in his skin form until he could at least get out of there. His wolf was done listening to those people. They were accusing him of being a liar, of taking money from the man who tried to kill him. His wolf couldn't stand it anymore. If Cutter didn't get out of there, his wolf would get free, and he couldn't be sure he wouldn't hurt them, or that he wouldn't enjoy doing it.

He rushed out of the room; his body throbbed from the imminent change and his mind was torn between his two forms. He staggered into a soft, luscious, delicious smelling body. A small squeak sounded, and automatically his hands reached out to steady her.

Lucie's big blue eyes blinked up at him, and she gasped as his body trembled, and he growled. They heard voices coming their way, and he allowed himself to be dragged into the janitor's closet. She shut the door firmly behind them and ran her hands up and down his chest as she made soothing noises.

"It's okay, we're okay," she murmured.

Her touch seared its way into his very soul. The urgent need to shift halted. Eventually, he calmed and under her ministrations his violent beast retreated, allowing Cutter to take back control. As his claws receded, unable to stop the natural urge, his arms slipped around Lucie and he drew her into a hug, partly for his own comfort and partly, so he didn't have to look at her worried countenance. She moaned against his chest, and he buried his head in her hair inhaling deeply. Her curvy body fit so snugly against his; he pressed against her even harder, cursing himself for his weakness but reveling in the warmth and pleasure she brought him.

"I'm sorry," he muttered into her hair.

"There's nothing to be sorry for," she murmured, rubbing her cheek against his chest.

"We shouldn't be doing this," he choked out, fighting his instincts and his horny wolf.

"The janitor won't be back for hours."

"No, I mean we shouldn't be together like this."

Her shoulders hunched in a shrug. "We're not doing anything wrong. People hug all the time. It's a free country. If it makes you feel any better, I'll go around hugging everyone I meet today, just to show you how normal it is."

His arms tightened around her as his wolf snarled at the thought. "Don't you dare," he warned her and was surprised when he heard a small giggle escape her.

"For a second there, I thought your wolf was going to get out and go on a rampage."

"He was," he said tightly.

"Maybe I should have been running in the opposite direction instead of pulling you into a small closet," she joked half-heartedly.

Cutter pulled his head back and cupped hers, directing her gaze to his. "Not you, Lucie. You never have to run from me."

Lucie smiled a little sadly before shaking her head. "And I swear, if my hedgehog ever goes on the rampage, I will never hurt you either."

He pressed his lips together to stop himself from chortling. "I'm glad to hear it, I heard that being pricked by a hedgehog will leave you in some discomfort for at least, oh, a couple of hours."

"More like three," she told him solemnly before grinning.

He had an unaccountable urge to kiss her twitchy little nose, but he fought it. Well, actually he had a strong urge to pull her pants down and drive his rock hard manhood into her wet heat, but that was a familiar urge that he was used to handling. This new one, the desire to do something sweet and intimate, that was something new and frightening. Having sex was one thing. That satisfied an itch that all shifters had. But wanting to do something cute? Wanting to snuggle after sex? That was alien territory for him. He hadn't even wanted to behave that way with his wife, not that it would have been overly welcome.

To her disappointment, he pulled away from her and stepped backward, hitting his head on a metal shelving unit. She winced as he rubbed his head, but at least the head pain distracted him from the pain in his pants. *Different kind of pain, but the pants one was definitely worse.*

Lucie folded her arms over her impressive chest, and he almost purposefully banged his head again.

"So what happened?" she asked gently.

"They think I had something to do with Clayton's and that woman's deaths," he blurted, happy to be able to talk to someone.

Lucie's mouth fell open in shock. "Mother of pearl! That's insane!"

"I know."

"You would never do that."

"I know."

"Those people are idiots."

"Oh, sweetheart," he laughed, "I know." Damn it felt good to have someone on his side.

"So what are you going to do?"

Cutter shrugged. "Nothing. I haven't done anything wrong, so there isn't any evidence against me."

That was kind of a half-truth. He still intended to look into Clayton's death. Whatever little faith he had in Diaz's abilities had completely evaporated during the meeting they just had. Cutter didn't trust the cat to give Clayton the justice he deserved. However, Cutter wasn't going to do it to exonerate himself; he was doing it for Clayton.

Lucie nodded. "They'll see that they're making a mistake soon."

"I hope so," he muttered.

"I'm sorry about what's happening, but I have to go," she told him reluctantly.

"Got a date?" he asked hotly, thinking of the lion shifter.

The warmth and feelings between them disappeared in an instance, and Lucie almost burst into tears at his abrupt change, but she stood her ground and jutted her chin.

"No, actually, I have work to do. I'm glad you're feeling better."

She ducked out of the closet with her head held high, and Cutter punched the wall. What the fuck was wrong with him? She provided him comfort and helped him, even though nothing he had ever done warranted that tender attention from her, and then he turned around and virtually slapped her in the face. *Couldn't he have just said thank you?!*

104

He shook his head as he tried to reach out to his wolf. His mood swings were just another reason why he forced himself to stay away from Lucie, why she couldn't be his mate. The sucker-punched look on her face said it all. How could he live with seeing that look every time he acted like a bastard? Because he would, again and again.

There was no point in dwelling on the matter. He'd been over it more than a thousand times, and every time he did, he came to the same conclusion – that Lucie was better off without him. So why couldn't he just let her go and be done with it?

"Fuck," he breathed, on seeing the fist-sized dent he just made in the wall.

He moved some cleaning products in front of it and made his way out the closet, making sure no one saw him. Could have been anyone...

*

"Move out of the fucking way, grandpa!" Cutter muttered furiously.

He swerved around the Buick, pushing down on the accelerator. The rain pelted his SUV, rolling down the screen in waves. The wipers squeaked as they worked overtime to clear the view of the road. Cutter growled and squinted through the glass. Even with his enhanced vision he could barely see anything.

Vaguely, he considered that maybe he should slow down a bit, but he was too pissed and too eager to get home. His run-in with Lucie had made him horny, and his altercations with various other people throughout the day had depleted his short fuse. He wanted to get home, try and get his dick into a more manageable state, and then crash in front of the TV while drinking as many beers as he had in his refrigerator.

He had spent a frustrating hour on the phone to his bank, yelling at them to correct their mistakes, and trying to return the money they had put in his account. But, no matter how much he screamed, it seemed that they didn't want to do that. They were adamant that the money was meant to be his, and that someone – they refused to reveal who in spite of all his threats – had purposefully wired it to him. The perky bank employee on the phone suggested that maybe he had a rich uncle who had died. Cutter hung up at that point.

His team – or at least, the three remaining team members – had caught another case. It was a murder-suicide, which pretty much solved itself, so he sent Wayne and Avery to deal with it. Realizing that other agents were giving him the cold shoulder and looking at him askance, Cutter left and went out searching for homeless people who knew his hedgehog victim. Apparently, false rumors of his involvement in Clayton's death had started to spread. It didn't take much for people to think badly of you. The Agency was worse than fucking high school he thought, grimly.

So, to recap, one of his oldest friends had just been murdered, his colleagues suspected he had something to do with it, he was being treated like a leper at work, he was no closer to solving his case, he'd managed to treat Lucie like crap, he was in possession of two hundred grand of unaccounted money, and it was raining. *T-fucking-riffic.*

Well, at least the weather matched his mood. *Miserable.*

Dale tried to entreat him to go out to the bar, but damnit if he wasn't sick of that place. Knowing his luck, he'd run into Lucie and Doctor freaking Perfect. No, his current situation called for drinking alone.

His wolf was still out of sorts and off balance about what happened earlier. The sullen beast was sulking and licking his wounds. He really had been ready to tear both Diaz and Primrose new a-holes… Thank every god in the heavens that Lucie had been there to stop him. Maybe he should say thank you to her. *With his dick.* Cutter scowled at the thought. He was too damn randy to be thinking about anything with any clarity at that moment. Although, if he spent the night with her, she might forget about a certain lion shifter…

Cutter let out a roar as he pulled into his buildings parking lot. His fucking neighbor, Wozniak, was in his space. He fought the urge to jump out and shred all the dickhead's tires with his claws. Hey, the idiot was driving a Volkswagen Beetle – what kind of grown man drives one of those?! They were sweet sixteen gifts to perky girls.

Ah, what was the fucking point? Tires screeching, Cutter pulled into the spot next to him and only dented the Beetle ever so slightly when he slammed his door into it. He didn't have time to call Wozniak out on it; he had bigger fish to fry.

He trudged up to his apartment, shaking his head, dislodging the beads of rain from his body. He made his way into his apartment and froze. *Something was wrong.*

Quietly he closed the door behind him; standing stock still, he sniffed. He couldn't scent anybody else, but there was still a strange smell in his apartment. Usually, the place smelled of his natural scent, sweat, beer, pizza, and the shower gel he used – *it was blueberry shower gel, okay?* He took great pleasure in spreading it all over his body – well, he took great pleasure in spreading it up and down one particular part of his body.

Tonight, however, there was a strange lack of scents. There wasn't a new scent; it was just that the old scents – the ones that should have been present – weren't as powerful. It was almost like they were neutered - like someone had been spraying deodorizing spray, purposefully to cover up their own scent. Shit, maybe someone had been there.

Cutter pricked up his ears, trying to detect foreign noises. He heard the ticking of his bedside clock and the gentle thrum of his air conditioning unit. The patter of rain strummed against the windows. Through the apartment on his left, he heard the whiny barks of Wozniak's dog and to the right the muted sounds of a TV. They were watching a game show if he wasn't mistaken.

Hesitantly, Cutter stepped inside the hall, making the way to his kitchen. He didn't really think anyone was there, but he needed to be certain. He left the lights off and moved through the dark with stealthy ease. He may have blindfolded himself numerous times when walking through the apartment when he first moved in to ensure that he knew the layout. It was a trick he'd learned from his army days when he went on black ops missions.

As he made his way into the living room, a faint metallic smell caught his attention. He ignored it for the moment and checked out the other rooms. Finding them all clear, he returned to the living room and sought out the origin of the strange smell.

Cutter knelt on the floor and peeked under his battered and scarred coffee table – something that came with the apartment.

"What the fuck?" he breathed.

He ran to the kitchen and found a dishrag. He used it to pick up the gun that was lying underneath his coffee table.

"Where the fuck did you come from?" he muttered, eyeing the piece.

Cold dread poured through him. This definitely wasn't his gun. He didn't leave it there. So, someone broke into his apartment and left it there. Someone who managed to do it without leaving a trace other than a weird lack of smell. Why would someone go to the trouble of doing that? *Someone was trying to frame him.* That had to be it, otherwise, why go to all that trouble?

What the fuck was he going to do? He knew what he should do; he should take it directly to the SEA and tell them everything. But would they believe it? It was a pretty unlikely story. His gut instinct, one that his wolf actually agreed with, was to dump it. But, no, he couldn't. He was a federal agent – he couldn't just dispose of potential evidence? What if it was the gun that killed Clayton and Marie? They needed to analyze it. It might lead to the real killer. Although, if it was that gun, clearly the killer was confident that it wouldn't.

Fuckity, fuck, fuck fuck! What if he…

His thoughts were interrupted by ferociously loud banging on his door. He looked at the door, trying to sniff out who was on the other side. He didn't have to wait long to find out.

"Open up, Cutter, we know you're in there," yelled Diaz.

"We're going to count to three and then we're coming in," added Primrose. "Don't make us use force."

His wolf howled. They were here to arrest him. If they wanted to talk, they would have asked him to come into the office. They were going to arrest him.

No, he couldn't allow that. If he were trapped in a prison cell, how could he prove his innocence? No, he wasn't going to let them take him.

The door burst open, shattering off its hinges. Cutter dropped the gun as agents streamed into his apartment. He ran for the bedroom as agents shouted out stop and don't run. Yeah, like he was really going to stop! *When did shouting that ever work?*

A gun fired a couple of times and bullets seared their way into his leg and shoulder. Blistering pain immediately burned through him. His whole body felt like it was on fire. The urge to stop and clutch at his wounds was immense, but his wolf pushed him on, driving him to escape.

He heard Diaz yelling, "What the fuck, Harvey?"

Cutter ignored it and slammed his way into the bedroom. He was out the window and down the fire escape before they even realized what he was doing. The moment his feet hit the ground, he shifted, tearing through his clothes.

His wolf pounded away from his building, whining at the pain coursing through him but not daring to stop for a second. He ran and ran, slipping through back alleys until the sirens petered out. He stopped, panting and whimpering. The rain was slick against his coat and blood dripped off him, mixing with the water and swirling down the drain.

His body was cramping, and the pain was only getting worse. His vision started to blur, and he feared the worst – they had used silver bullets. At that moment, the poisonous metal was making its way through his system, tainting his body. He wasn't sure if he could survive them.

He felt the pangs of sadness over death, but he gave himself a mental roar and told himself to get it together. He wasn't dead yet. He pushed himself to move, and, instinctively, he started making his way to the one place he wanted to be at that moment.

CHAPTER ELEVEN

Lucie waved at the car again. She clutched her umbrella and inwardly grimaced as she plastered a fake smile on her face.

"Please, just go," she hissed quietly through gritted teeth.

With one final wave, the BMW drove away, and Lucie sighed in relief. Fumbling in her purse, she searched for her keys.

It had seemed like such a good idea to walk to work that morning. How was she to know the heavens would part, torrential rain would fall, and she'd grudgingly agree to get a ride home from work with Rick rather than risk being swept away? She was in absolutely no mood for his flirty behavior, and his smiles and honeyed words had just served to irritate her.

Lucie immediately felt guilty. It wasn't Rick's fault she was in a bad mood; she shouldn't blame him for it. She was sure any other woman would find him charming - *any other woman who wasn't hung up on a moody, asshole wolf who was confusing the hell out of her.* Her hedgehog sighed. Earlier, she thought they were really getting somewhere until he turned stone cold in the blink of an eye.

She got it. He struggled with his beast and his moods. But surely if today had taught him anything, it was that she was capable of dealing with him when he was at his most deranged. Why did he persist in thinking that she couldn't handle anything he dished out? Sure, they'd fight now and again, most likely over his unreasonable behavior, but they'd make up, too. She didn't expect their relationship to be cupcakes and sprinkles every second of every day, so why wouldn't he give her a chance? Maybe she should kidnap him, tie him to a chair and smother him with love and kindness until he gave in and admitted he loved her. *She was veering into Misery territory again.*

She pushed the door open, shook out her umbrella and gladly stepped inside. Oh, she was looking forward to a nice, hot bath, a glass of wine, and then a bit of alone time with her battery operated boyfriend. Yeah, she was pissed at Cutter, but having been in close contact with his body, and being pressed up against his obvious arousal, had definitely riled her up and she could do with a little tension relief.

Lucie shucked out of her coat and frowned as her hedgehog snuffled uneasily. *Something was wrong.* She prickled as she sensed another presence in her house. Please no, not an intruder. Would they mind leaving quickly so she could get on with her night? She hesitated by the door, trying to scent who or what was there. She almost gagged at the blood mixed with what? Wet dog? And something else, something else much more enticing; mmmm, it smelled like fresh apple pie - Cutter's delectable scent.

"Lucie..." breathed a faint voice.

Oh no, Cutter.

Lucie rushed into her living room; she flipped on the light and squealed as she found Cutter, naked, lying on her couch and bleeding profusely. Her eyes flickered up and down his body, taking in every inch of muscle and a collection of wicked scars that adorned his torso.

"Cutter!" she wailed as she ran to him, kneeling beside him.

His eyes flickered open, barely focusing on her. "Lucie," he smiled faintly.

Gingerly, she pressed the skin around the two wounds on his body. "Cutter, can you hear me? What happened?"

"Shot... silver bullets..."

"Oh! Cheese and crackers!" Lucie bit her lip. "How long ago? I don't want to turn you over," and doubted she was strong enough to do so, "do you know if the bullets are still in you?"

"Think… hour… yes…"

"We need to get you to a hospital."

"No… can't… no…"

"Cutter…"

"You smell like… like the lion," he murmured. Even in his weakened state, he managed to look furious. "He didn't… he didn't touch you?"

"Of course not," she growled as forcefully as a hedgehog could.

He raised a hand and ran his fingers over her cheeks. She choked back a sob at the tingles his touch elicited. How would she cope if she lost him?

Cutter rubbed his thumb over her bottom lip. "These lips… these are all mine. So beautiful… all mine."

"You're delusional," she said dismissively, ignoring the thrill she got from his words. "We need a doctor."

"No… no one but you."

She thought of Rick. "I could ask…"

His eyes flashed to dull amber. His beast may be in agony, but he wasn't giving up without a fight. "No… not the… fucking… lion… he's a… a… fucker."

If Lucie weren't so worried, she would have rolled her eyes. *At least Cutter was consistent.* She dithered for a couple of seconds before jumping to her feet. "I'm going to…"

"Don't leave me!" he cried hoarsely as he moved to stop her. He gritted his teeth as no doubt pain shot through his body.

"Relax," she ordered authoritatively. "I have to get those bullets out. I need some tweezers. Wait here," she added unnecessarily.

She ran from the room to the kitchen, she set her kettle going before digging out some tweezers, bandages, and filling a bowl with water and searching for a new washcloth. Her hands shook, but she didn't falter. She'd worked in an ER before; she could handle gunshot wounds. Of course, she was always assisting a doctor, and she'd never worked on the man she loved before… but darn it, she could do this.

Lucie pulled on some plastic gloves and carried everything into the living room. She bit back a whimper on realizing that Cutter's breathing was slowing. "No, no, don't you dare." She slapped his face a couple of times. "You are not allowed to die on me, mister. We still have unfinished business."

Cutter wheezed out a chuckle. "Not… going… anywhere…"

"You better not," Lucie muttered as she set about cleaning the wounds.

He hissed at the pain but forced himself to remain still. He was struggling, and she could only imagine what he was going through. While she remained calm on the outside, her insides, and her hedgehog were quivering worse than jelly.

"Okay, baby, you're doing really well."

"Thank you… nurse…I get a… will I… get a… treat?"

Lucie gave him a wan smile. "I need to dig the bullets out; I have some painkillers, but they will make you drowsy and…"

"Just… just do it."

"This is really going to hurt," she warned him uncertainly.

"I can take it," he told her firmly as he dug his fingers into the couch, claws and all.

Lucie let out a deep breath before grabbing the tweezers and digging into his shoulder. Cutter's whole body tensed and a deep growl reverberated in his throat. She worked quickly and felt collected enough that her hands didn't shake. She wouldn't allow herself to mess this up. Soon enough, she found the bullet and then moved to his leg and found the second bullet.

She sat back on her heels panting as if she'd run a marathon. *Yeesh, that was the hardest thing she ever had to do.* Cutter relaxed back into the couch and closed his eyes.

The worst of it was over. The silver was out of his body and it meant that he could actually heal himself. She considered whether it was worth trying to stitch up the wounds, but decided against it. His shifter healing ability would take care of that pretty quickly. He would be in some internal pain for a couple of weeks, but outwardly, he would be okay.

Collecting herself, she ran to the kitchen and got a fresh bowl of water to re-clean the wounds. She was pleased to find that they had already stopped bleeding; his body was already repairing itself. She had once operated on a shifter who had been shot with a silver shotgun cartridge, and his stomach was riddled with pellets. They couldn't find them in time to prevent him from dying. His screams of pain haunted her to that day.

She worked diligently and soon had his wounds clean and dressed. She looked up to find him watching her.

"Thank you," he said, his voice already stronger.

Lucie bit her lip as she looked over her bloodied and clawed couch. She could care less about the piece of furniture, but she didn't really want Cutter to fall asleep on it. "Do you think if I supported you, you could make it upstairs?"

He thought about it for a few moments before nodding. She disappeared to turn down the bed for a few minutes and returned with some painkillers. She stood over him, tapping her foot until he took them.

Soon enough, they were struggling up the stairs. He grunted at the pain of trying to move his injured leg, and she puffed at the effort of trying to carry a huge wolf shifter. *Thankfully, she only had a small house.*

She arranged him on her bed and pulled the cover over him. "Not exactly how I pictured getting you into my bed," she whispered to herself.

Cutter chuckled, and her cheeks turned pink. Clearly, she hadn't whispered that quietly enough.

"Lucie," he reached out and snagged one of her wrists, pulling her down to the bed, so she perched on the edge. "Thank you, for helping me. I don't deserve it."

"Hush now," she soothed while plumping his pillows.

"If I'm going to die…"

"You're not going to die," she corrected him forcefully.

Cutter shook his head. "If I'm going to die, I need you to know… I really want to fuck you before I die."

Lucie pursed her lips at his extremely unromantic sentiment. "How lovely." She decided to put that down to the painkillers. With any luck, they would do their work, and he'd be snoring in a few minutes.

"Come on, sweetheart. Let's just do it, but I'm sorry, I'm not feeling my best, you're going to have to do most of the work. Climb on."

He started pushing back the covers, unveiling his taut, delectable body and his surprising erection that pointed at the ceiling. Lucie made herself look away as she grappled with him to pull the covers back up. If she looked, she might actually be tempted to, as he said, *climb on.*

Finally, Cutter gave in, but only because he fell asleep, and she covered him. She sighed as she watched him sleep. He really was perfect - so masculine and so roughly handsome. She reached her fingers to his body, tempted to trace the scars that graced his frame. To leave marks, those injuries must have hurt, and silver must have been involved, but they didn't detract one iota from his gorgeousness. Now he had another two scars to add to his collection. Her hedgehog whimpered in pleasure at seeing him in their bed. *Although, she really wished it hadn't been under these circumstances.*

Lucie dragged her feet to the bathroom and took a long, scalding shower as she worried about what had led him to her. She couldn't even begin to guess. Someone had shot him – *well, yes, obviously.* Someone who meant to kill him - given that they used silver bullets, that was a definite. Cutter didn't want to go to a hospital. That part worried her the most. As much as she would like to think that Cutter came to her instinctively because he needed her above all other people, she knew his actual first port of call would have been a hospital. If he didn't want to go to one, it meant he wasn't prepared to answer any cops' questions. That didn't bode well.

Whatever had happened, she needed to wait for him to be coherent to find out. She was sure it would be reasonable. She was a little uneasy about that. She was sure that Cutter was a good guy, but he was also kind of prone to being hotheaded and irrational. She just hoped that whatever the situation, it could be salvaged.

Her fingers traced over her lip where Cutter had touched her. He said she had beautiful lips. He said they were his. *He was delirious from pain.* With a sigh, she finished her shower.

Lucie pulled on some flannel pajamas and curled up in the recliner in her bedroom reading a romance novel. She felt too wide-awake to sleep and wanted to be there in case Cutter needed her. Her eyes flicked between her book and her patient until, surprisingly, her eyes drooped and she slipped into slumber.

*

Cutter jerked awake and sat up abruptly. Ignoring the unusual throb in his shoulder, he bared his fangs and reached for his gun. He patted the bed beneath the pillow and frowned as he found it empty, and discovered that the bed sheets were soft and silken under his touch – that made a change from itchy and scratchy.

His wolf stopped howling and instantly calmed as the smell of blueberries enveloped them. Cutter looked around the room and his eyes alighted on the huddled form of Lucie. She looked tiny curled up in the recliner.

The events of the evening flooded back to him and he rubbed his fingers over the bandages Lucie must have placed over his wounds. He remembered getting shot – *damn hard to forget* – but everything after that became a little blurry. He escaped his apartment, and realizing that his injuries were serious – nigh on fatal – he made his way to the first person he could think of.

Perhaps he should have bit the bullet – pardon the expression – and took his chances at a hospital or a free clinic, but, honestly, he wasn't sure if he was going to survive, and he wanted to be with Lucie. A million regrets had fluttered through his mind, but chiefly among those was the fact that he wouldn't get to see his son again, and that he had never given Lucie a chance. In the absence of Dean, who was living with his mother back in Georgia, he ran to Lucie. Plus, Lucie was a nurse, so it worked out well. The sharp pain lingered, but he already felt better.

Lucie. She really was an angel.

He had some vague recollections of calling her beautiful and asking her to climb on top of his dick and have sex with him. He wasn't certain whether they actually happened or whether he was just dreaming saying them. He had numerous dreams where he did both those things. He generally preferred to be on top, be he wasn't averse to the idea of Lucie riding him.

Fucking A. Now he was turned on and too tired and in too much pain to do anything about it.

He looked around the room for a distraction. His fingers curled into the bed sheets. He wondered how she got them so soft. It was like sleeping on a marshmallow. His wolf rumbled peaceably. The beast was just happy to have finally made it into Lucie's bedroom.

Lucie's bedroom...

Cutter groaned and scrubbed a hand down his face. He was such an ass. He'd broken into her house, bled all over her furniture, forced her to perform impromptu surgery on him, and now he was hogging her bed while she was banished to a cold, cramped chair.

Yes, why didn't she just sleep with him? There was certainly room enough for two.

Cutter felt an irrational wave of jealousy. Yes, there *was* room for two. The bed was huge. Who had she been entertaining in that big bed?

He inhaled deeply and was more than a little relieved that all he could scent was fabric softener, lavender, and the heavenly, blissful and sublime aroma of blueberries – Lucie's scent. Good, no male scents were present.

At least he hadn't actually broken into her house. Lucie had a spare key to her back door in a hidden rock that wasn't fooling even the dumbest of burglars. It had been disturbingly easy for him to get into her house. He needed to have a word with her about security. The next person who broke in might not have as good intentions as he did. While his intentions veered on the impure side, they weren't bad – per se. She needed bars on her windows, six locks on each door, an alarm system, and possibly even a guard dog. His wolf wagged his tail approvingly. He made a mental note to speak to her about it in the morning. As for the rest… he'd buy her a new couch, and he'd worship at her feet for saving his life. Hell, it was true – she really had saved his life.

He sighed as he watched her sleep; her pink lips were slightly parted as her chest rose and fell rhythmically. Cutter switched on her bedside lamp, and soft light illuminated the room. Lucie moaned, stretched and snuggled back down.

Carefully, he swung his legs out of bed, grimacing at the pain. Whoever the fuck shot him was going to pay. Judging by what he heard, he was going to guess that it was Harvey. However, it was just something he overheard as he was jumping out the window, and he had been shot twice. It was possible he had been mistaken. Whoever it was, they were using silver bullets, and that was strictly against SEA policy.

He tested his weight on his injured leg and deciding that it wasn't completely unmanageable, he shuffled out the room in search of a drink of water.

Lucie was still sleeping and snoring sweetly when he returned. He marveled at the many shades of pink adorning her bedroom. He had no idea so much pink existed in the world. A long line of stuffed toys, porcelain and wooden figurines, all in the shape of hedgehogs, of varying sizes were arranged on shelves that wrapped around the room. She also appeared to have a large toy house standing on a dresser. He peered at it and recognized it as something a female cousin also had when she was a kid. It was like a plastic dollhouse, only the dolls in it were actually animals. His cousin had a huge collection of them. She had families of cats, bunnies, squirrels, dogs – you name it she had it. He and his brothers destroyed several of them when they younger while pretending to be Godzilla. That earned him a thorough smack from his stepdad and a lost summer working for his uncle at his garage. Lucie's house, *naturally*, contained a family of hedgehogs.

Lucie was too cute for words.

She caught his attention as she shivered slightly. No, he couldn't have that. It wasn't fair for her to be sleeping in a recliner; she should sleep in her bed.

He leaned over and pulled her into his arms, easily lifting her. Her curvy little body felt phenomenal curled against him. She fit there so perfectly - like she was made for him. His wolf almost purred in agreement. He arranged her on the bed and slid in behind her, pulling the covers over them both.

He traced his fingers over her face, brushing away stray strands of hair. He hadn't forgotten the events that had led them to spend the night together, but at that moment, he was choosing to ignore them. Lying in bed with Lucie by his side might be the last peaceful, happy moment he had for a while, and he wasn't about to squander it. No, he was going to grab onto the little bits of joy he had in his life – like he should have been doing over the past year – and he was going to enjoy them while he could.

Because if that day had taught him anything, in the blink of an eye you could be seriously screwed.

CHAPTER TWELVE

Friday

"No, Delmonte, don't sleep on my chest… you know I can't breathe," murmured Lucie, sleepily.

She used her free hand to slap listlessly in that general area, but frowned when she didn't come into contact with an overly hairy, lazy cat. She was currently cat-sitting for her ex-husband, and Delmonte had a habit of curling up right on her chest during the night. The fact that he was an extremely large cat – *who managed to terrify foxes* – made breathing very difficult. Lucie was trying to teach Delmonte to sleep at the end of the bed, but it was hard to do, especially given that he was, in spite of his size, absolutely adorable, and Lucie constantly caved and let him do whatever he wanted.

The pressure on her body actually felt different to Delmonte's presence. The whole left-hand side of her body felt like it was being crushed. It wasn't exactly a bad feeling; it was surprisingly comforting – like being trapped in a big jelly. She assumed, anyway; obviously, that had never actually happened to her. *Sure looked like fun in Cloudy With a Chance of Meatballs.* Instead of being worried, her little beast was actually purring contentedly. In her half-asleep state none of this made sense.

And just what was that thing remorselessly digging into her thigh? She burrowed her free hand under the cover to feel it and… *holy Zeus!*

Her eyes snapped open. She was definitely awake now. She turned her head to find herself staring into the sleeping face of Cutter. The events of the previous night hit her like a tidal wave. Right – Cutter was shot. She took out the bullets. She put him in her bed. She just felt up his morning woody!

Dang rabbit! She literally just fondled a man in his sleep. She pulled her hand away ignoring the thrill she had felt at having his hard, silken length throbbing in her hand. Oh, she was a dirty girl!

Maybe if she could just slip out of the bed before he awakened. Hmmm, no dice. He was half laying on her, with one arm over her torso, and a leg casually thrown over her. Given that he was about twice her size, she wasn't going anywhere.

He must have felt her squirming because his arm tightened around her, and pulled her even closer to his body. His face was now only a whisper away from hers. She could feel his breath against her cheek. *It was surprisingly minty.*

Lucie smiled at his sleeping countenance; his brow was slightly furrowed, and he even scowled in his sleep, but waking up to his face beside her, despite the confusing circumstances, was downright lovely. If they were together, they could wake up this way every day. Cue dramatic, over exaggerated, wistful sigh. Maybe she should just enjoy this morning. Who knew if it would ever happen again?

Frowning, she craned her neck to look at her recliner. She remembered reading a book while she watched him sleep and then nothing. She must have dozed off. Yet, how does that explain how she managed to get all the way over to the bed? Did she sleepwalk over in the middle of the night?

Double dang rabbit! Her subconscious must have made her do it. Well, he didn't exactly seem to mind, not if the position of his body and the size of his, *ahem*, wood was anything to go by. She only worried about what else she had been doing to him in his sleep.

She really needed to get out of bed and get back to that recliner. Yep, pretending nothing had happened. That was the way to go. She began shuffling away with a more concentrated effort.

"Where are you going?" demanded the gruff, stern voice.

In surprise, Lucie squealed and whipped around to look at him, promptly head-butting him. Cutter grunted as she let out a wailing ouch. Did he have a metal plate in his head? It felt like he had a freaking metal plate in his head.

Cutter rubbed his fingers over her forehead. "You alright?" he asked in amusement.

"Yes, you just startled me," she hissed. "Are you okay?" she grumbled, remembering that she had actually slammed her head into his.

He snickered. "Yeah, I've had worse."

Lucie bit her lip as her hedgehog whined for him. She should be more sympathetic. He was virtually knocking on death's door the day before. "I'm sorry."

Cutter rubbed a thumb over her cheek as his lips curled upward. "You saved my life; you have nothing to be sorry for."

Lucie twisted onto her side, propping her head up on her hand. A flash of, what she suspected was, disappointment passed over his face as his arm and leg slipped away.

"How are your shoulder and leg?" she asked trying to be clinical over the matter, and trying not to stare at the hard lines of his gorgeous chest.

He shifted slightly and winced. "They ache, but I'm fine."

Lucie glanced at the clock on the wall. She had a million questions she wanted to ask Cutter, but if she wanted to get to work, she doubted she had time to ask them all. More than that, she actually wanted just to stay in bed all day ogling his fabulous form. But, no, she did need to go to work.

"I need to look at your wounds again before I go to work."

Cutter's face tightened. "You're planning on going to work," he said slowly.

"Of course."

"Can't wait to see your boyfriend?" he spat as amber rolled through his fiery eyes.

Lucie rolled her eyes – not *this* again. Even her sweet, patient hedgehog – who could forgive Cutter anything – was bored by this subject.

"Ugh! Give it a rest," she exclaimed angrily before flopping onto her back and throwing an arm over her face.

She tried - she tried really, really hard - not to giggle, as she felt soft, questing fingers tickling their way over her stomach.

"Stop," she whined without much conviction. "Don't, I'm really ticklish."

Telling him that was a big mistake. He was relentless as she writhed, wriggled, jiggled, squealed and snorted beneath. Her hedgehog was virtually rolling around in an excited ball.

"Stop, stop!" she begged. "I give in; I give in!"

Her wayward hand slapped at his shoulder, and he groaned.

"Peanut butter and jelly! I'm sorry!"

Lucie spun back over and started pulling off the dressing she had applied to his wound. She let out a breath of release as she saw that his skin had already knitted back together. He was an exceptionally fast healer. Still, it was best that she didn't hit him in any of his afflicted areas again. She pulled off the dressing completely and dropped it in the wastebasket before pulling down the covers and doing the same for his leg wound. She made sure the cover remained artfully draped over his boy parts. Yes, she'd seen them before, but if faced with them again she might not be able to restrain herself. With an apology to her battery operated boyfriend, it was nothing compared to the real thing.

"The good news is you don't need more bandages on your wounds. Just be careful when you shower – they're going to be tender for a while."

"Peanut butter and jelly?" he repeated before roaring with laughter.

Lucie blushed as she pulled the covers back over him. "It's how I swear."

"That would explain the times I've heard you shouting kitty whiskers and noodles." He rested an arm underneath his head, stretching out his body before her devouring gaze. "You're an adult, you can say fuck, you know?"

"It's not polite to swear," she told him loftily. "When I was a teenager, we had a swear jar in our house, so we found other ways to swear. Besides, I think the number of times you say the f-word more than compensates for me not saying it."

"Say another one," he teased playfully.

She gave him a small, shy smile. "Fishsticks," she cooed.

Cutter ran his tongue over his teeth. "Ah, yeah, talk dirty to me, sweetheart."

Lucie felt a fluttering in her nether regions. Crikey, this version of Cutter – the flirt – was dangerously sexy. And all it took for him to come out of hiding was getting shot twice with silver bullets. That realization had her arousal dimming. Yes, she still needed to get the low down on that situation.

She scooted up the bed and leaned against the headboard. "I really need to get up and get ready for work."

Cutter fixed her with a steely gaze. "Don't go; call in sick."

Lucie opened her mouth to ask why but the words caught in her throat as someone knocked on her front door and rang the bell. The twangs of Greensleeves sounded throughout the house.

He sat up, looking around the room. "Who's that?"

"I can't see through walls; I have no idea."

She jumped out of bed and slipped on her fluffy, thong slippers.

Cutter gave her a leery look. "You weren't expecting anyone?"

"No, but it's probably just my neighbor. Sometimes she pops by and asks to borrow milk or my wi-fi or my car."

"Mooch," he muttered.

"She's a college student living with her grandma; I cut her some slack, and her grandma makes me peanut butter fudge brownies. They're *transcendent.*"

Even if Mrs. Wilkerson didn't, Lucie doubted she'd be able to say no to Marlowe. The young woman was blessed; she was both beautiful and charming. She defied anyone to say no the twenty-year-old sweetheart. Once Marlowe had you in her grasp, she bewitched you until you gave her whatever she wanted. Her eyes were hypnotic. Hmmm, maybe she should keep Cutter away from her. She didn't want her wolf being enchanted by the lissome young Miss.

"What if it isn't her?"

Lucie shrugged. "What if it isn't?"

Cutter tensed as the surprise guest banged on the door with more gusto. Greensleeves assaulted their ears again.

He got out of bed and rose awkwardly, testing his weight on his injured leg and pretending he didn't see the disapproval on her face. "If it's someone looking for me…"

"Why would someone…"

"Just tell them I'm not here," he interrupted brusquely.

Lucie considered arguing, but decided against it and nodded. "You're going to have to explain this all to me." Without waiting for a response, she grabbed a bottle of eau de toilette and sprayed in liberally around the room to cover his scent. "Just hide and stay quiet."

"Why would I need to hide?" he asked as he pulled on her robe. "Why would they be coming into your bedroom?"

Lucie pressed her lips together to stop herself from laughing at the sight of him in her fluffy pink robe. It was a little short on him, only managing to fall below his butt, and it gaped open over his massive chest. Thankfully,

Lucie was a little hippy, and it made it's way around his hips with material to spare.

"Good point, just stay quiet."

Lucie ran down the stairs, squirting the flowery scent. She pulled the door open expecting to see the smiling countenance of Marlowe, but instead she almost choked at coming face to chest with Rick.

"Oh!" she exclaimed. "Rick, what are you doing here? I mean, uh, hi," she giggled nervously.

"Good morning, Lucie," he said in his deep, reassuring voice. "Did you sleep well?"

Self-consciously, she fingered the collar of her checkered, flannel pajamas, and dreaded to guess at the state of her hair. "Yes, thank you," she mumbled.

"I'm just on my way to work early and I thought I would drop this off." He pulled out her cell phone from his pocket and handed it to her. "You must have dropped it in my car last night."

Lucie grasped it. "I had no idea." She checked it for missed calls or texts. *None – big surprise.* "Thank you for this, you didn't need to go out of your way. You could have just given it to me at work."

Rick waved a huge hand. "It's no problem; I thought you might need it."

"Well, thank you," she reiterated awkwardly, while praying that he wasn't expecting her to ask him in for coffee or anything like that.

His nose wrinkled slightly, and he sneezed lightly, most likely an effect of the perfume. "It was my pleasure; I'll see you at work."

Faintly, she said goodbye too, relieved that he wasn't expecting anything more from her, and relieved that he hadn't scented Cutter's presence. She let out a long breath she didn't know she had been holding, waited until his car drove away, and then ran back into the house, clambering up the stairs.

Lucie flew into the room to find it empty, or at least, so she thought. Huge arms wrapped around her; her hedgehog mewled, but not in fright, no, this was pure excitement. Gently but firmly, he pushed her against the wall. He bracketed one hand on either side of her head as he stared down at her. She licked her lips and pressed her thighs together. His macho manhandling really shouldn't make her this hot. So why was she envisioning him throwing her onto the bed and ravishing her senseless?

"Were you hiding behind the door?"

"What did he want?" growled Cutter.

Great, back to this again. Way to douse her rampant desire. "Nothing, he was just returning my phone." She nodded over to the floor where she dropped it.

Cutter's eyes flicked in that direction before he huffed. "Why did *he* have it?" He emphasized the word he to an insane degree.

"*He*," she exaggerated the word too, "drove me home last night when it was raining. But as you well know, I didn't spend the night with him, did I?"

He leaned back a little, slightly pacified. But, just as swiftly, his eyes bulged and he thrust his face into her neck, sniffing and dragging his jaw over her shoulder.

"What are you doing? That tickles," she whimpered. "I'm ticklish all over!"

Cutter pulled back and leered at her. "All over?" he rumbled.

"Yes," she breathed as her whole body flushed. "Why did you do that?"

"I wanted to scent you to make sure he didn't touch you," he admitted looking a little sheepish.

Lucie glared at him with open-mouthed exasperation. "You could have just asked me!"

He snorted. "You get pissed every time we talk about him."

She tried pushing at his chest to get him to move, but he was solid as a statue. "Son of a monkey! Only because you get all jealous and whack-a-doodle about it."

"First of all, *son of a monkey* – that just makes me hot. Second of all, I'm just trying to protect you from him."

She folded her arms under her chest, jutting out her breasts to get his attention. When she got it, she kicked him for staring at her. She was sure she didn't hurt him, but he did let out a sarcastic ouch.

"Resorting to violence, sweetheart?"

"Trying to speak your language, snookums," she taunted in reply.

His smoldering eyes bore into her. "You keep up all this sexy behavior and, injuries or not, I will throw you on that bed and fuck you senseless."

Lucie leaned against the wall as her legs almost turned to pudding. She and her hedgehog wanted to scream: yes, please! "Don't make promises you can't keep," she moaned before she could stop herself.

Cutter shuddered and closed his eyes. "You're making this difficult for me."

"Humph, it hasn't been difficult for the past year," she grumbled, softly.

"You've no idea what the past year has been like for me," he murmured before shaking his head. "Getting back to my point, do you have any idea why he left his last job?"

"Who?"

"The fucking lion shifter!" snarled Cutter.

Oh right! She was distracted by their simmering tension, and Rick completely slipped her mind! "No, I don't know and I haven't asked him – that's how little I…"

"He had to leave because he screwed his boss' wife," he told her triumphantly.

"So?"

"So!" roared Cutter.

"Why should I care?" she asked in a bored voice. "I mean I feel for his boss, but it's really none of my business."

He pushed off the wall with a grunt and began pacing up and down her bedroom. He looked like an oversized, wild animal in her little pink habitat. *The male wolf has approached the female hedgehog; his growling mating call only heightens the arousal the small female feels for him.* She really had to stop watching nature documentaries.

"He's trying, almost successfully, to get into your panties..."

"Not successfully!" she objected hotly.

"That guy's a lion – you know about male lions, don't you?"

"Umm..."

He stopped and stood with his hands on his hips. In her pink robe, he looked like a very comical superhero. "They're all horndogs!"

"Not like wolves, hmm?"

Cutter clucked his tongue and started ranting. "Male lions have harems of wives. They're into multiple marriages, brainwashing, forcing women into becoming homemakers, kidnapping – the list is endless. You'd probably have to share him with six other women, and I'll bet he'd make you quit your job at the SEA."

"As long as I can be Tuesday," she retorted, cheerfully.

He gave her a look of disgust. "You're not taking this seriously."

"You're right, I'm not, because you're just being silly. I know there are some male lions that have harems, but not all, and they're not the only species of shifter that does. I don't think that they have to kidnap and brainwash women, however. Also, I don't know if Rick is one of them and, frankly, I don't care. Because, and let me make myself clear, I. Am. Not. Interested. In. Him." She gave him her sternest, no-nonsense nurse look. It was the one that said: *lay still and let me take your temperature with my rectal thermometer.*

Cutter looked a little stumped by her response, but he wasn't about to give up his anger at the lion so easily. "I don't like that he saw you wearing so little. He purposefully turned up at your house early to catch you just getting of bed." He looked her up and down from head to toe. "And look, he was rewarded by seeing you in your sexy nightwear."

Was he kidding? Lucie peered down at her pink and white, thick, flannel, checkered pajamas. The only parts of her that were showing were her feet, hands, head and a sliver of neck. "Sexy? These are completely shapeless, and there is very little of me left to cover."

"Humph."

Lucie was marveling at his comeback before something niggled at her. "How do you know how Rick left his old job?"

"Ugh…"

"Did you check up on him?"

"No…" The lie was obvious; guilt was written all over his face.

"You did, didn't you, why?" Lucie was more curious than anything.

"Well, after our last medical examiner tried to kill Erin and was stealing people's organs, I thought I should check him out."

She cocked her head to one side. "Fair enough."

Cutter relaxed a little on seeing that she didn't want to pursue that any further, but he tensed right back up at her next question.

"Are you going to tell me what's going on? Hard to believe but I don't find men bleeding all over my couch every night, and I'm kind of curious about what happened."

He sucked in a breath and hesitated for a few seconds before telling her, "I'm being framed."

Lucie waited for him to say more, but nothing was forthcoming. "You'll have to give me more than that, you can't just show up at my apartment almost bleeding to death, tell me someone if trying to frame you, and expect me just to say okay, well I'll leave you to it."

"It's a long story," he admitted with a wince.

She sat down on the recliner and prepared to listen. "Then you better start talking, because I really do have to get to work."

Cutter rubbed the back of his head and gave her a grim look. "I'm not sure I want you involved in this."

"I'm pretty sure it's too late for that."

"I'll have to go to the very beginning," he warned, probably hoping she would just give in and change her mind.

"I'm all ears," she told him warmly.

With a huff, he lowered himself to her bed and started, *albeit grudgingly*, talking. About four years ago, Cutter went undercover to try and take down Nicolas Maroni – a wolf shifter and crime boss in Ursa. He was into human trafficking, laundering money, drugs, contract killings... the list went on and on. He was suspected of kidnapping and torturing his business rivals to death. Cutter managed to get a job working for Maroni through a slightly unhinged old pack mate called Bruce who already worked for the wolf.

Clayton was his handler; only he and a few other agents at the SEA knew what he was doing. They suspected Maroni already had a mole in the SEA, so the operation was very hush-hush. They made a big show of making it look like Cutter got fired from the SEA. No one doubted that Cutter would do something that would warrant his dismissal.

For months, he worked to earn the trust of Maroni while feeding as much information as he could back to Clayton. Finally, just over three years ago, they had enough evidence to bring down Maroni, and the cherry on the top of the cake? Cutter found an informant willing to reveal the SEA mole. All he had to do was get his informant an immunity deal, and a promise of witness protection, and he would reveal all. *Sadly, it never got that far.*

Maroni found out that Cutter was still working for the SEA. He and his men caught him and locked him in a silver cage – about the size for a large dog. Maroni left his torture up to Bruce. Feeling betrayed, Bruce spent hours carving his skin with silvers knives before rubbing silver dust into the wounds. It was how he obtained his large collection of scars. Cutter felt like he was dying; over and over he wished Bruce would just give up and kill him.

Eventually, Cutter really was dying. Feeling cocky, Bruce opened up the cage, and with the last of his strength, Cutter launched himself at him. They fought, and through sheer force of will, Cutter was the victor. He wasn't at his full strength, but he just about ripped Bruce's throat out.

He managed to get out and find help. He virtually collapsed on top of a vacationing family's minivan outside of a Pancake Factory restaurant.

By the time he woke up in the hospital, it was to find that Maroni had been caught trying to flee. He was under arrest for a variety of different charges. Maroni wasn't talking, and no one would offer him a plea deal to talk. *They wanted him in prison for the rest of his life.*

They didn't find out who the mole was, though. When Cutter didn't check in, fearing the worst, Clayton orchestrated the arrest of Maroni and sent a tactical team to retrieve their informant. As soon as they stepped foot in the informant's house, it blew up, killing each and every one of the tactical team. The informant was already dead by that point. They found the remains of his body; his neck was broken. The killing of the tactical team was just plain vicious.

They suspected the mole tipped off Maroni to get out of town, but thankfully, Maroni didn't move quickly enough. And they suspected the mole of killing the informant before he got the chance to speak.

Lots of rumors abounded that Cutter was the mole. He was put through a rigorous investigation from II, but they could never prove anything. After everything he went through with Bruce, nobody honestly thought he was the mole.

Clayton was forced to retire; he shouldered the blame for the deaths of the tactical team. The old eagle was furious and couldn't let it go. Cutter figured he had been obsessing over the case for the past three years.

For a while, Cutter couldn't cope with what happened to him. He was a wreck until Gunner kicked him into gear and Cutter followed him to Los Lobos to start his life afresh.

However, then Clayton turned up in secret, someone murdered him, a woman who worked for Maroni went missing, the SEA suspect everything is linked to the Maroni case, and an unidentified gun was found in his apartment. Shortly before some very heavily armed SEA agents burst in and shot him with silver bullets. *Was that it?* Yeah, that felt like it.

Lucie chewed on her cheek as Cutter huffed impatiently, waiting for her to say something. She had no idea about any of this and here, she thought she knew just about everything about him! She was so naïve. Her hedgehog mewled in sympathy for her strong wolf. Nothing he had told her made her love him any less; actually, she may even love him a little more.

"So, you think Clayton was still investigating the case? Still looking for the mole?"

"Yes, I don't think he ever would have let it go. I told him over and over it wasn't his fault, but he couldn't help himself. He felt guilt for what happened to those agents, and guilt for what I went through. Hard to believe but he liked me."

She gave him a reproving look. "It's not hard to believe; you're surprisingly lovable."

Cutter grunted. "I think only you and Clayton have ever believed that, and he'd have killed me if I ever told anyone I think he found me lovable."

"Didn't Internal Investigations pursue the matter?"

"No, the guy in charge was adamant it was me, he just couldn't prove it."

"That's ridiculous!" she exclaimed passionately and she felt her eyes flicker to the blackness of her beast. "You wouldn't torture yourself!"

"He believed it was an extreme way of trying to prove my innocence," he said disgustedly.

"So maybe Clayton was onto something, and we have no idea what. Maybe Diaz can…"

Cutter silenced her with a fierce look. "Diaz already has a suspect; he won't investigate further. I'm almost positive the gun I found is the murder weapon."

"Surely that's circumstantial."

"I already have connections to all the victims, a lot of money in my bank account, and a murder weapon at my apartment. There's too much to explain away."

"You've been sewed up…"

"Stitched up."

"You've been stitched up. Now, what?"

Cutter clenched and unclenched his fists. "Now I have to figure out who's doing this."

Lucie walked over to stand in front of him. He watched her closely. She placed a hand on his arm; his muscle flexed under her touch. "I won't tell anyone you're here; you can stay as long as you need."

"Thank you," he murmured. "I knew I could rely on you. I'll leave as soon as…"

"No."

Cutter raised his eyebrows quizzically. "No?"

"No, with your injuries, I want you to stay here so I can monitor you." Plus, having him in her house brought her no end of personal satisfaction. She wasn't ready to let him go just yet. She probably wouldn't get another chance like this.

"I feel fine, a little achy, but fine. The bullets barely slowed me down. They haven't impeded anything if you catch my drift." He waggled his eyebrows about, and yes, she understood what he meant - heck, she woke up with the 'evidence' that morning, pressing against her leg. "I mean I can still fu…"

"Okay! But, sure, now you feel fine, but who's to say that your leg won't fall off in a couple of days time?" Lucie fixed him with a wide-eyed stare.

He let out a scoff of disbelief before his expression became much more uncomfortable. "Is that a possibility?"

Probably not, but she wasn't about to admit that and let him run around the city being hunted. "Who knows? Not that many shifters survive silver bullets. You probably only survived out of stubbornness."

"I don't want to lose my leg. I guess I better stay here."

He didn't say it very graciously, but she and her hedgehog were jumping for joy. They weren't exactly the best circumstances, but hey, beggars couldn't be choosers.

"Right, I am going to get ready for work, and when I get home tonight, we are going to have a long conversation about just what the heck we are going to do."

*

Cutter pounded his fist on the bathroom door. He knew Lucie could hear him. Even through the thick door and with the water running, she could hear him.

She told him she was going to work. He told her it wasn't a good idea. She insisted she had to go. He forbade her from going. She became all prickly over his high-handedness. He told her he would tie her to the bed if he had to. She got in a huff and ran into the shower. *Yep, he couldn't see how he could have handled it any differently.*

He was looking out for her; he was trying to take care of her, and she was just being downright willful. His wolf grumbled. If the beast had his way, they would have just tied her to the bed and completely skipped the argument. It would have saved time.

Lucie started singing in the shower. Cutter threw up his hands in defeat and stomped downstairs in search of food. Damn headstrong female who wouldn't do as he told her.

He was on his third bowl of sugary cereal as Lucie bounced into the kitchen. She looked pink-cheeked and radiant in a pair of blue slacks and a pale blue shirt with daisies printed all over it. She beamed at him and his ire at her rigid resolve to go to work melted. He defied any man not to give in to her sunny smile. Not that they would have the chance, he had an enormous and disturbing urge to kill any man Lucie smiled at. Spending the night in her bed, surrounded by her scent, and with her soft body pressed against his, had only made his desire for her skyrocket.

He returned her smile, and a delighted blush bloomed over her cheeks.

"You're not going to work," he growled, roughly.

Her face fell, and she pursed her lips. "Yes, I am."

"It may not be safe for you," he reasoned as his wolf barked at him to look for some rope. "People know that you, uh, you know, that we..." He trailed off uncertainly.

"Exactly!"

"What?"

Lucie poured herself some coffee in a to-go cup as she patiently explained. "If they're looking for you, and then I don't turn up at work, won't they be a little suspicious?"

Cutter snorted. "You're giving Diaz an awful let of credit to put those two things together."

"Besides, Rick has already seen me today. He knows I'm not sick."

"Asshole," he muttered under his breath. *The fucking lion was determined to ruin his life.* "I don't like it. I'm telling you to stay here."

Lucie scrunched up her face in displeasure. He really was concerned about her, and he wasn't just riling her up to get her to throw one of her soft curse words at him again. Okay, maybe that factored into it a little. Those cutesy little curse words made him all hot and bothered for some reason.

"Son of a mother trucker!" she murmured and Cutter bit back a grin as his wolf panted. "Look, I'll be surrounded by people; I won't be in danger. And if anyone asks me about you I'll… well, I'll fudging think of something."

"You said fudging on purpose to win me over."

She looked at him through her eyelashes. "Is it working?"

"Yes," he groaned.

"Excellent, now I want you to go lay down and relax. You're still healing; you need all the rest you can get. And you should probably stay away from the windows. There are a lot of curtain twitchers in my neighborhood." Lucie looked around the kitchen. "I don't suppose you've seen a cat running around here, have you? He's about the size of a small dog, has long white hair, and a cute, smushy face."

"Smushy, really? You're wasting your time with a cat. They're pets for ninety-year-old women or eleven-year-old girls."

"Cat hater," she teased.

"I saw him as I was coming in last night. I may have growled at him, and he may have run in the opposite direction."

"Oh."

"Sorry." He wasn't very sorry at the time. *Cute, smushy face his ass!* The beast saw him in his wolf form and growled – yes, actually growled – at him. Cutter almost had to take a bite out of the white, hairy monster before he skulked away.

Lucie didn't seem overly concerned. "It's fine. He's a natural explorer. He has a chip. If he doesn't come back by tonight I'll track him."

She picked up a banana and a granola bar for breakfast and started to leave. He stood up and pulled her to him, his hands rested on her shoulders. Damn, her nipples were hard and poked through her thin shirt, straining toward him. What he wouldn't give to rip her shirt off and feast on her beautiful orbs. He leaned a little more heavily onto his injured leg than he should have; the agony dispelled his mounting lust.

"Be safe," he told her. "Someone is out to get me; I'm sure of it. And if they killed Clayton and Marie Beauchamp, they wouldn't hesitate to hurt you, too."

"But I'll be at the office and…"

"And I still suspect an SEA agent is involved," he said, trying to hold back his fury.

Lucie paled and quieted. "I'll be careful."

"Unless I can persuade you to stay here," he suggested hopefully. His wolf held his breath.

"You can't."

Cutter grunted. Yeah, he wasn't really expecting that to work. He was loath to ask, but if she were mulishly insisting on going, then maybe she could help. "Can I ask you to do something for me then?"

"Yes," she replied immediately. Her face lit up, and he almost told her to forget it in that instant. The last thing he needed was for her to get overexcited, but if the last twelve hours had taught him anything, Lucie was more than capable of dealing with anything that he threw at her.

"I need copies of some case files."

"How do I get them?"

"Ask Jessie if she'll provide them. I need copies of Clayton and Marie Beauchamp's files. Jessie is working the cases, and I reckon she might trust me enough to give them to you. If she doesn't, and she tells everyone that you asked for them, then tell them where I am and tell them that I forced you to do it."

Lucie's brow creased. "I'm not going to tell them that."

Cutter shook his head; *this point was non-negotiable.* "Promise me you will, or I really won't let you leave this house. I will pin you down - my wolf's thrilled at the prospect." The animal really was; he was almost drooling over it.

"Like to see you try," she taunted.

"Would you?" He was genuinely interested; he wanted to know whether her ardor for him was still as strong as it was before all this mess started. And before she thought he was sleeping with a peacock shifter.

If she weren't careful, he really would drag her to bed and remedy the ache that had been building up over the last year. In fact, who needed a bed? The kitchen counter looked perfectly adequate.

Sadly, Lucie relented. "Fine, I promise to turn you in if they catch me, does that make you happy?"

"A little."

"Relax, and let yourself heal – I'll be back as soon as I can, and then, we'll try to figure something out."

"We? Oh, no, you're not getting involved in this."

"I already am involved and since I don't have enough time to argue about this further, let's put a pin in it and argue about it when I get home."

Reluctantly, he agreed and let go of her shoulders. "What am I supposed to do all day while you're at work?"

Lucie smirked. "Read a book, take your mind off what's happening, help yourself to my collection. They're about moody alpha males who fall helplessly in love with perfect, sweet women who are far too good for them, and then refuse to admit it because they're too repressed. You can probably relate."

Cutter gave her a sour look, and she blew him a kiss as she made her way to the door.

"Either that or listen to music or surf the web on my iPad. There are some men's clothes in the left-hand side of my closet and fresh towels in the bathroom – help yourself to both, and I'll see you later."

He grunted, and she escaped out the door before he really comprehended what she said. *Men's clothes?* His wolf snarled. What the heck was she doing with men's clothes?

Oh, his little hedgehog was going to have some explaining to do when she got home.

CHAPTER THIRTEEN

Lucie walked along the corridor toward Jessie's office. She wasn't doing anything out of the ordinary, but she felt as conspicuous as if she had a big neon sign over her head flashing the words 'up to no good.' Everyone seemed as friendly as usual, but was it her imagination, or were they looking at her a little funny?

She returned a hello to a penguin shifter from research. *Yeah, it was probably her imagination.* Or it could be the copious amount of perfume she was wearing. To cover Cutter's scent, she practically sprayed an entire bottle all over herself. Rick almost choked when she popped by his office to say hello earlier. Perhaps it might repel him a little – that wasn't a bad thing.

She felt like James Bond. Or maybe Don Smart might be more accurate. No, even he was a little too competent for her. What was the character from Spy Hard called? Oh, this was going to bug her all day.

Hopefully, she just wouldn't run into Diaz or any of his team. She had turned the matter over and over in her head, and no matter what, she knew she had to help Cutter. She didn't know Clayton, but she knew that Cutter had considered him a friend, and she saw that his death affected him. Cutter wouldn't have hurt him. He may bend the rules every now and again, but he was a good guy. And she wanted to find whoever was trying to frame him - even her hedgehog was gung ho about that. *He was her honey bunny, and whoever hurt him needed to pay!*

A part of her tried to be logical and tried to tell her that he needed to turn himself in, but the mushy, hopelessly devoted part - that would have gotten down on the ground and barked like a dog if he'd asked - scoffed at the idea. *She seriously hoped he never did ask her to do the dog thing.* She might be stubborn about some things with him, but ultimately, she loved him, and she wanted to help him. She just hoped that Jessie felt the same way. Not about the love thing, no freaking way, no, she just hoped Jessie wanted to help.

Lucie slipped into the squirrel shifter's office and gave the redhead a wave.

"Hi!" she squeaked with fake brightness. "I brought you a cruller. How are you? How's everything going? Strange weather we're having, right?" She cringed as the words fell out of her mouth. She may have missed casual by a tiny little bit.

Jessie raised an eyebrow as she took the cruller. "You okay? You seem tense."

Lucie's eyes darted around the room nervously. "So do you, do you have cameras in this room?"

The squirrel looked at her curiously. "Only ones controlled by me and I always have the microphones switched off. Have you heard about Cutter?"

"Sort of."

"Do you know where he is?" she asked, shrewdly.

"Perhaps."

"People are going bananas about him, they reckon he's a mole."

Lucie sucked in a breath. "What do you think?"

Jessie scrunched her nose, pushing her glasses up her face. "I don't think he's a mole."

She blew out a breath of relief.

"But I don't think it's a good idea for him to hide like this," she added, reprovingly.

"He thinks he's being framed," Lucie blurted. "And when they came for him last night they shot him with silver bullets!"

Jessie blinked at her. "Are you sure?"

"I had to dig them out of him – I'm sure." She shivered and her beast whimpered on remembering the pain etched into his stoic face.

"They shouldn't have done that, that's against SEA policy," Jessie muttered half to herself. "What do you want from me?"

"Copies of the files, please," said Lucie with a pleading look.

Jessie thought it over for a few beats. "Okay."

"Thank you."

Jessie downloaded them onto a memory drive and handed it to her, just as Diaz and Primrose strode into the room along with an unpleasant looking wolf shifter. She had just enough time to stash it in her bra. She didn't really think they would, but if they asked her to empty out her pockets, they definitely wouldn't find it *there*.

The wolf shifter gave her a dismissive look. She recalled doing his physical. He was a member of Internal Investigations and a cranky patootie to boot.

"What are you doing here?" demanded Primrose.

Diaz ignored the hyena shifter. "Hey Lucie, you okay?"

"Yes, absolutely, one hundred percent okay – terrible weather we're having." Her hedgehog huffed at her. Never mind Spy Hard, she was at the Abbot and Costello level of competence. Reel it in, she thought.

"Sure is," agreed Diaz with an easy smile. "Have you seen Cutter recently?"

"I saw him at work yesterday. I heard he punched a hole in the wall of the janitor's closet on level seven."

She didn't enjoy doing it, but throwing him under the bus for that minor thing might actually lead them to believe that she wasn't willing to cover for Cutter. Aside from that, she knew he had been the one to create that huge hole. It was the janitor's closet where they had their brief interlude – the odds were good that he did it.

"Not since then?" prompted Diaz.

"No, is everything okay?" she asked with ridiculously big, innocent eyes.

"Of course," Diaz smiled.

Lord, he had a good poker face. Primrose just looked unimpressed, and maybe it was because she was feeling guilty anyway, but she could have sworn the hyena shifter didn't believe her.

The II agent stepped forward and fixed her with a frosty smile, and she shuddered involuntarily. There was something very odd about him. "You'd tell us if you had, wouldn't you?"

"Well, yes, is there a reason I wouldn't? Is something going on?"

"That's none of your concern," snapped Primrose.

Lucie's eyebrows shot up. *Blistering barnacles, what had her panties in a twist?* She was usually so calm and professional.

Diaz winked. "Nothing to worry about."

"Well, I better go. Bye everyone." She walked away uneasily, forcing herself not to look at Jessie. If a look passed between them, the others might be suspicious.

She didn't realize her hands were shaking until she reached the elevator, and her fingers trembled over the button. There was no way she was going to admit it to Cutter, but both Primrose and that II agent freaked her out. If she said anything to him, she suspected that he really would try to tie her to the bed, and that definitely wasn't her thing. Although, she could see the benefit of tying Cutter to the bed - that idea seemed like a lot of fun.

Her hedgehog huffed as she scented whiskey, stale beer, an abundance of body spray, and lemon pledge for some reason. *Dale.*

"Hey Lacey, how's it going."

"Actually it's…"

"Have you seen Cutter today?"

"No, have you?"

She noticed his eyes were bloodshot and roved up and down the corridor as he talked to her. He was another wolf shifter who creeped her out. He turned up in odd places at odd times. In particular, he kept showing up in the medical bay. She found him there again yesterday. He claimed he wanted to see Helga about a massage, but when the six-foot-two she-bear entered the room, he fled in the opposite direction.

"Nah, he seems to be AWOL. Tell him I'm looking for him if you see him, will you?"

"Sure."

"Thanks, Lacey."

"Actually it's…"

Dale walked past her; his arm brushed against hers and – ugh – he sniffed her.

He gave her a look of interest that she hadn't seen before. Or at least she hadn't seen it aimed in *her* direction before.

"You know that color looks nice on you, brings out your eyes." This was followed up with an unnerving, slightly leering look.

"Umm, thanks," she mumbled pressing the elevator button again.

"Are you free this evening? Maybe we could go for a drink together."

Her hedgehog sniffed. "I can't, I have plans with a friend."

And if she hadn't, she would have made plans. She regretted she wasn't ballsy enough to say that out loud. Isis or even Avery would have. Although, Dale probably wouldn't have been offended. She bet women rejected him all the time. His personality certainly seemed to suggest that was the case.

"Another time, Lacey." He shrugged and walked away.

"Actually it's… oh, what's the point?"

Lucie almost leaped into the elevator when it arrived; only when the doors closed did she relax and fish out the memory stick from her bra. Her heart was pulsing wildly in her chest. Well, at least James Bond had nothing to fear from her. She was not cut out for deception.

*

Cutter alternately grunted, growled and frowned as he pawed his way through Lucie's wardrobe. She had a lot of male clothing – a disturbing amount for someone who was single. His wolf prowled unhappily. *Who the fuck did it all belong to?* At first, he was elated to think it might be her father's or her brother's, but he had the impression that she didn't have close relatives.

Worse still, it was all too big for him! He was six-foot-three with a wide chest that would make a superhero envious, and yet, they were too big for *him*. The clothes were designed for someone at least three inches taller and at least five more inches on their chest. Who the fuck was this giant who dared keep clothes at his hedgehog's house?

Her phone started ringing, and Cutter ambled downstairs to listen and see if whoever it was would leave a message. He was still wearing the pink robe and was surprised at how comfortable it was. Truthfully, he was loath to take it off.

Two people had already rung and left messages today. The first was from someone called Malcolm, telling her he had extended his honeymoon by a week and asking her if she would continue collecting his mail. The second was from her dentist confirming an appointment.

The phone stopped, and Lucie's chirpy recording echoed in the quiet house. "Hi! I'm not in right now, but if you leave a message I promise to get back to you as soon as I can." Beep!

"Hi, Lucie, it's Xander."

Cutter and his wolf snarled – in the same way they did when Malcolm's voice came through. With any luck, it would be the same kind of message – from a *married* man.

"I haven't heard from you in a few days, call me, okay? Anyway, I'll be by on Saturday. I can't wait to tell you about Italy. Love you."

How long he stared at the machine, he couldn't say. He tuned out his irate wolf and focused on looking at it, memorizing every inch of it. His first instinct was to rip it out of the socket and hurl it across the room. But no, he could be reasonable. It wasn't the machine's fault. He didn't hate the *machine*. He hated *Xander*. Xander who had just come home from Italy. Xander who was threatening to visit on Saturday. Xander who loved Lucie. *Fucker*.

To his irrational mind, the fact that Lucie had spent the better part of a year throwing herself at him, and he had spent that time rejecting her, was irrelevant. No other man had any right to claim he loved her. Was he selfish? Yes. Was he an asshole? Yes. Did he care? No.

The phone rang again, and he almost snatched it up, ready to yell at Xander that Lucie wasn't interested. But, instead, he dug his claws into his palms and waited to hear the message.

Followed by Lucie's greeting message and the beep, a much more welcome voice tickled his ear, had his wolf prancing like a puppy, and made his manhood stir. "Hi, it's me. If you're there, pick up."

Cutter grabbed the phone. "Lucie," he breathed. "Are you okay? Are you hurt? Did that fucking lion try anything with you? Do you need me to rescue you? Answer that last one first."

"Cheeses, that's a lot of questions."

He snickered. *Cheeses*. Seriously, the dumb curse words made him ridiculously hot. He was so twisted.

"Okay, umm, let me get this straight. In answer to your questions:

absolutely not, fine; no and definitely no. How are you? How are your shoulder and your leg?"

"What? Oh, yeah, fine."

Apart from a few twinges when he tried to use his afflicted arm or leg too much, he barely even noticed. While obsessing over his predicament, and those fucking clothes in Lucie's closet, he'd pretty much forgotten about his injuries.

"I don't want to talk too much over the phone – there are ears everywhere…"

Cutter groaned; she'd been watching too many spy movies.

"But I managed to get what you needed."

"Good. I guess there's only one thing left to ask - why do you have men's clothes in your wardrobe?"

Come on – she already told him what he needed to know about the case. Now, he had to move onto the second thing that was bugging him. He had his priorities.

"That's not important," she sighed down the phone.

"Disagree."

"Look I'll be home as soon as I can."

He pursed his lips. "Humph, just be careful. Has anyone asked about me?"

"A few people," she admitted, reluctantly.

"I don't like you being there alone."

Lucie giggled indulgently. "I'm not alone; I'm surrounded by people."

Cutter snorted. "Yeah, that's what Erin thought right before she ended up being chased through the building by the last crazy medical examiner. You should stay away from the new medical examiner, just in case."

"Umm hmmm, try to stay out of trouble, and call my cell phone if you need me.

"Ditto, sweetheart."

They hung up. His wolf grouched at him for not broaching the topic of Xander. But Cutter decided he wasn't going to - it was none of his business, and Lucie didn't have to explain herself to him. No, he had bigger things to worry about. He was going to take the high road and just delete the phone message. There – problem solved... for now.

At that moment, his whole future was in the balance. He worried that he wouldn't be able to sort this mess out. He worried about what would happen to his son if he went to prison. He worried about Lucie being in danger.

He needed a distraction. He should shower and dress. But first, he needed to look through Lucie's underwear drawer. For men's underwear, naturally. He wasn't looking through her underwear because he got a perverted pleasure out of imagining her wearing them – *no siree*. The fact that he always went commando seemed to have slipped his mind at that moment.

*

"Hey!"

Lucie screamed and spun around to find Avery leaning against the wall and Wayne smirking, sinewy arms folded over his chest. She cursed her hedgehog senses as she pressed the heel of her hand into her heart; why did she not sense they were there?

"Hey, guys." She smiled weakly.

Avery looked around. "Whatcha doing out here?"

Lucie shrugged exaggeratedly, almost cracking her shoulders. "Just getting some fresh air. Ha ha ha."

She took a deep breath and started choking as she inhaled two lungfuls of cigarette smoke. That probably wasn't the best excuse given that she was standing next to the smoker zone.

Avery raised her eyebrow. "Really?"

"Actually I'm thinking of taking up smoking again. I used to smoke but then I quit. I gave up after my divorce because it was getting so expensive, and given that I couldn't rely on my husband's income anymore, I had to choose between smoking and wine, and I decided to give up smoking. But now that I'm in a new job, I have more money, so I'm thinking of starting again. So, I decided to come out here and inhale some cigarette smoke so that I could get acclimatized to it again."

Phew, she may have just pulled this off. Hard to believe that she hadn't prepared that speech in advance, or that she hadn't ever smoked.

"Wow, that was a weirdly detailed explanation," mused Avery.

Wayne pulled a pack of cigarettes and a lighter out of his back pocket, tossing them both to Lucie. "Here, have one on me."

She fumbled as she caught them. "Oh, umm, thanks."

They both watched as she struggled to get the packet open. "Uh, don't think that you have to keep me company."

"We're on break," explained Wayne.

Finally freeing a cigarette, she tapped it against the packet – *she'd seen people do it in movies.* She placed the cigarette between her lips and started flicking the lighter.

After a few moments, Wayne pulled the cigarette from her lips. "Wrong end; I guess it's been a long time since you had one." Lucie blushed as he turned it around and put it in his own mouth, quickly lighting it and taking a drag.

"That your boyfriend on the phone?" asked Avery.

"Sort of."

"Something's going on with Cutter."

"Oh?" she squeaked, feigning surprise.

"Yeah, you don't happen to know what, do you?"

Both Avery and Wayne looked at her closely.

"Me?" Her voice sounded like she had inhaled a tank of helium.

"Nobody will tell us anything," grumbled Wayne, stamping out his cigarette with a little more force than necessary.

Avery scowled. "All we know is that Cutter isn't here, and Diaz, and some guy from II, want to know where he is. He's not answering his phone, and the director told us to butt out of it."

"I don't know why you think I know anything."

Avery snorted as Lucie squirmed. "We're not idiots. We can see that they think Cutter had something to do with the recent deaths."

"There're lots of rumblings around the building about II trying to arrest him," said Wayne in disapproval.

"Do you two think he had something to do with the deaths?" Lucie asked, timidly. Her hedgehog grumbled; wasn't it better not knowing?

Avery laughed in surprise. "Cutter? Nah. I can't see him going to the effort of covering up a conspiracy."

"He's more likely to beat the person up and then grumble about how the guy had it coming," agreed Wayne.

The lioness gave her a shrewd look. "But if I were Cutter, I'd go to the person who cared about me most if I wanted to stay hidden."

Lucie flushed and looked at her feet. "I don't know what to say."

"Well, wherever Cutter is, I just hope he gets the message that he can count on us if he needs help."

"Yeah, I hope he gets the message, too," mumbled Lucie.

Avery bit her lip. "Be careful, Lucie, if things really are bad…"

"Just stay out of trouble," intoned Wayne in a deep voice.

"I will."

She left the two agents as quickly as possible, lest they change their minds and decide to grill her about Cutter's activities. She spent the afternoon trying to avoid Rick and glancing at the clock every ten minutes. She almost cried with relief when the clock finally hit 5pm.

The SEA didn't really close at 5pm, but most workers had the day shift, and there was a nominal crew of nightshift workers – most of which tended to be vampires and nocturnal animal shifters who couldn't get on with being awake during the day.

Lucie grabbed her purse and was almost out the exit when she was waylaid by Rick, dressed in jeans and sporting a genial smile. *It was such a shame that he really did nothing for her.*

"Hey, Lucie, you fancy getting a drink together?"

She flustered. "Oh, umm, I can't. I have plans with a friend."

He nodded, but she could tell he didn't really believe her. Well, that was his problem. She moved past him.

"It's not doing you any good to pine after someone who doesn't want you," he told her, harshly.

Lucie paused and looked back at him over her shoulder as her beast wailed in furious outrage.

The lion shifter softened a little. "You're better off cutting ties with Cutter, considering the situation."

"Situation?" she asked innocently, clutching the memory stick Jessie had given her in her palm.

"Haven't you heard the rumors?"

"Only that people are looking for him," she lied, surprisingly effectively.

"He's wanted for questioning for two murders."

Rick sneered as he said the words. *Apparently Cutter couldn't count on Rick to be on his side.*

"Oh, my," she muttered inching to the exit.

"I'm sorry to have to tell you."

He really did look apologetic, and she felt a little guilty for lying to him, but she didn't have time for this, but, perhaps, this was the time to nip Rick's interest in the bud.

Lucie forced herself to look sad. "It's fine. And I know you're right, I shouldn't pine for someone who doesn't want me. I'm trying to get over that, but I wouldn't want to rush into something with someone else either while I'm still in pine city."

"I understand that I need to be patient."

She faced him and bit her lip. "But, can you understand that even if you are patient, it still doesn't mean that the result you want is the one you'll get in the end?"

Rick looked at her as if she were an alien – one with six heads, red skin, and tentacles. "You mean, even if you weren't in love with the wolf…"

"I don't think I'd want to be with you either; I'm sorry," she said softly, with as much regret as she could muster.

He raked his fingers through his hair. "Wow, I've never, ah…"

"Never been rejected by a woman?" *Why was she not surprised?*

"No, not by a woman like you."

"A woman like me?" she repeated incredulously.

"Well, uh," he stammered, realizing he may have made a mistake, "one of your ilk."

"Ilk?" she squeaked as her hedgehog growled.

The lion held up his hands in surrender. "I'm not saying this right. Pride lionesses can be cold and haughty, they really make lions work for them, and they reject men out of spite, but shifters like you…"

"Are usually grateful that handsome predators like you are interested in them?" she interrupted in a mixture of amusement and amazement.

"Quite frankly, yes."

Arrogant dillweed! "So you assumed I'd just swallow the whole 'looking for a mate' schtick, and I'd be falling at your feet to let it be me?"

Rick chewed on his cheek. "You're angry."

Talk about Doctor Perceptron, she thought, snarkily.

"No, just flabbergasted, to be honest. The men I've dated could hardly be considered prince charmings, but they've never expected me to be grateful to be with them."

"I didn't really mean…"

She held up a hand. "I'm glad I could give you this new experience of being rejected by someone of my *ilk.*"

"Lucie, I'm sorry."

"We can still be friends, Rick, but no more flirting," she told him, firmly.

"You're right. Lucie, really, I didn't mean to offend you."

"It's fine," she replied snippily.

Actually it was fine; while she was a little put out by his egotism, this whole confrontation actually solved her problem. She managed to rebuff Rick's advances without even coming out of it as the bad guy. *Win-win situation.*

"Great, see you tomorrow?"

Lucie frowned. "Tomorrow?"

He smiled. "At the softball game."

Right… sugar puffs! She'd forgotten, so much happening and all that… he stood watching for a reply.

"Yes, see you then," she said absently.

*

He watched as the chubby little hedgehog shifter left the building. She looked around self-consciously to make sure no one was watching her. The dumb bitch didn't even glance in his direction. Hedgehogs really were a lesser, pathetic species. How Cutter could even give her the time of day was mind-boggling. A wolf and a hedgehog together, was there anything more grotesque?

He knew Cutter was hiding underneath the hedgehog's skirt. He'd run like a coward, straight into her waiting bosom. He could just burst into her house and kill them both, but no, he wanted Cutter to suffer.

Let the traitorous wolf have his fun with the hedgehog. It will be even more delicious when she's dead. Three years is a long time to wait, but, finally, Cutter will get what is coming to him.

CHAPTER FOURTEEN

"Cutter! Cutter, come on, baby, wake up."

Lucie came home to find Cutter snoozing in her bed. At first, pleased that he was taking some much-needed rest, she was soon horrified as he started violently yelling, and lashing about on the bed. Her animal howled at her to help him.

She grasped his shoulders, clinging to the scorching, sweat-beaded skin as he thrashed underneath. Unable to control him, she straddled his waist, pushing her weight down on him.

"Baby, you're having a bad dream, wake up," she pleaded.

Lucie yelped as his fingers roughly clamped onto her ass and with a lurch toward her, his eyes snapped open. Violent amber eyes regarded her with confusion. He blinked, and slowly the amber tinges seeped away.

"Lucie?" he choked out.

She pushed his shoulders back down to the bed. "Hush, it's okay, you were having a bad dream. You're okay; you're fine."

"Lucie," he groaned more forcibly.

Instead of removing his hands they were kneading her buttocks, manipulating her fleshy orbs. She licked her lips as she felt heat pooling between her legs. He rocked her over his stomach. The material of her panties rubbed against her sensitive folds, making her wet and needy. She needed to get out of there before she did something embarrassing like scream 'take me now.'

"Do you need anything?" she whimpered, barely able to concentrate.

Cutter pushed her down his body until she pressed against his arousal. "You."

Lucie squealed as he flipped her onto her back. With a flash of claw, he ripped through her clothes and pulled the tatters away from her body. Her hedgehog mewled in joy.

"What are you doing?" she asked breathlessly.

His lips curled into a feral grin. "Can't you tell?"

He snaked down the bed and parted her legs before she even roused the energy to pretend to protest. She almost darted off the bed as he swiped his tongue over her drenched slit, but she stayed grounded thanks to his fingers firmly, yet gently, digging into the flesh of her thighs. He suckled on her clit, licking and biting it before burrowing his tongue in her channel.

Lucie's fingers dug into the sheets as she cried out in ecstasy. It had been so long since she felt pleasure like this – *not that she had ever felt pleasure quite like this before.* Nothing could compare to the decadence a simple flick of his tongue afforded her. Her body started tightening as he plunged a finger inside her and teased her clit. She could feel it, the burning need for completion, growing, expanding, hurtling towards the stars, until...

The son of a nutcracker stopped.

She wailed. "Why did you stop?"

Cutter bared his fangs and crawled up her body, settling his large frame between her thighs. His hot erection teased her entrance as his lips descended on hers. He scorched her with his kiss, plundering her mouth and dueling with her tongue. She wrapped her arms around his neck, deepening the kiss, wanting to inflame him the same way he did her.

Their first kiss. She almost giggled into his mouth as she realized he had kissed her down *there* before he had kissed her mouth. Well, no one could accuse them of being boring.

She whimpered as he pulled away from her swollen lips. They'd never been used in such a brutal yet sensual way. That was who he was – harsh but passionate. He kept her away from him for a year, fearing that she couldn't handle his rough nature, but he was so wrong. Without it, he wouldn't be him, and she loved every lip-smacking, yummy, perfectly imperfect inch of him. She wouldn't want him any other way.

"Do you want me?" he demanded, throatily.

"Yes," she moaned trying to lower her hips towards his straining manhood.

"I want us to come together during our first time," he rumbled.

And with that declaration, he drove himself inside her. With a slow yet determined motion, he didn't stop until he buried himself to the hilt. She gasped at the satisfying feeling of fullness. She hitched her legs around his waist and nodded at him that she was okay, and he started stroking inside her with hard, fast thrusts.

Neither of them would last long; they were both too worked up, too desperate to unleash the release that had been bubbling for the past year. He pounded and crashed against her body, mercilessly filling her over and over. He was so big he hit every sweet spot, every nerve ending. She loved how tight she was around him, how her muscles stretched and strained to contain him.

His breathing grew harsher, and his movements became even more ferocious. They raced toward their mutual climax. With a bellow, Cutter drove inside her one final time and exploded, triggering her release.

She screamed his name as her hedgehog howled in happiness. She shook her head from side to side, ignoring the urge to sink her sharpened teeth into his neck. She wanted to claim him, to take him as hers, but she resisted – for the moment. Instead, she lay back on the bed, panting and shivering in orgasm.

With a groan, Cutter collapsed onto her waiting body, pillowing his head on her breasts. She clutched him to her and whispered the word 'mine.'

*

"No regrets?" Lucie asked, uncertain as to whether she would like the answer.

She lay atop him, listening to the steady beat of his heart. His hands skimmed up and down her back, massaging her skin. She felt exhausted, satiated, and thrilled, all at once. After their first coupling, they made love two more times. Their second time, he flipped her onto her front and entered her from behind as his fingers wormed their way under her body and stroked her clit. The last time was less frantic and more sensual; he had her ride him as his hands and mouth caressed her breasts.

"Fuck no," he answered firmly. "You?"

"Jinkies no."

His big body shook with laughter. "Don't start with that dirty talk or I will have to have you again."

"Hmmm, haven't I worn you out yet?"

"Not even close," he growled at the suspected challenge.

"Your bullet wounds didn't affect you, did they?"

She couldn't hide the worry from her voice. Silver bullets were not to be sniffed at. She would advise anyone else to wait at least a week before even attempting intercourse. She was desperately thankful that Cutter didn't need that long.

"What do you think?" he replied cockily.

"Mmmm, I don't think so, but then I have nothing to compare it to."

"Perhaps we should keep having sex and you can rate my performance," he suggested.

Lucie pretended to ponder his generous offer. "It could be like a study of how long it takes for a shifter's sexual prowess to return after getting shot by silver bullets. Alright, in the interest of science, I will make this sacrifice and have lots and lots of sex with you."

Cutter chuckled. "You're so selfless, sweetheart."

"Darn tofind.'" She traced the scars on his chest with her index finger. "What was your dream about?"

He tensed under her slightly. "About being in the cage; the torture."

"Do you have nightmares often?"

"Most nights," he admitted. "It's why I sleep alone."

"Bad dreams are hardly…"

"After it first happened, I woke up screaming one night. I was, uh, married at the time. My wife tried to wake me, and I almost strangled her. I came to my senses and stopped, but the damage was already done."

Lucie already knew about his marriage and divorce, vaguely; she wasn't privy to any of the finer details, however. "She left you?"

"Not at first. We had separate rooms. But, when it became clear that I wasn't getting better, she found someone else."

"Bitch." Lucie's hand flew to her mouth as Cutter started roaring with laughter, almost dislodging her from her perch on his body. "Cheese and rice! I can't believe I just said that!"

"I appreciate the sentiment," he guffawed as he actually wiped away a tear and rearranged her on top of him. "But, don't think badly of her. We shouldn't have gotten married in the first place – we never really loved each other. She wasn't just thinking about herself. She did what she had to, and I don't blame her for leaving."

"Humph." Yet he married *that* woman, and Lucie struggled to get him to go on a date with her.

"Last night was the first time in over three years that I hadn't slept alone."

"I'm sorry about that," she murmured, flushing.

"Why are you sorry?"

"I shouldn't have gotten in bed with you like it; I was very…
presumptuous." *Honestly, she didn't just go crawling into any man's bed!*

"You didn't. I woke up and carried you to the bed."

Lucie sat up to look at him. She straddled his waist, and he rested his hands
on her hips. "You did?"

Cutter grinned. "Yeah."

"Why?"

"Maybe I wanted the company. Besides, I seem to sleep really well with
you beside me."

Not that she wanted to discourage this, but… "How do you know? It's
only been one night."

"You're right; maybe I should do a study of my own. I should sleep next to
you as much as possible to see the effects it has on me – you know, for
science."

"Mmmm, I love science," she cooed.

"Who do those men's clothes belong to?" he asked unexpectedly, nodding
his head in the direction of her closet.

"Oh, they're just my ex-husband's," she replied dismissively before leaning
down, and flourishing butterfly kisses on his neck.

Cutter sighed in distracted contentment for a moment before coming to his
senses. "Why the fuck do you have your ex-husband's clothes?"

"He stays over when his partner is away on business. He doesn't like to be
alone."

She sped up her kisses, hoping to get away from the obvious questions that
were about to blast in her direction. *No such luck.*

"Your spare bedroom doesn't have a bed," he hissed. "Tell me he sleeps on the couch."

"Ummm…"

"He sleeps in your bed?!" roared Cutter.

Lucie yelped as he shot up, wrapping his arms around her as they sat nose to nose.

"He's gay!" she blurted.

"Are you just saying that to make me feel better?" he asked suspiciously.

"No, he really is gay. It's why we got divorced. By that time, we were more like roommates anyway." *Not that they were ever really passionate at the start of their relationship.* "But, when he finally realized and then clued me in on something everyone else had already noticed," *all their friends had seen the signs months ago apparently!* "We got a divorce. We're still close friends. Maybe it's a little weird that he shares my bed…"

"A little?!"

"But given that we have zero sexual attraction to one another, we don't see it as a big deal, and neither does his partner."

"I still don't like it," he muttered grumpily.

"Then I'll tell him he can't stay here again."

Cutter actually appeared surprised. "Just like that?"

"Just like that." Maybe the arrangement was a little weird, and she wasn't about to argue over such a small matter. Her ex hardly ever slept over; it wasn't worth getting riled up. Besides, giving into this would work in her favor if she wanted him to do something for her, like… like get married. Hmmm, maybe that was asking a bit much.

"Well, good. Uh, thank you."

Lucie sighed and leaned her forehead against his. As much as she had enjoyed their passionate lovemaking and unusual pillow talk, they couldn't put off what needed to be done forever.

"What's wrong?"

"Apart from you technically being on the run for murder?"

Cutter groaned. "Right. Yeah, no more enjoying ourselves. We need to get down to business."

CHAPTER FIFTEEN

Cutter skimmed through the files that Lucie had acquired for him on her laptop. He didn't know what came over him when he had woken to find Lucie straddling him earlier, but he was glad he gave in to it. He couldn't imagine anything more perfect than the time he spent with Lucie in her bed. It wasn't just the sex – it was *her.* Being with her, talking to her, he came alive with her. His wolf howled in agreement.

He'd been a fool. His wolf was also in agreement on that front. However, he was still worried about hurting her. He still didn't think they should be together in the long run. Sure, she soothed him now, but what would happen if something really happened to piss him off? What would happen if he had a really bad nightmare? She may think she can handle it, but would she feel different when waking up to find his paws wrapped around her throat? No, it was too risky. He'd give her as much of him as he could, and then he'd walk away and let her get on with her life.

In the meantime, he needed to make things clear with her before she got the wrong impression and started picking out wedding centerpieces.

"Lucie, I," he bit his lip, unsure of how to proceed.

Lucie, having donned a tight pair of shorts and a vest after he destroyed the clothes she had on, frowned at him as she snuggled and petted the monstrous Delmonte. The white beast had returned while they were enjoying the last moments of their post coital bliss. The animal let his presence be known by jumping on the bed and hissing at Cutter. The fact that Lucie immediately jumped off him to give the feline intruder a kiss and a cuddle didn't bother him whatsoever. *Mental harrumph.*

"Uh oh, I know that look, that's the 'we just had sex but I'm dumping you look.'"

"I'm not dumping you," he grumbled, "and how exactly do you know that look?"

Lucie rolled her eyes. "I guess you're about to give me some spiel about how wonderful, magnificent, incredible I was in bed – all true, of course."

"Of course," he agreed wholeheartedly.

"But that you think we should just be friends because you're in no position to be in a relationship."

Cutter rubbed the back of his head. Well, yes, that was pretty much the topic of conversation he was trying to broach.

"It's okay, don't get your pink, fluffy robe in a twist over it," yes, he was wearing her robe again – it was comfortable, "I get it. This is hardly the time to play Romeo and Juliet. In case you hadn't noticed, I was really horny, too. It was great, and I wouldn't say no if you wanted to do it again. So, thanks."

"Uh, you're welcome?"

His wolf was just as baffled as he was by her response. Shouldn't she be begging him to reconsider? Why did he feel like he was the dumpee? Could it be that his little hedgehog wasn't as enamored with him as he thought?

Cutter watched as she went back to petting and cooing the feline horror. *Stupid cat.* He pulled his pink robe – what? It is really comfortable – around him more tightly, and glared at the laptop screen. His wolf let out a feral growl as he came across the crime scene pics. The fucker who did this was going to pay.

Huffing, he slammed the laptop shut and rested his hand on top. Lucie raised her eyebrows but didn't say anything, not about that, anyway.

"Are you hungry? I'm famished," she declared.

He had to admit he hadn't eaten much all day, and their vigorous bedroom activities had depleted his energy somewhat. *Although…*

"What are you offering?" he asked, waggling an eyebrow suggestively.

"I don't really want to cook; I was thinking about ordering Chinese."

"I guess," he said sullenly, "if nothing better is on the menu."

"Chinese it is," she laughed.

"Won't it look weird if you order enough for two?"

Lucie shimmied over to the phone and pulled out a menu. Her ass jiggled mesmerizingly in her tiny, tiny shorts – they barely provided full cheek coverage.

"No, I usually do. I can never decide which dish I want so I always order too much, and then I have the rest for lunch the next day."

She put in an order for various dishes before pulling out a pad of paper and a fluffy, pink pen. "Okay, we need a plan of attack."

"We need a pen that looks like it was barfed up by a parrot to make a plan?"

"Yes, we do."

Cutter tapped his fingers on top of the laptop. "I don't think you should be a part of this. It could be dangerous."

"But, couldn't you argue that I've already helped you, so I'm already in danger?" She said it with such a sweet smile – it didn't seem to match her words at all.

"No one knows I'm here; you'll be fine, but maybe I should go before…"

"No, no, no, no, no!" she cried, raising her voice ever so slightly. "We've already been through this. It's best that you stay here given the severity your injuries."

He gave her a leer. "You didn't think they were severe when you were trying to suck me dry with your pus…"

"I helped you," she interrupted, blushing, "and lied to my bosses for you - you are not ditching me."

"It's not about ditching. I'm… I'm no good for you."

His wolf whined at him; he wasn't just talking about the messy situation in which he found himself.

Lucie snapped her fingers in his face. "Hey, you zoned out there for a moment. Look, I'm a big girl," his eyes automatically dipped to her abundant breasts stretched in her tight, tight vest. She snapped her fingers again with a sigh. "I decide what's good for me – not you. And as with all the things that came before you - ice cream, cake, nachos, reality TV, and bikinis - I have decided that, in spite of popular opinion, they and you are good for me."

Cutter nodded, and he had only one thing to say about that, "Bikinis are *very* good for you – but not in public, only in my company. In fact, you don't have to bother wearing anything at all in my company."

She ignored him and started scribbling on her notepad. "Okay, so we guess Clayton discovered something, something that apparently dragged him to Los Lobos and made him need to speak to Sadie Beauchamp."

"Yes."

Lucie started chewing on her pen but grimaced and spat out a feather. "Any idea what?"

"No."

"I see," she rubbed her lips together, "now what?"

Disappointed by the end of the bikini discussion, and sporting an erection that was downright uncomfortable, Cutter thought it best to try and throw himself into the case.

"I don't think we'll get anywhere with Clayton, and according to the file, Sadie Beauchamp only arrived in town a few weeks ago, so no one really knew her. However, Marie and her boyfriend only arrived a few days ago. Apparently, the night Marie died, he was in police custody for attacking a police horse."

"Charming," she murmured.

"According to Diaz's notes, the boyfriend is a drug dealer and user. He wasn't forthcoming about Marie, and wasn't exactly cut up about her death, or that her sister was missing. Diaz suspects the asshole knows something but won't help. I wouldn't mind talking to him."

"Do you know where to find him?"

"LLPD arrested him outside the Slippery Newt; it's a bar on the other side of town. I'll try there first."

"We'll," she corrected him, cheerfully.

"I'll," he rumbled in a much less cheerful tone.

Lucie gave him a beatific smile. "You can't go alone; it might be dangerous. What if you get into a fight with him?"

Cutter almost burst into hysterical laughter at the thought of his mild-mannered little hedgehog getting in the middle of a fight between him and a drug dealer. His beast, on the other hand, reverted to his desire to tie her to the bed to keep her out of trouble. *Wisely, he kept both reactions to himself.*

"You're not an investigator."

She nodded and seemed to take that on board. "Well, maybe Wayne or Avery…"

"I don't want to drag them into this." It was bad enough that he had pulled Lucie into the madness, possibly endangering her and ruining her career.

"Well then, I'm all you've got," she declared, gleefully.

"But it might be dangerous," he reiterated for what felt like the fiftieth time, although he doubted she was going to listen to him – *why start now?*

"Ha! Danger's my middle name… well, actually it's Martha but you get my drift. And, what other choice do you have?"

He folded his arms over his chest and almost thrust out his bottom lip like a petulant child. "I don't like it."

"You don't have to like it."

"Well, just stay out of the way."

"If we're only going to talk to him, it won't be an issue. I mean, you're going to be low-key, right? You're still recovering from your injuries, and you're a wanted man remember?"

Cutter smirked. "Wanted man? This ain't the wild west, sweetheart. But don't worry, I can be subtle."

*

"I don't think you're being very subtle," said Lucie standing back in the middle of the rooftop. His little hedgehog wasn't keen on heights. He felt better with her being away from the edge, too. He was already paranoid about her getting hurt, he didn't need to add tripping and falling off a roof to the list of things he needed to worry about.

Cutter looked back at her over his shoulder. "Really? Huh."

The coyote shifter in his paws, wriggled, squirmed and squealed again. Cutter gave him another shake and told him to, "Shut the fuck up."

Okay, maybe dangling the good-for-nothing dickhead, upside down, from the top of a building, wasn't the subtlest option, but he could be doing something a hell of a lot worse.

Luck was with them – well, a tiny bit of luck in comparison to the events of the past week – and they found Marie's boyfriend, Max at the Slippery Newt. They followed him back to Sadie's apartment. It was still a crime scene, but no SEA officer guarded the door, and they caught him breaking in and looking for anything he could steal and sell. It was his belief that everything in that apartment was rightfully his since Marie was dead. He was taking Sadie's belongings so he could sell them – to make up for future loss of earnings that Marie's death caused him. On hearing that garbage, Cutter didn't think twice about dragging the slimy coyote up to the roof and giving him an airing over the side of it.

"Where's Sadie?" barked Cutter.

"That judgmental bitch? How the fuck should I know?"

"Did you ever meet Nicolas Maroni?"

The coyote stopped struggling against Cutter's steely grip on his legs. "No."

His wolf huffed. He didn't even have to scent him to know that was a lie.

"Try again," he rumbled, throatily.

"Fine, I may have done a little business with Maroni back when we were in Ursa. But Sadie, she worked for him in one of his clubs. He whored her out to his friends."

"Give me a reason not to drop you?"

"You can't kill me," whimpered the coyote.

"Please, even I'm starting to think he'd be doing the world a favor!" called Lucie.

The coyote let out a grunt of frustration. "I know that Sadie was banging someone from the SEA."

Cutter pulled him over the ledge and dumped him on the rooftop. He loomed over the shaking coyote. "How do you know?"

He tried to scramble away, but Cutter put a boot on his chest. At least he and Lucie's ex shared the same shoe size, even if the clothes he was wearing were baggy.

"She told Marie; Marie told me."

"Who was it?" demanded Cutter.

"I don't know."

"Not helpful."

Cutter reached down to pick him up again, and the coyote squealed. "I don't know their name but I saw them."

"Keep talking."

The coyote stammered through his speech, "I was thinking I might be able to get some money out of her, so I followed Sadie the other night when she went out to meet him and…"

"And?"

"It wasn't a *him* – it was a *her*." The coyote imparted the information in a whisper as if it was the most shocking news he had ever told anyone.

"Her?"

"Yeah, some uptight-looking blonde hyena, tall and skinny, dressed in a business suit. They met outside the park and got in the hyena's car; they argued, and then they started making out, and then Sadie left."

"What were they arguing about?" asked Lucie from his left elbow. Her curiosity had drawn her closer to them.

"I don't fucking know; I can't hear through car doors."

He gave Lucie a look of derision that was soon wiped off his face as Cutter snarled at him. "Anything else?"

"That's all I know."

Cutter stared at him for a good couple of minutes, and when the coyote didn't add anything, he nodded. "Stay out of trouble, or I will come back, and I will drop you next time."

*

"Are you thinking…?"

"Yes," he replied curtly. "Primrose."

After leaving the coyote on the roof, ignoring the urine smell that emanated from him, they were returning to Lucie's house. Cutter fidgeted in the passenger seat. He didn't know why, but it felt wrong to allow himself to be driven by a woman. He could stomach another man driving, but with a woman, he felt the need to be in the driver's seat. His wolf concurred – *he should be in charge*. It was probably his asshole alpha tendencies trying to push forward. The only reason she was driving was that it was her car, and she wouldn't go anywhere unless she drove. She muttered something about his driving skills being only surpassed by the contestants on Wacky Races.

However, he couldn't deny that watching her drive definitely had perks. For one thing, she had only thrown a sweater over her outfit and was still wearing her deliciously barely-there shorts. An expanse of creamy leg flesh jiggled every time she worked the pedals. He had to fist his hands to stop them from creeping over to caress her. The last thing they wanted was an accident.

"I know she's a bit…ummm…"

"Of a total bitch," he supplied.

"Yes, but I can't imagine Primrose would be the mole. What he said, it's a big surprise, isn't it?"

"I know, the idea that she would…"

"Yeah, who knew she was gay? I always envisioned her just not having any girly parts, and plugging herself into the mains to power down each night."

"That's not what I meant," he sighed. "I was still talking about her being the mole."

"Right, but you don't know for certain she is."

"No, but I have a theory. Sadie worked for Maroni; she met Primrose; they fell in love or whatever. After the arrest of Maroni, Primrose kept Sadie, and somehow Clayton found out that Primrose was the mole. Clayton was trying to persuade Sadie to testify against her, so Primrose killed Clayton and made it look like Sadie disappeared."

Lucie pulled into her garage and turned to face him. "Why kill Marie? And why would Sadie need to disappear?"

Cutter slumped a little in his seat. "Okay, so my theory doesn't quite cover everything."

"Are you thinking what I'm thinking?" she asked as she chewed on her plump bottom lip.

"Fuck, I hope so," he said as he ran his hand up her thigh. Hey, they were parked now, where was the harm?

Lucie gave him a mock look of outrage. "Not about that! Well, yes, but later. We need to talk to Primrose."

She didn't slap his hand away, so he took that as an invitation to leave it there and started tapping his fingers against her thigh.

"Yeah well, if I turn up at her house I'm as good as in prison."

"Not me though."

The rhythm of his fingers stopped as he glared at her. "Oh no, you're not going to her alone."

She widened her eyes and licked her bee-stung lips. How can one innocent, little hedgehog disarm him so thoroughly with hardly any effort at all? His wolf moaned impatiently, and his manhood strained his pants. Funny, when he first donned them, he was sure they would be too big for them. He had visions of running around and them falling down, baring his ass to the world. Now they felt like they were fucking strangling him.

"What if I were surrounded by dozens of SEA agents?"

Hmmm. His fingers started moving again, gradually working their way up her leg as they tap-tap-tapped. "You mean at work on Monday?"

"Or sooner, like tomorrow at the softball game."

Fuck, he'd forgotten about that. He was actually due to play. Lucie attended all the games but was only a reserve player. She was hardly gifted when it came to sports, but she was a team player, and always prepared to help. Although, he did have to admit that watching her run was a heavenly, pant-tightening experience. It was a wonder she didn't knock herself out with her magnificent assets. He smiled at his lewd thoughts.

"I'm not sure that's a good idea. If she's the mole, then she will be dangerous."

"There will be a crowd of people – not just agents, but also their families, the other team, and all their families. The place will be heaving. What are you doing to my leg? It feels like morse code."

"Oh, it is; I'm sending you a message."

Lucie leaned over, so her lips were inches from his. "What does it say?"

"Lucie, get over here and fuck me," he murmured against her mouth.

"So romantic!" she whispered playfully. "So, it's settled then; I'll talk to Primrose tomorrow."

"No, it's too dangerous. I forbid you from…"

He forgot his objections as her lips met his.

CHAPTER SIXTEEN

"I can't believe I let her talk me into this," Cutter grumbled to himself.

With a snort, his wolf – *and only company* – agreed. Of course, at the time when she was suggesting it, the fact that she was shimmying into her pair of little, white shorts she always wore for softball games didn't help.

Ugh, that was it, that was his kryptonite – *shorts*. For some reason seeing her in them sent him wild and turned him into a bumbling idiot. Yeah, seeing her naked was great, too – that was a no-brainer. But there was something about shorts. Maybe it was the hint of her nakedness underneath, the way they barely skimmed her ass cheeks, and the idea that he could just snake a finger inside them and find his prize...

Cutter shook his head. He needed to start dressing her in muumuus.

He had tried railing at her not to go to the game, but that didn't work. Instead, she had teased him with a saucy wiggle of her hips, and asked whether he was afraid she would get hurt, or afraid that she would have a good time. Frankly, neither option appealed to him.

As a compromise, Lucie suggested borrowing her neighbor, Malcolm's van. Since he was still on vacation, he wouldn't need it, and he wouldn't mind if she borrowed it. That way Cutter could hide in the back of it and still be near the game in case she needed him.

Grudgingly, he agreed to that plan. He wouldn't have if Lucie had actually given him all the facts. It wasn't a van – *it was an ice cream truck* – and now Cutter was being assailed by numerous, chubby children all demanding ice cream. He was pretty sure that Lucie was going to find the whole thing hilarious.

After sending away another couple of kids with a scowl, he grabbed the binoculars Lucie gave him and spied on the softball game. He easily spotted Lucie; no one filled out that uniform quite like her. What the… That fucking wildebeest shifter just put his arm around her!

Cutter roared and grabbed the door handle but froze before he made it outside. His wolf pushed at him to hurry – punish the shifter who dare touch their female!

No, no he couldn't. It pained him to do the right thing, but he needed to stay where he was. He tensed, sweated, and trembled as he waited for his wolf to back down, but eventually, he did.

She only had one stipulation for him coming along – that he didn't get out of the van. He was going to honor that.

He only had one stipulation – he had to be as close to her as possible. Also, if anyone thought to pat her butt in some kind of sporting fashion, he would be out of the truck and ripping their throats out before she could say nutty fudgkins. Okay, that was two stipulations.

At least the wildebeest had only touched her shoulder; he guessed he could let him live. Now he…

Bang, bang, bang, bang! "Open up and sell us ice cream!" cried a belligerent pre-pubescent voice.

Oh, fuck this! Cutter opened the door to the assembled moppets and let out a mighty snarl.

*

Lucie found herself sitting next to Avery and Wayne while munching on a hot dog. Both the lioness and gator shifter were preparing to bat, but since Lucie was only the third reserve, she threw caution to the wind and braved the wares of one of the food trucks that were idling nearby.

"How's it going?" she asked in between bites, ignoring the hungry look on Wayne's face.

"Apart from the fact that our Alpha team has practically fallen apart, and our current leader is wanted for murder? Not much," replied Avery sarcastically.

Lucie waved at Cecile; the swan shifter was holding a bat and flirting outrageously with a very smug-looking Rick. She looked around at the assembled SEA agents, and frowned upon realizing that a certain squirrel shifter was conspicuous by her absence.

"No Jessie today?"

Wayne bared his fangs. "That asshole II agent, Harvey Blue is practically trying to work her to death. She can't even go to the fucking can without him pouncing on her!"

"The director and Harvey had a screaming match over it," Avery told her confidentially. "And now, the director has been advised to take a paid vacation while Harvey handles the case."

"Jiminy crickets!"

"Harvey has completely taken over the investigation; Diaz is just there for the ride. Apparently, he was putting too much effort into actually interviewing witnesses and not chasing Cutter, so Harvey went to his boss and persuaded him that Diaz wasn't capable of handling the case on his own."

"How do you know all this?"

Avery shrugged. "I got Diaz drunk last night and gave him a booby hug."

"A booby hug?"

Avery grinned. "Sure, let me show you."

The lioness pulled her to her feet and wrapped her arms around the little hedgehog shifter, she pressed out her boobs and rubbed them against her in a circular motion, softly but firmly. Wayne and a few other agents were virtually salivating when they parted.

"Oh! A *booby* hug."

"You should try it, with your endowments the guy would probably give you his kidney."

Lucie's cheeks pinked under her friend's frank gaze. She was hardly shy about sex, but Avery was always so blunt and unabashed about carnal matters that even she blushed. Isis, on the other hand, was downright filthy when she wanted to be, and almost made Lucie melt with embarrassment.

"What are people saying about Cutter?" mumbled Lucie, trying to change the subject.

Wayne barked a laugh. "Honestly, nothing worse than usual."

Mental phew!

"Just in case Cutter is interested, wherever he may be," Avery gave her a significant look that made her blush from the prickles of her hedgehog right down to her baby pink painted toenails, "we have made a little headway with our hedgehog case."

Avery explained that they found a homeless man who witnessed a wolf shifter searching through their victim's makeshift home. They believe it was their killer coming back to find something; he scared the shit out of the homeless guy, who was too afraid to return. And, after Avery flirted mercilessly with the lead technician, he did a more thorough workup on all their evidence, and the DNA on the toothpick they found was a match to someone called Bruce Knightley. Unhelpfully, he was apparently already dead.

Lucie eyed Primrose, sitting apart from other agents, and decided to make her move. "Well, thanks for the info."

Avery winked. "Sure, I hope wherever Cutter is he's hanging in there."

"Yeah, me too."

Her eyes flicked over to the ice cream truck, and she actually felt the blood draining out of her face when she saw Cutter outside of the truck, jamming his finger in the chest of a tough-looking male. Not as tough as Cutter, of course. Even with the distance between them, she could sense Cutter's rage. Her hedgehog snuffled and decided that no doubt the other male deserved it. Lucie was a little less certain but decided just to let him handle it. *But she would have plenty to say about him getting out of the truck later.*

Instead, she steeled herself and approached Primrose. Was it her imagination, or was the air colder around the aloof hyena shifter?

"May I sit here?" asked Lucie brightly, and without waiting for an answer.

Primrose pursed her lips. "Why would you want to?"

"Well, I, we don't really know each other, I thought we could be friends."

The hyena shifter sneered. "Have you heard from Cutter?"

Lucie licked her lips as her hedgehog growled at the other female. "Uh, not recently, why do you ask?"

Primrose glared. "Like you haven't heard."

"I've heard rumors, but I don't give them any credence," she said, hotly.

"Look, you seem like a nice if gullible woman. If you know where he's hiding, give him up. He's a sly bastard, and smarter than he appears. People thought he was dirty back in Ursa, and all this just goes to show that things haven't changed."

Primrose stood up to leave, clearly bored with the conversation. Lucie wanted to scream at the hyena that she had no idea what she was talking about. Her beast was all for shifting and pricking her without mercy. However, she was actually trying to get information. "So you knew Cutter back in Ursa, right?"

"Sure, everyone did," snorted Primrose.

"So, do you really think he killed Clayton?"

She hesitated for a moment. "It doesn't matter what I think; it's the evidence that matters."

With that, Primrose stalked away, viciously grabbing a bat from Lake. The normally calm Lake muttered curse words after the frosty hyena shifter.

Well, that went well. She turned to the ice cream truck in time to see Cutter punching the other male. *Oh, pumpernickel!*

*

Lucie pulled Cutter into the truck, ignoring the string of obscenities he was currently leveling at the bleeding panther shifter.

"Son of a squeegee, what were you thinking? Anyone could have seen you!" she cried when safely ensconced inside.

Cutter's whole body throbbed as he clenched his fists. His blazing amber eyes eagerly looked past her to the door, which she was currently blocking.

"The fucker had it coming," he hissed.

Lucie threw up her arms. "For what?"

"I told his kid to shove it and…"

"You told a kid to shove it?" she repeated incredulously.

His jaw ticked. "Not in those exact words."

Was he kidding? "Worse words than shove it?"

Cutter ground his teeth impatiently. "His fat son was badgering me about giving him ice cream, and I told him over and over that I wasn't going to sell him any, so I gave in, and yeah, I told the little asshole to fuck off, and suddenly I'm the bad guy?"

"Yes! He's a kid and you're a grown man; you should know better!"

He growled. "A grown man with anger issues - he's lucky I can control myself as much as I do. The dad got in my face so, you know, nature took its course." Cutter clenched his fist and pounded it into the freezer. "That

180

guy tried to push me around, and I don't take crap from anyone."

Maybe she should have been disturbed by his outburst, and even scared by his display of violence, but she wasn't. Her little hedgehog whined, and she realized it was out of concern. "Why are you so angry?"

"Ugh, I don't fucking know!" he hollered. "It's something all my shrinks have been trying to figure out for years. Father issues cause my stepdad slapped us around, being kicked out of my pack for being too aggressive, serving overseas in the army, the whole torture thing – take your fucking pick!"

He smashed his other fist into the freezer, giving it a matching dent. He barely had time to prepare as Lucie threw herself at him, mashing her lips against his. He stood rigid for a few moments in disbelief, before he opened his mouth to her probing tongue, and slipped his arms around her.

After a breathless exploration of his mouth, she pulled away and lavished kisses on his neck, licking and biting his skin. His erection pressed against her stomach, and she rubbed her breasts against him.

"What are you doing?" he groaned.

"You're frustrated," she breathed in between kisses. "I'm giving you an outlet for your anger."

One hand settled on her ass while another reached up to massage her breast. "Usually I punch things."

"Mmm, this is more fun." Her fingers found his belt and started tugging it open.

"Aren't you afraid I'll hurt you?"

"I'm not so easily breakable, whatever you got, I can take it."

Lucie almost jumped for joy as she freed him from his pants and smoothed her hand up and down his fat length.

"Here? Now?" he asked in disbelief. *He really wasn't getting with the program.*

Her hand stilled, and she pouted. "Well, if you don't want to?" She gave him a firm squeeze, and he let out a sensual snarl.

"I want to," he growled.

Thank Merlin's beard for that!

He crushed his lips to hers for a bruising kiss before pulling away and spinning her to lean over the counter. She squeaked in delighted surprise as he dragged her shorts down her legs. He leaned over her back, kissing and nipping her neck; his body pressed against her, and his manhood rubbed against her buttocks.

"Stop teasing me; I need you, too," she pleaded.

And in a way she did. She needed to do this for him; she needed to calm him, needed to take away his pain. Her beast was a soothing, timid little creature while his was a gruff, unmanageable beast. They needed each other.

Thankfully, he didn't keep her waiting long.

Grabbing her hips, he pressed himself inside her with one, inexorable push. She let out a keening cry as he started driving himself inside her with a passion. Her fingers scrabbled and scraped over the counter as he pounded her. Her head rolled from side to side as heat bloomed in her womb.

His hands slid underneath her shirt, rubbing the soft globes of her breasts and tweaking the nipples through her bra. She moaned as electric pleasure shot straight to her girly parts.

"So close," she gasped and pushed her hips back against him.

With a roar, Cutter buried himself inside her so deliciously deeply and exploded. His hands grasped her breasts almost painfully, and the added sensation sent her flying over the edge. She yelled his name as her beast barked in pleasure, and her body writhed and pulsed in his arms before she collapsed, panting and moaning.

Cutter rested his head on her back. "Was that okay?"

"Oh, yes, definitely," she cooed from her slumped over position on the counter. She felt boneless.

"I didn't hurt you..."

"Heavens no, not even close. I told you, I don't break so easily. That was... wonderful. Did I hurt you? I mean, your wounds..."

"Of course not," he snapped and pulled out of her; she winced at his sudden departure. Even soft, he was still pretty darn big.

"Lucie, I..."

Ugh, there was that apologetic tone again. She sighed; he was about to give her the 'that was great, but we're just good friends blah, blah, blah' speech. Her hedgehog huffed in disappointment. She really wasn't in the mood.

"I'm fine, Cutter. I'm fine."

She leaned down and pulled up her shorts. He really needed to stop worrying. She'd been horny for a good year now, so she was currently letting her girly parts do the thinking for her. While Cutter worried he was taking advantage of her, he couldn't be more wrong. She'd pursued him for a year, and now that he was in dire straits, she was going to take full advantage of his dependence on her to ravish his body over and over. While she couldn't deny that she would dearly like for their relationship to be long term, there was no way she could regret what they were doing, and he was silly if he actually thought he was the one in charge of their couplings. Not that she would admit it to him - *alpha male and all that.*

Feigning nonchalance, she dipped into the freezer and pulled out a cherry flavored popsicle and started licking it suggestively. "So, what next?"

Cutter watched her with ill-concealed hunger. "I'm going to need a few moments."

Her eyes took a slow, lingering tour of his body. "You don't look like you need recovery time," she teased with a wink.

The way he looked away almost in embarrassment was adorable. Although, she suspected his reaction had more to do with misplaced guilt than

183

anything else.

He cleared his throat. "Did Primrose say anything?"

"No, that woman's more repressed than a... than a... oh I can't think of anything." After her earth-shaking orgasm, she was having trouble thinking at all. "But she didn't say that she actually thought you were guilty."

"Yeah, I didn't think she'd help."

"Avery told me that the II guy, Harvey Blue has taken over the investigation."

"Fucker!" snarled Cutter as he zipped up his pants.

Sigh, what a pity – she was actually enjoying the view. "He creeps me out."

"No big surprise, that guy's an asshole. Speaking of which, who was that fuckwit you let hug you?"

What was he talking about? Lucie gave him a frown in between licks.

"The wildebeest!" he grunted, tapping his foot. "I could scent his unwashed ass all the way over here."

"Oh, Geoff? He's happily married with three kids, and he was just helping me because I almost slipped and fell on my behind."

Cutter looked like he wanted to argue, but visibly, he held himself back. "Well, good. I don't like seeing other men hug you. But I have to admit, I enjoyed your hug with Avery."

"Mmmm, me too," she said as she threw away her popsicle stick and started licking her fingers a little more zealously than she should have.

His eyes widened with lust before he scowled. "You probably shouldn't do it again," he said grouchily and with obvious jealousy.

Silly wolf, hadn't she told him over and over he was the only one for her? Although, she had to admit a little possessiveness wasn't entirely unwelcome. Her hedgehog growled disapprovingly.

"So what now?" she asked, changing the subject.

"We'll follow Primrose; maybe she'll lead us to Sadie."

Lucie giggled. "Are we going to follow her in an ice cream truck?" She traced her fingers over the two fist-shaped dents in the freezer. "Not sure how to explain this to Malcolm."

"I'll think of an excuse for your precious Malcolm."

"Oh, for the love of…"

"And with any luck, Primrose will be looking for black SUVs, and she won't think twice about a friendly neighborhood ice cream truck."

Cutter slid into the driver's seat, and Lucie took the passenger seat, huffing and clucking her tongue.

"By the way, Avery wanted me to pass on a message about a case you were working on before… you know…"

He turned to face her sharply. "You didn't tell her that I was hiding out with you?"

"No, don't worry - you're safe. She guessed it, and she wouldn't tell anyone."

"It's not me I'm worried about, they could throw you in jail for helping me."

Worry etched his handsome face and her hedgehog virtually swooned. Maybe he was a little crazy, but he did care about her. It made her heart bloom with tender love and her shorts wet with excited need. Did they have time to… *uh oh, no they didn't.* There was a steaming pile of danger marching their way.

"I'm pleased that you care, but maybe we should get going because it kind of looks like there's a lynch mob heading our way."

Lucie pointed out of the window to the six, overly large, bullish men heading their way. The one in the middle leading the charge was the panther shifter Cutter punched – identifiable by the streams of blood on his face. They all looked similar with their thick bodies, flat noses and small, squinty eyes. Perhaps they were brothers and panther shifters – *that was one hell of a litter.*

Cutter being Cutter, he just bellowed with laughter and cracked his knuckles. "Don't worry, sweetheart, I can take them."

"Won't that draw attention to you?"

He creased his brow at her comment. It wasn't that she didn't think he was capable of winning a smack down with six angry panther shifters – *per se.* It was just that she didn't exactly relish the thought of watching her honey bunny get hurt. He was always blathering on about how he couldn't stand the thought of her getting hurt, so why would it be any different for her?

Thankfully, whatever deity was watching out for hedgehog shifters, decided to throw her a bone.

"Hey, look!" she cried pointing in the opposite direction. "Isn't that Primrose's car leaving? The game must be over."

"Ah, shit!" exclaimed Cutter throwing the truck into drive and peeling after Primrose. He huffed as he drove past the jeering panthers. "I could have taken them," he muttered petulantly.

Lucie rubbed his shoulder. "Of course, you could," she cooed, stroking his ego. "They wouldn't have known what hit them."

His lips curled upwards, and he rubbed his cheek against her hand as he drove.

CHAPTER SEVENTEEN

They followed Primrose for about an hour. She seemed to be driving aimlessly and doubled back on her route several times. At first they thought she had spotted them, but they reaped their reward when she ended up at a storage depot.

They watched as she drove inside the depot, using a key code for the gate, and waving at the guard who was watching a Golden Girls rerun.

Cutter drove around the outside of the depot until he found a quiet and unobserved spot to park. There only appeared to be one camera at the front gate, so the security guard wouldn't be an issue, and given the height of the fence, Cutter was, *for the first time that day*, pleased that he was driving such a ridiculous vehicle. It was extremely handy in the circumstances. Lucie, on the other hand, didn't seem to share his enthusiasm.

He opened his arms. "Just jump, sweetheart, I'll catch you."

Lucie was crouching on top of the truck chewing on her lip. "What if you don't?"

To get over the fence, all he had to do was climb onto the roof of the ice cream truck and jump over. The stupid truck was the right height just to vault on over. Lucie wasn't thrilled with this plan, but her concern over his wounds was soon shot down and, reluctantly, she went along with it, and had allowed Cutter to help her climb onto the roof. Since he had already taken the plunge over the fence, however, her nerves seemed to be getting the better of her.

"I will."

Her bottom lip quivered in fear. His little hedgehog really wasn't good with heights. His wolf yowled, wanting to leap back up there, wrap her in his arms, and promise her that he would always be there to protect her from pesky heights. *Sappy, right?* If this were anyone other than Lucie, he'd already be barking at them to jump, and his wolf would be sneering scornfully. It might not always show, but he had a lot of patience for her.

Lucie was wringing her hands. "Won't it hurt?"

"No, you won't hit the ground."

"I mean you, won't it hurt you when I land on top of you and turn you into a pancake?"

Cutter let out a deep belly laugh and actually had to slap his leg. It wasn't just her comical words; it was the serious mien of her face as she said them.

"I'll be fine," he said through a few last twitches of laughter.

"Your funeral, wolf," she muttered as she inched to the edge of the roof and shakily stood up. "Maybe I should shift and try and crawl through the fence."

"You're not getting naked outside," he told her sternly, "and besides, you're light as a feather, hedgehog."

"You're a good liar, I know I'm chubby."

"C'mon sweetheart, you have a perfect figure – you're just fishing for compliments."

"Oh, snot buckets! Here I come."

Lucie closed her eyes and with something akin to a belly flop, jumped off the truck. Cutter caught her, naturally, and hardly even buckled under her weight. He wasn't kidding when he said she was as light as a feather to him, or that her figure was perfect. Okay, maybe she packed a few extra pounds than his previous females, but boy were they packed in all the right places.

Reluctantly, he set her on her feet and took her hand. Sniffing the air for the hyena's scent, he inclined his head and set off running in her direction. Lucie puffed and panted alongside him, but never once complained or told him to slow down. It was perhaps unfortunate that it was such a large storage depot. He did consider offering to carry her, but the sight of her jiggling, as she ran, was already pretty distracting, having her warm body pressed up against him would make him completely forget their purpose for being there.

He slowed as Primrose's scent intensified; it was coming from a storage lockup with a slightly ajar door. Moving quietly they approached and just as Cutter tried to glance inside, Primrose appeared with a gun trained on them.

Instinctively, Cutter stood in front of Lucie, shielding her, and whipped out his own gun. Or at least, the gun he had liberated when he tussled with the coyote the previous night. Primrose stared at him coldly as his wolf trembled, waiting to pounce.

"Where did you get that gun?" asked a sweet voice from behind him as she tried to poke her head around him to look.

He pushed her back with his free hand. "Not important. You better start talking, Primrose," he ordered harshly.

"Me?" she spat. "You're the one wanted for murder."

"So call it in, tell them you caught me. Do it; I won't shoot while you make the call."

Primrose narrowed her eyes but didn't make a move. Perhaps she was afraid he would shoot, but, he suspected that she didn't want the SEA to turn up. They stood watching each other, resolutely still. He could hear Lucie shuffling from foot to foot behind him. Their standoff was interrupted by a moan floating to them from the storage lockup.

"Who was that?" he demanded roughly.

Primrose's eye twitched, and her arm shook ever so slightly.

189

"Prim?" came a tremulous and weak voice.

Lucie sucked in a breath before she evaded his grasp and walked past both him and Primrose and straight into the lockup. Slowly Primrose lowered her gun, and he did the same.

"Cutter," called Lucie.

He followed Lucie and found her standing over Sadie Beauchamp. The bobcat shifter was lying on a cot. She was pale and shaking.

"Fuck," he breathed.

Lucie pulled back the dressing to a wound on her stomach and sucked in a breath at the bloody sight before her.

"I thought she was getting better," mumbled Primrose as she stood next to him. Her usually hard eyes were frightened and brimmed with tears. "I took out the bullet and she seemed to be okay. She was fine last night, but now she…"

"She has a fever," said Lucie, gently, "and her body can't cope with both the fever and healing the gunshot wound. She needs antibiotics. We have some at the SEA building."

"You can help her?" asked Primrose, wonderingly.

"Yes, but you have to promise not to turn Cutter in."

Cutter looked at her in surprise, but the biggest surprise of all was when Primrose agreed to that without even hesitating.

Primrose fished a pen and paper out of her purse. "Write down what I need and I'll go get them."

Cutter grabbed one of the boxes piled in the corner and sat down heavily, watching Primrose warily. It occurred to him that Primrose could easily break her word and come back with a dozen agents to take him by force, but he doubted it. She seemed to be genuinely concerned about Sadie; he couldn't sense any deception on her part.

Primrose gave Sadie a kiss on her temple. "It's okay, babe, everything's going to be okay." She strode to the door and looked back at Cutter and Lucie. "I better be able to trust you."

"Same here," grunted Cutter as she nodded and left.

Sadie seemed to have drifted off into a fretful sleep. Cutter grabbed Lucie and pulled her back to sit on his lap, ostensibly to comfort her, but really it was for his sake. There was a slim chance that a dozen agents would come bursting through the door any moment, and this could be his last chance to be near Lucie. *He wanted to savor every moment.*

*

Primrose returned with the medicine, and thankfully no tactical team came storming into the lockup like a bunch of Tarzans on speed. True to her word, Primrose didn't tell anyone. She encountered no problems obtaining what she needed. No one even considered questioning her. *They wouldn't dare.*

Lucie gave some pills to Sadie and within a couple of hours she was stable again. Lucie redressed the wound, and they were all relieved to note she had stopped bleeding and was starting to heal. Primrose held Sadie's hand and intermittently stroked her cheek throughout.

"You better start giving us some answers," rumbled Cutter.

"How did you find me here?"

"We followed you."

Primrose groaned. "Please don't tell me you were in that stupid ice cream truck."

Lucie nodded sheepishly.

The hyena shifter let out a noise of disgust. "You know I saw it, and I thought it was weird, but I just assumed... I can't believe how dumb I was."

"Lucky we did," growled Cutter, as his eyes dipped to Sadie's sleeping form.

Primrose watched the gentle rise and fall of the bobcat's body as she breathed. She turned her accusing eyes on Lucie. "Would you have refused to help her if I said I was going to turn Cutter in?"

"No," admitted Lucie. "I could never do that."

Cutter squeezed her shoulder, feeling inordinately proud of his selfless, little hedgehog.

"I believe you," sighed Primrose.

"Now, what the fuck is going on? What happened to Sadie?" demanded Cutter. His beast was practically burning with eagerness.

"She was shot," deadpanned Primrose.

"Why, though?" encouraged Lucie.

Primrose looked down at her girlfriend unhappily. "Sadie and I, we met when I was just starting at the agency. She worked at a coffee shop. We dated for a while and things, well, we were happy, and I thought she was my mate but… my parents are ultra-conservative; they couldn't accept me being gay. I was ambitious, really ambitious when I was younger, and kind of a bitch…"

Cutter snorted, and Lucie kicked him.

"I started to believe that being with Sadie would hold me back, so I broke it off. I made it easier, I acted like a screaming asshole so that she wouldn't miss me. I moved away, accepting a job at another branch."

Primrose paused as Sadie's breathing hitched, but continued as she calmed. "It wasn't until a few years later that I heard from her again. I moved back to Ursa with a promotion, and she called me out of the blue. She'd been hurt – badly - by a man but she didn't dare go to the cops, she wanted my help…" Primrose couldn't hide the bitterness from her tone.

Lucie placed a hand on the hyena shifter's shoulder. She flinched a little at the contact but didn't ask her to move away.

"What happened to her?" murmured Lucie.

"It was all Marie's fault!" she snarled. "That fucking moron Marie and her shithead boyfriend owed money to Nicolas Maroni – *lots* of fucking money. The bastards stole a shipment of his drugs thinking they could sell them. Maroni found them high off their asses before they even had a chance to get out of the city. He was going to kill them, and since they didn't have any money, and neither of them was in a fit state to earn it, Sadie stepped in and offered to work off the debt. I don't think she realized how bad it would be at the time."

She ran a finger down Sadie's cheek, as angry tears threatened. "He had her work in one of his clubs, *servicing* his friends, letting them abuse her however their perverted minds wanted. The way they treated her…"

Primrose choked, caught between indignation and sadness. She allowed Lucie to give her a hug, and even nuzzled her neck.

"I knew I had to get her out of there, but I was so afraid of them hurting her even worse. Sadie told me that Maroni had someone on the inside of the SEA – you'd be amazed at the things she overheard. She didn't know exactly who, but she was the one who persuaded your informant to speak to you. Sadie fed me as many tips as she could, and I did as much investigating as I could, tipping off the SEA anonymously…"

"All those tips - they were you?" interrupted Cutter, incredulously.

She nodded. "I did what I could, and I really thought that when you had all your evidence that it would all be at an end, and we'd be free. But then, all those agents died, they tortured you…" she trailed off gloomily. "At least Sadie was free. But I worried that the mole would come after her; you and Clayton didn't know how much she actually knew about Maroni, but I wasn't sure about anyone else. I got a transfer out of Ursa as soon as possible. I've been moving from branch to branch ever since, taking Sadie with me, but making sure I hide her. I always made sure people hated me enough never to ask about my private life. I was paranoid, and I didn't risk us living together, but at least I was happy." Primrose smiled slightly.

Cutter's wolf prowled. Story time was all well and good, but didn't she forget a few things? "What about Clayton?"

Primrose grimaced. "The old eagle just suddenly showed up. He somehow found out where Sadie was, and then he turned up at the diner where she was waitressing. He kept asking her all these questions about Maroni, about the men he made her…" She paused as an angry tremor coursed through her body. "Sadie just wanted to forget it ever happened, so she told him to get lost, but he was persistent, and after we argued about it, she agreed to meet him and talk. I was planning on going with her, but…"

"Clayton was killed," supplied Cutter, grimly.

"Yes."

"And then someone came after Sadie?"

"Yes. Her bitch little sister was in town, crashing on her sofa. Her asshole boyfriend got himself arrested, so the stupid girl went to a bar and brought home some random guy who offered her drugs. When he got to the apartment, he killed Marie and tried to kill Sadie. He shot her, but she managed to shift, jump out the window and run down the fire escape. She came to me, and I brought her here."

Cutter felt a spark of almost excitement. They were getting closer to an answer; it was tantalizingly within reach. "Who was the guy?"

"One of Maroni's old men, Sadie told me he looked different, his neck was covered in scars, and he could barely speak, but it was him. She isn't sure of his name."

"That doesn't sound like any SEA agent I know," said Lucie in disappointment.

Cutter tried to smile, but it must have come out as more of a scowl. He was half disappointed, but also half relieved.

"Does Sadie have any idea why Clayton suddenly looked for her?" he asked Primrose who shook her head in response.

"But at least we know it's one of Maroni's men doing this," offered Lucie optimistically. "We just need to catch him, right?"

"I wouldn't even begin to know where to look," he started despondently. "I need to think about this."

"You're not going to tell anyone about Sadie," barked Primrose. It was probably meant to be a question, but it came out as an order.

He opened his mouth to snarl at her but, much to his chagrin and his wolf's fury, Lucie hugged her tighter.

"We won't, of course, we won't," his little hedgehog soothed. "Maybe the two of you should come home with us?"

Cutter gave her a cutting motion across his throat that just made her frown.

"I appreciate the offer," said Primrose, "but I'd rather stay here. I have portable heaters, and the bathroom is just down the way. The owner of this place is easily bribable; a number of married men end up living here after their wives kick them out," she told them scornfully.

Primrose pressed herself against Lucie, enjoying the comfort the small shifter provided. Cutter stepped up to the intertwined women and forced them to pull apart. He put his arm around Lucie and tucked her into his side, placing his big body between the two women. *What?* Was he getting all jealous and territorial just because they were hugging? *Nuh-uh, no way.* His wolf howled – the beast was all for being jealous and territorial.

"Take care; we'll be back in the morning to check on her, right?" mumbled Lucie whose face was currently planted in his chest area.

Cutter gave her a sour look but agreed when she looked up and gave him the full force of her big baby blues. With that, he dragged her away before his little hedgehog decided that Primrose needed another hug.

*

"Well, at least we're making progress," offered Lucie as Cutter hauled her over the fence. He did consider just asking Primrose to give them the code to get out, but this was more fun. He cupped her ass cheeks, giving them a light squeeze that was totally necessary.

"Yeah, we eliminated our only suspect," he replied gruffly as she scrambled onto the roof.

He clambered up the fence with ease, reveling in the impressed expression on her face, and more than a little self-satisfied at the hint of arousal he scented.

"But we have this new suspect – the scarred man."

Finally back in the ice cream truck, Lucie tried to inject him with some optimism. A lost cause as far as he was concerned.

"Yeah," he muttered.

"You were hoping it was going to be the mole?"

Cutter sighed. "Yeah, there're just too many things that don't make sense, and I just... I don't know how it all pieces together."

"Let's go home and get some rest, it's been a long day already." And it was still early afternoon. Lucie stared out the window, pensively.

"Sadie will be okay, thanks to you," he murmured, guessing the direction of her thoughts.

"Primrose would have taken her to the hospital in time. I just can't help but feel... anger at what happened to her."

His wolf whimpered helplessly as Lucie shivered. "Maroni's in prison."

"Yet, she's still in danger."

Cutter pressed a chaste yet tender kiss to her temple, and she wiped away a tear.

He started driving home and after a couple of nose blows, she said, "I forgot to tell you Avery's message. She wanted me to update you on the hedgehog's murder."

"Fuck, I'd forgotten all about that."

Lucie proceeded to relate the progress Avery and Wayne had made, informing him about the DNA on the toothpick belonging to someone called Bruce Knightley.

Cutter pondered that name; it certainly sounded familiar.

CHAPTER EIGHTEEN

Cutter and Lucie let themselves into her house through the garage, sneaking in like thieves in the night. Except they weren't thieves, and it wasn't night. Lucie laughed at acting so stealthily around her own house, but Cutter grunted and growled until she gave in.

As they approached the door to the kitchen, Cutter froze, and his wolf growled lowly. He scented unknown males. Lucie bumped into his back.

"Wha…"

Cutter spun and clamped a paw over her mouth. She peered at him wonderingly before the saucy minx kissed his palm.

Caught between a disapproving frown and slack-jawed lust, he snapped into action as he heard a crash in the kitchen. With a snarl telling her to stay where she was, he crashed through the door, taking two preppy-looking male shifters by surprise.

The smaller male - a raven shifter - let out a yelp as Cutter threw him against the refrigerator. Multitudes of colorful fridge magnets scattered across the room.

"Eric!" roared the larger male — a fucking lion shifter Cutter noted, before body slamming him.

Cutter was kneeling on the lion's neck before he heard his hedgehog's disgruntled squeak.

"Oh my god! Baby, no, that's Xander."

His wolf howled in outrage before, with renewed murder in his eyes, he started applying more pressure.

"Cutter, stop!" she yelled.

With an enormous amount of regret, and a monumental effort to contain his wolf, Cutter backed off as Lucie and the raven shifter twittered over Xander. *Fucking Xander.* If he started telling Lucie to her face that he loved her, Cutter would fucking murder the cat!

Lucie, wisely, took a step away from the two males and placed a hand on Cutter's trembling chest. Perhaps she sensed his displeasure, or it might be the constant, low rumble emanating from his mouth.

"What are you guys doing here?" she asked, training her eyes on Cutter.

The raven shifter inspected Xander's neck. "Didn't you get our message?"

She cocked her head to the side. "No, what message?"

"I left you a message on your answer machine telling you that we were coming by," rasped Xander.

Lucie raised an eyebrow at Cutter and pouted her lips together. Yeah, she was mad, but all he could think about was how kissable she looked at that moment.

"No, for some reason I didn't get that message."

The raven looked over Cutter appreciatively. "New boyfriend?"

"No," blushed Lucie.

"What's it to you?" demanded Cutter, clinging to his outraged beast.

The two males gave each other significant glances, and in unison they said, "New Boyfriend."

Cutter bared his fangs. "Who the fuck are you?"

"Cutter!" Lucie gaped at him. "This is Xander, my ex-husband."

She wiggled her eyebrows up and down. She might as well have said 'hint, hint.'

"You better be as gay as she said you were!" ground out Cutter.

"Cutter!" Her voice went up about two octaves in shock. The two males just stared at him in surprise.

What? He wasn't ripping them apart for intruding or declaring their love for Lucie – even though his wolf wanted to. His mood was actually kind of mild. That was probably due to her hand still innocuously placed on his chest. *Yep, it may be hard to believe, but this was a mellow kind of rage.*

"I promise you I'm gay," said Xander with only a hint of amusement. "I have a boyfriend and everything – this is Eric."

The raven shifter pouted as he pulled Xander to his feet. "The *boyfriend* – but I prefer the term life partner."

Xander snorted. "Yeah well I prefer you not bringing takeaway curries into the house, but we don't all get our way."

They smiled at Cutter, who seethed in return.

Lucie was chewing on her lip so hard it was almost raw red. "Umm, what brings you guys by? I thought you weren't back until next week."

Xander smiled. "We cut our visit to Eric's parents short."

Eric nodded. "My mom won a trip on a Caribbean cruise at bingo."

"How lovely! Millie must have been thrilled," gushed Lucie.

"So we came home early, and we thought we'd swing by to pick up Delmonte, regale you with our trip to Italy, and treat you to dinner," said Xander.

Eric grinned. "Of course, if we knew you had company…"

Lucie flushed a delightful shade of pink over her neck and face, and if they didn't have intruders – *or company, whatever* - Cutter would have instantly delved into her shirt and investigated how far reaching the flush was. Fuckers, ruining his fun.

"Well," she began, shyly, "we're just going to get changed, how about we order some takeaway when we come down? Not Indian," she added on seeing the moue of distaste on Xander's face.

The other two men agreed and watched as Lucie tugged on Cutter's hand, leading him away from the kitchen.

Xander frowned as Cutter passed him. "Hey, is that my sweater?" Cutter snarled. "Nope, never mind, my mistake."

She didn't speak a word as they walked upstairs; she didn't utter a peep as she pulled him into the bathroom, and not a syllable passed her lips as she started stripping out of her clothes. He expected recriminations for attacking and then snarling at her friends, but nothing came, and it made him extremely nervous.

"Aren't you going to yell?"

Lucie slipped off her oversized t-shirt. "I'm sorry, I forgot they had a key."

"What's happening?"

Torturously slowly, she pushed her shorts down her legs and kicked them away. She bared her sweet mound to him, and he could see the glistening, pearly evidence of her arousal clinging to her curls. "I'm getting naked."

"I can see that," he replied, a little more hoarse than he would have liked. "You never told me your ex was a lion shifter."

"Because it makes no difference."

His wolf almost swooned as she unhooked her bra and let it flutter to the floor. Was there a lack of oxygen in that room? Because it felt like there was a lack of oxygen.

Lucie stepped into the shower and turned on the spray. She squirted some shower gel in her hands and, never breaking eye contact, she let them wander over her breasts.

Cutter swallowed as he watched her hypnotic movements. Just moments ago, his wolf had been furious, but the tension was almost fleeing his body; it was being replaced by a much more pressing and enjoyable feeling. "Wha... what are you doing?"

"Having a shower. Aren't you going to join me?" She batted her eyelashes. *Minx.*

"Won't they be waiting for us downstairs?"

"They'll keep."

One hand travelled down her stomach to tap her clit; she let out a breathy moan. Within seconds, he was pulling off his clothes and pinning her to the wall of the shower. He plunged two fingers into her tight sheath and she rippled around him.

"So wet, so ready," he crooned against her mouth. "Ready for me."

"Yes, only you, always you," she babbled as his fingers pumped in and out of her.

She pushed her hips against his hand as tiny claws sliced through her fingers into his shoulder. He pushed his palm against her sensitive nub, making her arch against him, crushing her plush breasts against him. He dipped his head and laved each of her creamy orbs with his tongue. Her bucking motions against his hand went wild and she grasped his head, clutching him to her. He sucked as much of her flesh into his mouth as he could before releasing it, and nipping little love bites around her nipple.

"Going to... almost..." she panted.

As he felt her cresting, he thrust a third finger inside her, and she came, jerking against him almost violently. He withdrew his fingers and drove his aching manhood inside her; her orgasm made her almost painfully tight, and he fought the urge to come straight away, and let her milk the essence from his body. Determined to last, he gritted his teeth and held still as her inner muscles clamped and suckled at him.

When she finally calmed and slumped against his body, he gripped her hips and began rocking in and out of her body. Soon enough, her legs were wrapped around him, and she was racing toward another climax. As she screamed in ecstasy, Cutter roared and spilled himself inside her.

For the first time in his life, he had an urge to sink his teeth inside the quivering woman he held in his arms and make her his forever.

*

Once Cutter relaxed, dinner was actually quite a pleasant experience. Xander and Eric bore him no ill will, although they couldn't help chuckling as he scooted his chair right up next to Lucie's, and dropped a proprietary arm over the back. He was hardly the chattiest of wolves, but he listened, and he laughed, and he didn't do anything crazy like hit anyone – *again*.

She was thankful that the SEA had not made the hunt for Cutter public. It might have been a bit tricky trying to explain why Cutter's face was currently plastered all over the TV for being a wanted fugitive.

Delmonte made an appearance partway through dinner, cuddling up to his owners, fawning over Lucie, and spitting at Cutter. Xander and Eric fussed over the oversized cat, telling him how much they missed him, while Cutter rolled his eyes and returned the hiss the animal gave him.

When it came to saying goodbye, Xander gave Lucie a big hug and told her how much he liked her new boyfriend. Lucie didn't have the heart to correct him, so she just said thank you.

Lucie found Cutter in her room, sitting on the edge of her bed after she waved a final goodbye to her friends. She only hesitated briefly before pushing her way onto his lap. What? Who knew when she'd have the opportunity again? Her hedgehog agreed – enjoy every moment while she still can. She quivered excitedly as she felt his arousal, thick and hard beneath her buttocks. Cutter let out a martyred sigh and wrapped his arms around her.

She curled her fingers into his sweater. "What are you doing hiding up here?"

"I didn't want to watch those bozos pawing at you," he admitted, gruffly.

"They're gay bozos – and they're not bozos! We were hugging goodbye – it's what friends do."

"I don't do that with my friends," he replied sullenly.

Lucie giggled. She imagined watching Cutter and Gunner hug would be a strange sight to behold. Although, she certainly didn't want him to start hugging Isis or Avery; her little beastie growled at the thought of those long-legged felines touching her wolf. *Maybe she could see where he was coming from.*

"They're like brothers to me. Xander's family aren't exactly thrilled about him being in a relationship with a man, Eric's live in Canada, and I don't have any family so we all kind of stick together."

Cutter cupped her face, bringing her gaze up to his luminous green eyes. "You don't have family?"

Her face dropped unhappily. "My parents died when I was ten; after that, I went through a few foster homes."

"I had no idea," he muttered, tensing in annoyance. Her hedgehog mewled. Annoyance at her? Surely not.

"I ended up at a really nice home with a lady called Mae – we called her Aunt Mae. We stayed close until she died a couple of years ago. I do keep in touch with a few foster brothers and sisters, but they don't live in Los Lobos anymore."

Cutter stroked her cheek and in a surprisingly cutesy move, kissed the end of her nose. "I'm sorry, sweetheart, I should have known."

Oh, her little honey bunny! He was angry at *himself* for not knowing.

Embarrassed, he cleared his throat. "What's with the animal dream house?" He nodded at her little doll house – or rather, hedgehog house – and also her pride and joy. Hey, kids' toys aren't just for kids.

"Oh, I used to have one when I was little, but after my parents died I went into foster care, and I couldn't take it with me. I used to love it, so after I got a job, I bought one. I still play with it now. You're never too old."

"I have a son," he blurted abruptly.

"What?" Her head snapped up so quickly she swore she got whiplash. "You do? I never heard that, and I thought I knew everything a stalker could about her prey. How am I just hearing about this? What happened?"

Cutter chuckled hollowly. "There's not much to tell. After Annie got knocked up... uh, after she found out she was pregnant, we got married. It didn't take long for us to realize that had been a mistake, but we both loved him, so we tried to make it work for his sake." He let out a long breath. "And then there was the whole Maroni thing... After that, she was... she was scared of me... and she was scared I'd hurt our baby. So she left me, took our baby boy, found someone else, and joined his pack."

"I'm sorry."

"I don't want your pity," he snapped.

To his surprise, Lucie bopped him on the head. "That's not what it is you dummy."

Cutter tried to bare his fangs at her, to show her he was a big bad wolf, but he couldn't help the smile that lifted the corners of his mouth. She imagined she was the first hedgehog ever to hit him, although it was only playfully.

He rearranged her slightly, so she was straddling him and resting her head in the crook of his shoulder. "Things are better now. Now, I talk to my boy on the phone, and I visit when I can. But after that, I knew I wasn't meant to be anyone's mate. How could I be with someone that I could hurt?"

Lucie stiffened in his arms as a sliver of disappointment eked down her spine and deflated her inner animal. "Is this your oh-so-subtle way of reminding me that there's no future for us?"

"Lucie…"

"Don't. I already told you; I care about you, but I'm fine with whatever we have right now, you don't have to worry about me. But, to be clear, I'm not afraid of you. No matter how much you're pushed, I know you wouldn't hurt me, right?"

She traced a finger around his collar, grazing his skin, and he shuddered ever so lightly.

"No, I wouldn't… not permanently anyway."

Hmmm, not the most romantic declaration but she'd take it… for now. "I'm sorry about your son."

Cutter shrugged as he started running his hands up and down her back. "His name's Dean, and his stepdad's a good guy. He's better off with him. I'm not exactly a good dad. Annie said I'm incapable of being firm with him - I just keep giving him treats when he's naughty."

Lucie let out a hoot of laughter. "You, not firm? Merlin's beard!" The idea of the Agency's grouchiest wolf shifter – a crown that took a lot of grouchiness to obtain – not being firm, was just downright hilarious. "How old is he now?"

"Four," he muttered.

She could tell he was a little put out by her humorous reaction… which just made her laugh even harder. Boy, how would he be if they had some terrible little ankle biters running around? *Literal ankle biters – she was a menace when she was young.* She felt a twinge and her hedgehog snuffled. Not that she was certain they would have any kids… *sigh.*

"Do you miss your wife?"

Cutter looked at her like she was insane. "No, definitely no. I'm sorry I don't see Dean more often, but it's better than him seeing the worst of me."

"I'm sorry."

"Fuck, don't feel sorry for me!"

"You're right – I'm not sorry at all. Happy now?"

"Very."

"Good." They sat in silence for a few minutes before Lucie had to put a stop to that. What was the point of having a mouth if you didn't flap it around? "Are you thinking about Clayton?"

Cutter grunted. "I have this feeling like I'm missing something important, but I don't know what." He was sitting, pondering as Lucie started humming. "What was the name that Avery gave to you earlier?"

"Oh? Umm, Bruce Knightley, I think."

"Bruce… Bruce Knightley." He rolled the names around his mouth before his whole body went rigid, and he shot to his feet. "Mother fucker!"

CHAPTER NINETEEN

Lucie held up the freshly printed picture. "So this is Bruce Knightley?"

Cutter plucked it from her hands and studied it distastefully. Lucie fidgeted on the hard kitchen chair. When he leaped up from the bed, she had taken a mighty tumble to the floor, and, frankly, her ass still smarted. He apologized profusely, rubbed her cheeks repeatedly, and even went so far as to kiss it better. At that point, he got a gleam in his eye, and she put a pin in their activities while he explained what had him so riled.

Seeing her squirm, Cutter pulled her onto his lap. One hand massaged her behind while the other clutched at the photo.

"Officially, yes, but he never went by that last name. I knew him as Bruce Connors. He preferred his mom's last name."

At Cutter's insistence, Lucie called Jessie on her cell phone. Surprisingly, Jessie was at work and Lucie chastised her for working such long hours, and then felt like a heel for asking Jessie to help her with something work related. Jessie didn't mind, and she e-mailed Lucie a picture of Bruce Knightley.

"We kind of grew up in the same pack," explained Cutter, grimly. "Bruce's dad was a real piece of work - treated Bruce's mom like crap. He wasn't allowed to join our pack. Every so often she'd turn up, black and blue, dragging Bruce with her - they'd stay for a while, and then his dad would show up, and his mom just ran right on back into his arms."

Her heart twisted. "So, this is the Bruce who got you a job in Maroni's gang and then tortured you?"

His eyes narrowed even more. "Yes."

"That... that butthole!" exploded Lucie. Her irate hedgehog was definitely in agreement on that.

"Whoa, steady, language," commented Cutter, surprisingly amused at her outburst.

"I thought he was dead."

"I thought he was too, but if his DNA is showing up at murder scenes, he's probably not quite as dead as I thought he was."

"So maybe he's the one who tried to kill Sadie."

He nodded. "It would make sense, I did try to rip his throat out, he might have had a bit of trouble healing that, and he might have scars."

Lucie jumped up, ready for action. "We need to show his picture to Sadie; if she can identify him, maybe we could take this to the director."

"Maybe." His amber infused eyes didn't stray from the photo. Perhaps he was trying to divine his location just by looking at his image, that or make Bruce's head exploded with his mind – *either way*.

"You don't sound excited."

Cutter opened his mouth to bare his fangs. "I'd rather find him and rip his throat out again."

His wolf was close to the surface, perhaps too close. He might not be able to think rationally. She needed to calm him, so she resumed her seat on his lap and kissed his neck, nibbling on his collar bone and nipping his chin. *Ah, the sacrifices she had to make.*

He tried to remain stoic, but he crumpled at her teasing onslaught. "Fine, we'll do it your way, call Primrose, and let her know we're on our way."

To show that there was no shame in defeat, she gave him a thorough kiss before grabbing her phone to call Primrose. There was just one problem – Primrose didn't answer. Lucie kept trying, but she didn't get an answer.

"Maybe she's in the bathroom," she suggested uneasily. "Or maybe they're both asleep – it's getting late."

Tersely, Cutter told her to try again. She did. No answer.

"I don't like it; I'm going over there," he declared.

"I'll get…"

"No."

"But…"

Cutter gave her a 'don't fuck with me' stare. Usually, she'd ignore it and just carry on with whatever she was doing, but for some reason she actually thought he meant it this time.

"I don't know what we might be walking into, and I sure as hell am not willing to risk you."

"But…"

He softened but only marginally. "Please, Lucie, stay here. I love how stubborn you are – even though it bugs the hell out of me, but please, do as I ask. I don't want to lose you."

Son of a motherless goat! How could she say no when he admitted to loving a part of her, and then actually saying something sweet?

"Okay."

He pressed a kiss to her lips. "I'll call you as soon as I know something.

"Just be careful," she pleaded, following him to the door and wringing her hands.

"I will."

He gave her one last meaningful look fraught with some emotions she really didn't want to identify at that moment. Maybe later, when she had him in her bed, and completely at her mercy. For now, she looked to the skies and begged the hedgehog deity to watch over him.

But in the meantime, perhaps some more earthly help would come in useful.

*

Cutter raced to the storage depot. His wolf was furious at leaving Lucie behind, but even the unreasonable beast knew it wasn't a good idea to bring her along. A thought reinforced when he arrived to find the fence hanging limply from its hinges and the guard in the office shot dead.

He abandoned the car and proceeded on foot to Primrose's storage lockup. The rest of the facility was eerily silent, making the cries and yells from Primrose's even more conspicuous.

Moving quickly and silently he sidled into the lockup. Sadie was huddled in a corner, crying while Bruce kicked a naked Primrose. She must have tried to shift, but he overpowered her. He was too bent on his task, too enthralled by the whimpers she admitted, and the pain he caused to notice Cutter's arrival. *Sick fucker.*

Cutter didn't even bother to pull out his gun. He wanted to enjoy this; he didn't want it to end too quickly. A sentiment his itchy-pawed wolf agreed with. The sooner they got started, the better.

"Bruce!" he roared.

The other wolf stopped and slowly turned to look at him. He wasn't nearly surprised enough to see him.

"Cutter," he rasped, his voice only a distant whisper of what it used to be.

Cutter surveyed the angry scars on Bruce's neck. They really looked like they hurt. He should have taken his fucking head off.

Bruce smirked. "About time, I was beginning to think I'd never get a chance to kill you. I mean I would have been happy just to gun you down in the street, but my brother reckoned that would look bad for him, so I had to wait, and it has been fucking hard."

Cutter looked between the two women. Sadie didn't appear harmed – just shaken. Primrose on the other hand looked bad. She had managed to crawl over to Sadie, and the two hugged. Every instinct he had told him to rip the wolf apart - his own beast was virtually tearing himself apart to get out – but he didn't want anyone else to get hurt.

"Why now?" Cutter growled.

"Why not?" Bruce ran his tongue over his fangs as his eyes sparkled amber. "You know how long I've been wallowing in a fucking Mexican hospital waiting for this to heal?" He stroked his scars. "I lost three years of my fucking life thanks to you; they say I'm lucky to be alive, I don't feel lucky."

"Should have stayed dead then."

Bruce chuckled horribly. "Everyone thought I was, my brother saved me though, got me to safety."

"How'd you find them?" Cutter inclined his head at Sadie and Primrose.

"You're not the only one who's been talking to Marie's boyfriend. My brother suspected the girlfriend was Primrose, so he had a tracker on her car, and when he found out she stole that medicine, he figured it out and had me come down here to sort the mess out."

Cutter's muscles twitched and grew. "Your brother works at the SEA?"

Bruce smirked. "You have no idea, do you?"

"He our surprise mystery guest tonight?"

The other wolf's expression turned downright feral. "Nah, he has his hands full on the other side of town dealing with a prickly little brunette."

Cutter tensed as red-hot rage poured through him. Bruce just babbled on, apparently uncaring as to the danger he was in.

211

"This isn't how I wanted it to go down. I had plans to kill Lucie slowly in front of you. But then this bitch had to ruin it," he sneered at Sadie. "She should have died when she was supposed to. Still, never mind, killing you will still make me feel better."

Cutter was barely listening. His wolf howled ferociously, and his blood boiled. *Lucie.* His Lucie. No, he wouldn't let her down – she needed him. He roared savagely as his muscles and bones started twisting and reshaping themselves. He didn't even try to fight the shift.

Bruce's eyes widened slightly in fear. Fucking stupid wolf! He had no hope against Cutter to begin with, but now that he had threatened his female, he'd be dead within seconds. He lunged at the other wolf with a bloodthirsty snarl.

*

Lucie fretted. She paced, she tried to watch TV, she ate a whole box of *Fortunate Charms* – they were a cheap knock off breakfast cereal of which she was an addict – but nothing could soothe her or her worried beast.

She made the right decision in calling for backup. He may want to run around playing action lone ranger wolfman or some gobbledygook like that, but she wasn't giving him the opportunity to get killed – he still had to give in and admit he loved her – he wasn't getting off that darn easily!

She almost jumped up the wall in her agitated state when Greensleeves flooded her living room. Jeez, was that Cutter?

She ran to the door and on opening it she… froze. What was *he* doing there?

"Hello, Lucie." It was the II agent, Harvey Blue, smiling genially while pointing a gun at her. "Get back in the house."

CHAPTER TWENTY

Cutter growled and swiped at Bruce, who whined and tried to limp out of reach. *Pathetic.* Their fight must have lasted all of ninety seconds, and his opponent could barely stand. The other wolf was a masterpiece of cuts and bites; there was barely an inch of his thick fur that wasn't matted with blood from his many wounds.

With a pitiful huff, Bruce dropped to the floor and painfully rolled over, baring his belly in an act of submission. Cutter prowled around his prone body. Would the honorable thing be to let him live? This woeful wolf that had tortured him and killed fuck knows how many others. Did Cutter care about honor? No, he cared about Lucie – and time was ticking on. He needed to get to Lucie, and the easiest way to do that was to kill Bruce. It was the most efficient way to ensure that he was taken care of.

Perhaps sensing what was coming, Bruce shifted back to his human form. He panted and began pleading for his life. Cutter's wolf ignored him and prepared to rip out his throat – and this time he'd make damn sure he was dead.

"Cutter!"

The wolf growled as Wayne barreled through the door. The gator shifter had a gun trained on Bruce. "I got it."

Cutter growled at him. The miserable excuse for a wolf shifter was *his* to kill.

"Cutter," snapped Wayne, forcefully. He pulled out a set of handcuffs. "Step back and let me put these on. Please?"

With a monumental effort, Cutter backed away and wrenched control away from his animal. He shifted back to human, ignoring the blood streaks over his naked body.

Wayne slapped the cuffs on Bruce, who was groaning in pain. The gator shifter gave him a totally accidental kick that set off a fresh set of moans. "Lucie called me; she was worried."

"Lucie's in danger."

"Go, I got this."

"Call her; warn her," he ordered as he started running.

For three years, he had wondered what he would do if he ever got his hands on Bruce. At the time, he thought Bruce was dead, so they were just fantasies. He enjoyed thinking of the ways he would make the bastard scream, and inflict some of the pain he had felt. The old Cutter would never have left him alive for Wayne to deal with. But that was the BL portion of his life – *Before Lucie*. The only thing that mattered to him at that moment in time was her - he wasn't going to lose her. He couldn't bear it. He finally admitted the truth that he had spent a year running from. *She was his mate.* And lord help anyone who stood in the way of him claiming his mate.

*

Harvey checked his phone and scowled. He was standing over Lucie as she sat on her couch; his gun waved aimlessly in her direction, but he wasn't focusing on her. Maybe she could rush him and take the gun. Women on TV did it all the time. And women on TV also fought crime and chased bad guys in four-inch heels. In other words, TV wasn't based on reality.

She was perhaps a little miffed that Harvey hadn't bothered to tie her up. Was she really so harmless that she didn't even rate being tied up? Maybe it was the fact that her favorite color was pink, or the fact that she liked to knit that made her seem so non-threatening. Yeah, she did have to admit that she probably wouldn't get very far against a wolf shifter. Well, physical strength wasn't going to help, so maybe she needed to distract and conquer him with her rapier wit. *Raspberries!* She was going to die. Her hedgehog took the opportunity to curl up into a ball – she was too timid for her own good. She had to do something. Maybe if she stalled for time, Cutter would come back and rip this guy to shreds.

"You're the mole, right?" she blurted.

Harvey grunted, and she took that to mean yes, I am the scum sucking, traitorous hound that doesn't deserve to breathe the same air as other SEA agents.

"You fed information to Maroni."

"I see you are well informed, has Cutter been whispering sweet nothings into your ear as he fucked you?"

She flinched at his language – which was odd because Cutter swore like a sailor, and that never bothered her. Her reaction amused Harvey, though.

"Or are you his crime-fighting partner? His little sidekick – Robin to his Batman," he sneered.

She preferred to think of them as Mulder and Scully but, you know, without the aliens. Not that she was going to get into that conversation with him.

"You sold out your fellow agents…"

"It wasn't quite like that…"

"Then what was it like?" How on earth could he justify what he did?

"Like I have to tell you. What did you do with the picture Jessie e-mailed you?"

Lucie blinked at him in surprise and Harvey gave her a superior smile.

"It seemed prudent to monitor Jessie's communications," he explained, smugly, "given her loyalty to Cutter. Unfortunately, I couldn't tap her cell phone without her noticing. E-mails though, technically belong to the agency. I guess the picture was for Cutter. Where is he right now?"

"I don't know."

"You're lying," he said, blandly. "Tell me the truth, or I will really make Cutter suffer. You've seen his scars; a lot worse things can happen."

"He went looking for Primrose." She conceded the truth to him; she just didn't go into all the details.

Unease pooled in her stomach as his face brightened. Oh no, it was never a good sign when the bad guy looked pleased.

"With any luck my brother will have already killed him."

"Your brother?"

Lucie jumped as he burst into laughter. "You really didn't figure it out, and to think I was worried about Cutter. Bruce Knightley - my brother. Different mothers. He's the reason I informed to Maroni in the first place. The dumb fuck owed the man thousands in gambling debts. In return for his life, I had to feed that pig Maroni information. The things you do for family. Not that it was hard to do. Maroni, in spite of Bruce's debt, gave me plenty of money – the information was worth more than any gambling debt."

She pursed her lips. "You outed Cutter when he was undercover and got those agents killed."

He wasn't remorseful in the least. "I had no idea Cutter was undercover until my boss got drunk and spilled it to me. Worse than that, I found out an informant in Maroni's crew was going to out me. So I gave Maroni Cutter and killed the informant."

"You didn't have to kill that tactical team!" She bit her lip – what was she saying? *He didn't have to kill anyone!*

"That wasn't on purpose – I set the bomb to destroy the house, I didn't know they would be there. Bad timing."

She gaped at him – like a fish caught in headlights. "That's all you can say?

Bad timing?!"

Harvey shrugged unconcernedly.

Since he was feeling so chatty… "What about Clayton?"

"I suspected Clayton knew something when he pulled some files from the archives. My old boss let me know. He keeps me up to date on things on the proviso that I don't mention his drunken slip about Cutter to anyone. He'd get fired for that."

Harvey lowered his weapon; his finger was still on the trigger, but it wasn't pointed at her.

"I didn't really think much of it until I saw Clayton in town – I just saw him by accident outside a Hola Sunshine of all places." He shook his head ruefully. "So I had my brother follow him. My brother has spent the last three years recuperating in Mexico, and he is more than keen for a little payback. Dumb eagle never knew he was being followed. Knowing that he was meeting up with that whore Sadie, I decided it was time to take out Clayton and Sadie and have Cutter take the blame. I tried to get Cutter arrested back in Ursa, but it wouldn't stick. Fucking asshole has more luck than a bloody leprechaun."

"Did Clayton and Sadie even know anything?"

He snorted. "I doubt it, I asked Clayton but the stubborn fuck refused to tell me anything. I think he was just grasping at straws. But I wasn't willing to risk prison. Do you know how many years I'd get for the deaths of those agents?"

Not enough, she thought heatedly.

"As for Sadie, she knew even less, but I couldn't risk her staying alive, so my brother tried to kill her – not successfully," he let out a growl of irritation, "but by now I'm sure he has righted that."

He gave her a smile – *ugh, it was horrible.* "I have to say I am impressed that Cutter managed to get away after I shot him twice. We figured he'd come running to you, but we thought we'd give you two lovebirds a few days together before we killed you. It would make your loss even more devastating for him. Sadly, the photo sped up our plans a little."

Harvey had a moue of distaste on his face. "My brother had this big idea to torture you in front of Cutter, to make him suffer, but luckily for you, it's going to be a shot to the head. Cutter will have the blame for that too. Lovers' spat, maybe?"

"There's just one problem with that," she said quietly before her eyes slipped over his shoulder as if looking at someone who wasn't there. "Cutter!" she yelled.

He spun around, raising his gun and firing wildly at her refrigerator. Poor thing never hurt a fly!

But Lucie took the distraction to shift, her limbs shortened and she shrunk to her tiny beast. Immediately, she burrowed under the couch cushions. Thanks to Delmonte, the back of her couch had a small hole that the huge cat somehow managed to squeeze into. Another reason, other than Cutter's blood stains, why she was getting rid of it.

She scrabbled and scrambled to get inside as he yelled, bellowed and roared and started tearing apart the couch. His claw-tipped fingers scraped dangerously close to her belly. *Oh, fiddlesticks, this was a bad plan!* She didn't know how long she could hide.

Lucie squeaked as windows crashed, and she heard a pair of ferocious roars. Lord the house was under attack!

*

Cutter drove like a madman – or mad wolf. He had a few cop cars chasing him at one point, but he drove fast enough and erratically enough to shake them. Lucie's little compact could really move when pushed.

As he neared her house, he saw the ambulance and the SEA cars. His wolf howled in agony as his chest tightened to that point that he thought his heart might explode. The director and Jessie were standing outside with twin grim expressions.

He jumped out the car and ran to them, ignoring the fact that he was naked and splattered in dry blood. They didn't seem to notice either.

"Lucie," he choked out.

"We haven't found her yet," Jessie informed him, softly. "The scent of blood…"

The squirrel shifter appeared to be on the edge of tears, and the director laid a hand on her arm in comfort.

Cutter watched as paramedics pulled Harvey out of Lucie's house on a stretcher. His hands were handcuffed, but it was clear from the deep gashes lacing his body that he wasn't going anywhere. *Fucking Harvey, he should have known.* Avery and Isis trailed after him wearing matching blankets and sporting twin feral expressions.

He ignored them all. He didn't care about anything other than finding his hedgehog.

"Lucie? Lucie?" he bellowed as his wolf pushed at him to hurry.

He sniffed; he could scent her delectable blueberry scent. He let his nose guide him; he ran into the house, throwing people out of his way. He threw himself at the couch, the frame was intact but the cushions had been mauled and stuffing was strewn across the blood-splattered room.

"Lucie?"

He strained and heard a snuffling. He almost cried with relief as a tiny hedgehog ambled out of a hole in the couch. His wolf roared in happiness as he snatched up her prickly little body in his hands, cradling her tiny frame. Her white tipped points tickled his palms.

"Fuck, Lucie, you are never allowed to scare me like that again, do you hear me?" he barked a little more forcefully than he intended.

The hedgehog's nose twitched.

"I'll take that as a yes," he sighed, rubbing her rounded tummy.

He was never going to let her go. *Mine.*

CHAPTER TWENTY-ONE

After safely ensconcing Lucie at a hotel – a good hotel that the SEA was paying for – with a SEA agent guarding her door – who was on pain of death if he dared leave his post – Cutter helped wrap up the case.

He wasn't allowed to question either Harvey or Bruce. Apparently they feared he wouldn't be subtle and might rip their heads off or something. Well, they weren't wrong, but he was pretty sure he could find a subtle way of doing it.

Apparently, as soon as he awoke, Bruce started telling them everything. He was probably too afraid to go another round with Cutter.

Avery and Isis informed him that Lucie was worried about him and called Avery after he left to find Primrose. Avery was at the bar with Wayne and Isis, so she sent Wayne to look for Cutter while they went to talk to Lucie.

As they arrived, they saw Harvey's car parked down the street and approached with caution, at the time fearing that he had just come looking for Cutter. But when they heard him roaring, they shifted and crashed through the window.

Cutter was relieved Lucie was okay, although he was a little miffed that he didn't get to be her knight in shining armor. But, he figured he had years ahead of him to save her, over and over. In pretend, naturally, because she wasn't allowed to be in a dangerous situation again – ever. In fact, he didn't want her crossing streets without him, and if she thought she was allowed to leave the house without him escorting her, she had another thing coming. *What, too much?* He didn't care.

Primrose was going to be okay; she was already starting to heal. Sadie refused to leave her side. Everyone was just shocked to witness Primrose displaying tender emotions. It was just so… *strange*. Like watching Darth Vader stop to pet a puppy or something.

Harvey wasn't talking, but they had enough evidence to arrest him anyway with the testimony they had from Bruce, and for attacking Lucie. Plus, when they really dug, they were confident they could link him to the murders in Ursa.

The director was immediately taken off his enforced vacation. He didn't rub it in his boss' nose for listening to Harvey… well, not much anyway. The director did, unsurprisingly, berate Cutter for not giving himself in, but given that the guy framing him was the SEA agent trying to catch him… the director wouldn't punish him. But, he insisted that Cutter take a week vacation to recuperate. *For all their sakes.*

That was fine with him. The old Cutter, *BL Cutter*, might have argued and insisted he needed to stay, but he had something better to do. He had a hedgehog to woo.

He even finagled a week's paid vacation for Lucie. About a week in bed together would be about right for the two of them. They needed to make up for lost time.

He'd been so scared of hurting her that he'd run from her like a coward. All it took was getting shot by his colleague, framed for murder, and nearly losing her to a crazy wolf for him to realize that he needed her. Shame all that hadn't happened a year ago really.

He now knew that he did actually deserve her. Well, maybe he wouldn't go that far, but he was selfish enough that he was going to keep her, and that was that.

*

Lucie was kind of sorry she missed seeing Isis and Avery tearing into

Harvey. She was sure the look on his face would have been priceless as the tigress and lioness tore him a new one. But, she was just pleased that it was over.

So why did she feel sad?

Because it meant she no longer had an excuse to keep Cutter in her bed. He was now free to go and do whatever he liked. *Bummer.*

Her hedgehog perked up as she heard arguing outside.

"What the fuck? Were you sleeping?" roared an irate but very welcome voice. Her hedgehog mewled in happiness.

"I was just resting my eyes..." came the muffled reply.

"What the fuck are they teaching you at the academy? Forget it, fuck off, I'm here now."

Her handsome wolf stomped through the door, looking every bit a wild romantic hero, and the first thing he said, "Why the fuck was this door unlocked? Anyone could have walked in here!"

"Not with the guard outside," she reasoned, patiently, as she ran into his arms.

"The fucker was sleeping!"

She snuggled against his chest and felt gratified when he slipped his arms around her and held her tightly. She was wearing a SEA t-shirt that one of the agents had given her. Her own clothes had been destroyed by Harvey when he threw his temper tantrum, and Cutter hustled her out of her house so quickly she didn't have time to grab something. The thin material was inadequate to hide the puckered points of her nipples, hardened by her arousal at the arrival of Cutter. She tried to pull away in embarrassment, but he wouldn't let go.

Cutter clung to her, and she couldn't deny that there wasn't anywhere she would rather be at that moment. Of course, his own arousal was almost digging into her stomach at the moment. It was a warm and naughty pressure that made her thighs clench instinctively.

With a sigh and a disappointed whimper from Lucie, he let go of her and led her over to the bed, so they were sitting, side by side.

He gave her a searching look, and she felt an urge to fill the silence but she stopped herself.

"Thank you for everything you've done for me," he said, softly.

"You don't have to thank me; I'm your friend."

He scowled at the word *friend*. Did he not even want to be friends with her?! Did her disappointment know no end?

Lucie looked away from him, afraid she might do something girly like break out into tears. "You don't have to stay here though; you could actually go back to your apartment."

"I don't want you to be alone," he replied gruffly.

"Seriously, it's fine."

"You haven't got another man coming by, have you?" he accused in a harsh tone.

She didn't even bother to answer; she just rolled her eyes and pouted.

He hooked a finger under her chin, forcing her to look up at him and into his amber laced eyes. "Listen to me." The steely dominance in his voice was startling, and sent her nether regions almost into convulsions. "I want to be here." He took a deep, steadying breath. "I love you, Lucie, and I have since the moment I met you."

She sucked in a breath at his unexpected admission. She had hoped that, at least, she might get a 'let's be friends who sleep together' speech. She just assumed that down the line, after doing *that* for about five years, she would blackmail him – or perhaps tie him down and sexually torture him - before she finally got the L-word.

"I love you, too," she gushed.

He leaned in for a kiss but jerked away when she slapped his arm. "What the fuck?"

"If you love me, then why in hell's mini golf course have you been running from me?" Her hedgehog was all for swooning directly into his big, strong arms, but Lucie had a little more reserve – just a little, though. *Not too much.*

He smirked at her choice of words before sobering.

"Sweetheart, I'm an asshole."

"Okkaaaayyyyyyy." Not the reaction she was expecting; she assumed he was going somewhere with this.

"Even before the whole Maroni blowout, I was an asshole. I'm moody and angry all the time; I turn into a dick at the drop of a dime, and I have trouble controlling my rage. I've taken anger management classes so often I know them better than the teacher does. Added to all that, I have fucking night terrors where I wake up trying to strangle people or trying to shoot the wall. Would you inflict me on a person you love? I just thought I would make you miserable."

Ugh, he was insufferable! "Do you really think I haven't been miserable this past year?"

"I kept thinking that you'd find someone better than me, and they'd make you happy," he said distastefully, as if the idea of that ever happening was akin to eating a burger made out of worms.

"Well, I haven't found anyone else and I never well. I'm miserable without you, so I might as well be miserable with you – not that I think I will be."

He looked at her ruefully. "No, I don't think you will be either."

Wow, he was full of surprises. First of all he threw her the L-word without any prompting, and now he was admitting that being together wouldn't be on par with the Titanic sinking. "What made you change your mind?"

Cutter began stroking her hair. "The other day, when you woke me from my dream, all the pain, and anger, I just let it go as soon as I saw you. And when you sleep beside me, I don't dream. These past couple of days, in spite of everything, I actually woke up feeling happy. I want you to be my mate, and I want you to know I'm not lying when I say that I fell in love with you when I met you. I haven't even looked at another woman this past year."

Lucie frowned. "But, aren't you forgetting someone?"

Cutter raised his eyebrows.

"The peacock shifter," she said, hoping to keep all emotion out of her voice. Which was no easy feat when her mind and hedgehog automatically reached for the word hussy instead of peacock.

His face darkened, and she immediately felt chagrin at bringing it up and ruining the moment. She started to climb off the bed, and his arms wrapped around her, pulling her onto his lap. He clutched her tightly and possessively.

"Uh-uh, sweetheart; I've been trying to explain about that ever since it happened. Now, you are finally going to sit still and listen." He rubbed his thumbs in circles over her ass trying not to snicker at her pout. "Nothing happened with that girl."

She stared at him for a few beats. "Aaaaannnnddd?"

"And?" He looked at her genuinely perplexed.

Lucie's eyes flashed black to her little beast. "Really? After putting me through the ringer about Rick and Xander, that's all I get?"

"Fine," he growled. "I got really drunk and she made sure I got home. I don't remember the night, but I know I didn't have sex with her. I haven't been with anyone else since I met you. You are the best sex of my life, and I love you. Happy now?!"

"Yes," she answered, mollified, completely unmoved by his surly tone. "I haven't been with anyone either since I met you."

"Thank fuck for that," he exclaimed, letting his head drop onto her shoulder. "I want to spend at least the next two days with you naked, and I just don't have time on my schedule to hunt down and kill any asshole who dared touch you. Not that I wouldn't have. Besides I did a pretty good job of scaring them away from you."

"Scaring who away?"

"The assholes that dared to covet what is mine," he told her proudly.

Lucie didn't know whether to hug him or slap him. No wonder the guys who had tried to get close to her over the past year now actively ran when they saw her. They must have been terrified that Cutter was planning to come after then. Of all the… Oh, what was the point in arguing? His possessiveness was actually a turn-on. She nuzzled his neck. "Mmmm, you're my big, bad wolf."

"I can't promise things will be easy with me. I can't promise I won't hurt you. I can't promise…"

She raised her fingers to his lips. "I'll settle for a promise to love me and to always put the toilet seat down. As for the rest, we'll fudge it as we go along."

"Fudge," he muttered. "You're just trying to turn me on."

"I don't have to try," she cooed.

"No, you don't."

With a roar, he flipped her onto her back. He stood at the edge of the bed as she wriggled about. She settled down and leaned up on her elbows. He looked pensive and uncertain, almost like he didn't know what to say. Luckily, he had a mate who was rarely lost for words.

"Are you going to stand there all day enjoying the view? Or are you going to get over here and bond with me? Of course, if you don't think you're up to it because of your wounds…"

"Well, that sounds like a challenge." Cutter gave her a wide, toothy grin. His face was etched with hungry desire. Her hedgehog trembled in delight.

Within seconds he was out of his clothes and crawling up the bed; her t-shirt was but ribbons as he sliced it away from her body. She panted and gasped as he sensually attacked her; his hands and mouth were everywhere, licking, sucking, massaging – barely an inch of her escaped his onslaught. She writhed and clutched at the bedcovers as her pleasure curled tighter and tighter, desperately seeking release. And just when it was in reach…

He stopped. *Holy cow – he was such a son of a mother frogging tease!* Disappointed, she started unraveling.

"Don't stop," she begged, breathlessly.

He chuckled and nipped her thigh with his sharpened teeth. "Sweetheart, we have all night. No need to rush. I want this to be special."

"There's every need to rush," she grumbled. Her climax tucked her tail between her legs and started skulking away.

He spent a few minutes massaging her legs, running his fingers over her skin. It was a peaceful kind of pleasure, as opposed to the earth-moving kind she experienced from an orgasm. It was actually kind of nice. She relaxed and watched him, enjoying seeing his large, dark hands, manipulating her creamy skin. His hands worked their way up to her breasts, kneading them lightly, not enough to make her come, but enough to give her satisfaction.

By the time he had finished and was settling between her legs, her eyes were closed, and she was virtually purring. But, feeling his throbbing manhood pressing against her clit was enough to reignite the fire within.

"Are you ready for me?" he asked smugly.

"I'm always ready."

"I love you."

"Me ooooooohhhh!"

He thrust inside her, and she let out a wailing moan. Lord, she hoped the people in the room next door didn't think she was dying. *Could you die from too many orgasms?* Only one way to find out.

He didn't stop until he was fully sheathed, and when he was, he took her mouth in a greedy kiss, swallowing the moans and whimpers she let out as she adjusted to his size. She wrapped her arms around him as he rocked inside her, filling her over and over.

She tilted her hips and pushed against him, meeting his strokes and taking him deep – so deliciously deep – inside. He couldn't hold back for long; his movements became more insistent and driven by his beast, by his need to claim her, he began driving himself inside her passionately. It was too much, the feel of him inside her, the way he rubbed her sweet spot, and the way he grazed her clit – it was all too much.

"You're mine," he growled as his pulled her against him, roughly impaling her.

"Yes!" she squeaked as she shuddered around him.

"Say it!"

"Yours, all yours," she whimpered.

Cutter threw back his head and roared, "Mine."

He forced himself inside her almost violently, and she screamed his name as the orgasm tore through her body like lightening. His fangs sliced through her neck, and she pushed her teeth into his. Her little beast howled in joy as he finally became her mate. Their intertwined bodies throbbed and pulsed, as the mate bond formed and they felt each other's love and desire.

Satiated, she lay back on the bed and sighed as her mate licked the wound on her neck lazily. Proudly, she ran her fingers over the little bite marks she had left on his neck, and giggled as he let out a rumbling snarl. They wouldn't be quite as obvious as the mark he had left on her, but she didn't care. She knew he was hers, and that was all that mattered.

Mine.

EPILOGUE

One week later

Lucie ran her hand over her fiancé's ass.

"What are you doing? People can see us," Cutter grumbled, more than a little embarrassed.

She leaned up onto her tippy-toes and brushed her lips over his. "Oh, lighten up, they're all grown-ups. No doubt they've seen men being fondled before. Besides, how am I supposed to keep my hands off this ass, it's divine!"

Cutter groaned as all his so-called friends burst into laughter. *Bastards.* Just wait until they had mates who worshiped their bodies.

Lucie batted her eyelashes over her enormous blue eyes, as her lips curled up sweetly. Oh, never mind fondling his butt, if she kept looking at him like that he might just drag her down to the floor and have his delightfully wicked way with her right then and there.

Cutter wasn't known for being demonstrative when it came to women. Actually, he'd never even kissed a woman in public before Lucie. The furthest he could manage was hand holding with his ex-wife. His aversion to public displays of affection was one of many things that Annie couldn't stand about him. Looking back, it really wasn't a surprise that they didn't stay together for very long, or that Annie was still wary of him when he came to visit. Thankfully, she seemed to be thawing, though. *That was thanks to Lucie.*

On their week off from work, he had taken Lucie to visit his son. Cutter practically puffed out his chest as he remembered seeing them coloring pictures together. Although, he wasn't exactly pleased that, under Lucie's influence, Dean seemed to love pink now. That was something he better grow out of. Lucie had been delighted to meet Dean, and his pup had taken to her quickly. Even Annie had warmed to Lucie and told Cutter he was lucky to have her. He wasn't going to argue with that. Of course, after meeting Dean, Lucie had a soft gleam in her eye and Cutter was a bit concerned about what that meant. He would worry about that later.

Not much had happened at the Agency while they were away. *Other than Dale being arrested for stealing drugs from the medical bay.* Apparently, the arrest was pretty welcome after being caught by Helga. The she-bear caught him trying to pilfer some pills and she went berserk. Dale admitted that he had been trying to steal some since he arrived there. His father had cut him off, and he needed extra money; he was planning on selling them. He also admitted to drugging Cutter the night they met the peacock shifter twins. It certainly explained why he couldn't remember anything. Dale wanted him to have a good time, but he was kind of heavy with the dosage. Cutter wanted to tear him apart for almost ruining things with Lucie, but, his little mate was teaching him the art of forgiveness, so he guessed he would only beat Dale to a pulp if he ever saw him again – *much more civilized than killing.*

Primrose took a leave of absence from the Agency; they weren't sure if she was coming back, but she actually seemed happy – which was creepy and odd – but they wished her well. To compensate for her absence, Isis was transferred to the Alpha team. After the time she spent diabolically scheming to get a place on the team – back when Erin first arrived - it was kind of a welcome surprise when she got there for doing nothing.

Weirdly enough, the money that appeared in Cutter's account was his. It had nothing to do with the case. *His mom won the lottery!* She gave all her kids two hundred grand. Her bank made a mistake when transferring the money and sent it in two batches. His mom was peeved that Cutter never called her back about it; apparently she left him twelve phone messages about it. But, Cutter checked his answer phone as frequently as he threw on an apron and baked cupcakes – so, never. The money was a welcome surprise though. He put half in a college fund for Dean and the rest was being put toward the new house they were planning on buying. Or a new car. Or a cruise to the Mediterranean. They hadn't decided.

At the insistence of his wolf, and to the surprise of his friends, he pulled Lucie up for a lingering and passionate kiss. She moaned into his mouth, and his wolf almost purred at the feel of her pressed up against him. Okay, so the floor might be a bit too public – no need for anyone else to get a look at her heavenly body – but could they make it out to their car?

"Hey, look who's back!" called Avery happily.

Wes, Wayne, Lake, and Diaz – *who he was trying not to think of as a scumbag* – all called out hellos.

Cutter grunted as Lucie broke their lip-locked state to turn and see. He almost pouted. Surely what they were doing was more interesting?

Grudgingly, he looked up to find his polar bear boss, Gunner, and his human mate, Erin grinning at him. Heat dusted his cheeks. He didn't know why – it's not like he was doing anything wrong – but he suddenly felt a little self-conscious.

Gunner and Erin were holding hands and sporting matching looks of contentment. Gunner nodded at him and gave Lucie a speculative look, before maneuvering Erin onto a chair. Erin shook her head as he virtually lifted her up. Previously, Cutter had almost found Gunner's protectiveness of his mate, and his need to be near her, insane, but now, he totally got it. His wolf was practically pawing the ground when he didn't know exactly where Lucie was. He didn't even like her going to the bathroom on her own, but he found out the hard way that women didn't like men going into the ladies room. *That ostrich shifter had a mean right hook.*

Ignoring the delighted look on Erin's face, Cutter slipped an arm around Lucie's waist, and she snaked one hand into his back pocket rubbing her fingers over his ass. Okay, yeah, he had to admit he had a pretty fine ass. Could he blame her for wanting to touch it?

Lucie and Avery started grilling Erin about the honeymoon, who in turn responded by turning bright red and giggling. Apparently it had been a *very* good honeymoon.

"You're back," said Cutter to Gunner.

"Yep."

"Good time?"

The polar bear smirked. "Yep. So, you and Lucie?"

"Yep. Drink?"

"Sure."

Cutter nodded. That was the end of the honeymoon discussion as far as they were concerned. "Erin, drink?" he offered.

Erin put a spare hand against a heated cheek; the other was enveloped in her mate's big paw. "Just mineral water for me."

Gunner nodded and squeezed her hand.

Lucie's eyes widened excitedly. "Oh my god! You're pregnant!"

Erin looked a little flustered while Gunner beamed proudly.

"How did you know?" she croaked.

Lucie jumped up and down. "Lucky guess, congratulations!"

Avery and Lucie hugged her while the men gave Gunner some hefty back slaps and, to Avery's aggravation, told him well done.

"Shouldn't Erin get a well done, too?" she asked peevishly.

"Good point," agreed Diaz. He moved to hug Erin but almost ignited under Gunner's heated glare and stopped. Gunner repositioned himself, so his arm was wrapped around his mate.

Lucie started asking Erin dozens of questions about the baby. When was it due, had they thought about names, how were they decorating the nursery… Erin was flushed but happy with all the attention she was getting. Cutter, on the other hand, listened to all her questions with alarm, and almost considered bolting when Lucie gave him a hungry look.

But she just rolled her eyes and laughed. "Don't worry, stud. I'm not quite ready for us to have a baby yet either."

Cutter let out a long breath, and everyone laughed. Their revelry halted when Gunner's phone started chirruping and, with a sigh, he answered it.

"Hey, Jessie, how come you're working?… Aha… I'm sorry… yeah, I'm back… it's okay… no, Jessie, it's fine… where is it?"

Erin's face fell as she realized he was being called to work, and Gunner gave her an apologetic look.

"Sure, Jessie, and, by the way, Erin's pregnant."

Everyone present could hear the squeals of the excited squirrel shifter.

Gunner chuckled into the phone. "Okay, I will, don't work too late." He hung up and kissed Erin's temple. "I gotta go, babe, I had a call. And Jessie says congratulations."

Erin looked up at him beseechingly. "Must you? It's our last night before we have to go back to work."

Gunner opened his mouth to respond, but was cut off by the heavy tread of stiletto boots and an irritated, shrill voice.

"Freaking hell! This weather is awful. Never mind cats and dogs, it's raining fucking elephants out there!"

Everyone tried not to laugh at Isis' bedraggled state. Her long red hair was soaking and rat-tailing down her back while dribbles of black mascara ran down her cheeks. To the unmated males' delights, her tank top was almost see-through, and her nipples were hard nubs, trying to poke through the material.

Isis saw Gunner and Erin and gave them a half scowl, half smile. "Welcome back."

"Erin's pregnant!" gushed Lucie.

Isis raised her eyebrows. "Seriously? Congrats, we're all hoping the baby takes after Erin, right?"

There was a chorus of oh yeah, and a few people said definitely.

Gunner ignored them and focused on his unhappy mate. "I'm sorry, babe, I'll be as quick as I can, I just need to go over to the Shelley Cemetery and look around. Apparently LLPD requested the SEA send someone over."

Lucie elbowed Cutter in the stomach and inclined her head toward them. Gunner could easily have ordered any of his team to go in his place, but since they were off duty he wouldn't be cruel. Cutter rolled his eyes and huffed. In spite of his wolf's objections about wanting to spend the night with his own mate, Cutter would volunteer to go instead. Being mated to someone who was sweet and selfless was really hard sometimes!

Unexpectedly, he didn't have to be nice. Someone else beat him to it.

"Oh, stop with the big, sad eyes," snapped Isis. "I'm already wet through, and since I'm the rookie member of the team, I'll go."

"You will?" asked Gunner in frank surprise.

"Sure, consider this my baby gift to you... because you won't be getting anything else."

"Thank you, Isis," said Erin with feeling.

"Yeah, yeah, save your mushiness; I'll see you tomorrow."

Isis gave a wave of her manicured hand and stomped out the door, dripping water as she went. Erin snuggled against Gunner happily, and Cutter allowed Lucie to lead him away from the group. He brought her fingers up to his mouth and kissed her ring finger – right over the engagement ring he had given her earlier that day. Asking her to marry him was a no brainer, and after he heard that Xander never actually bought her a ring... he just had to make sure she got the prettiest one imaginable.

"I was going to volunteer before Isis did, you know that, right?" he murmured.

"I know, and I'm proud of you."

Cutter raised an eyebrow. "You are?"

"Of course, you're my bad-ass wolf with a big heart of gold. I love you."

He smirked. "Of course you do."

Lucie bit her lip. "Actually I'm glad Isis volunteered; I thought that we could slip away and have a noisy night at home."

"Not a quiet night?"

"Oh no, with the things I'm going to do to you, I doubt you'll be able to stay quiet for long."

Her fingers ran along the neckline of her shirt, and she pulled it down slightly, giving him a peek at the lacy, red concoction currently lucky enough to cradle her two perfect breasts. *Was it wrong to be jealous of a bra?*

Cutter groaned. "Pretty," he choked out as his brain was suddenly deprived of an awful lot of blood.

"You should see the matching shorts," she teased. "All for you."

"For me?" he gulped.

She bit her lip and fluttered her eyelashes. "For your paws only."

She rubbed her breasts against his chest, and he let out a lusty growl. "Fuck, what are we waiting for?"

Without a backward glance at their friends, Cutter grabbed her hand and dragged her giggling frame out of the bar. And when she didn't move quickly enough, he simply picked her up and slung her over his shoulder, which only made her giggle harder.

In his defense, he had a lot of lost time to make up for. He allowed his fears to control him and spent a whole year running from her, and now he needed to make it up to her.

Now she was his, forever, and he never intended to let her go.

Mine.

*

Isis growled as her four-inch heels sank into the wet, muddy grass. Probably not the best footwear for hauling ass around a cemetery but, hey, they made her legs look amazing. Plus, she really hadn't been intending to do this when she dressed that morning. Stupid LLPD – couldn't they handle anything on their own?

She slapped her torch against her palm as the batteries spluttered and died. "Piece of fucking junk."

Terrific. Alone, in the dark, in the middle of a graveyard. Yep, it was the start of every bad horror movie she used to love - she'd been a total addict when she was a teenager. Good job she was a kick-ass tigress, or she might be a little creeped out at that moment.

And where the fuck were the LLPD? Wasn't this their party?

Her tiger let out a wary yowl as she heard a twig snap to her left. Why was there always a random twig for the bad guy to step on and spook the heroine?

Isis rested her hand on her gun. Her first choice would be to shift and let Ms. Kitty – *that's what she called her tiger* – loose. But humans had an unfortunate habit of screaming and wetting their pants whenever she let her frisky feline loose. *And they called her a pussy!* If any of the idiot LLPD were stomping around, she didn't want to give them a heart attack accidentally.

She couldn't hear any other strange noises, but the wind was starting to whip up something fierce. So much for the glorious Los Lobos nights. She scented the air and almost gagged at the smell of rotting flesh. *What the crap?* Okay, yeah, it was a cemetery – but the bodies were in the ground right? Oh, it was *that* kind of horror movie. Well if it came with Rick Grimes from the TV show, she'd be okay with that.

Isis was considering cutting her losses and just turning round. She'd never admit it to her friends, or her mother – who had an unhealthy interest in her daughter's sex life – but a nice, warm bath beckoned. And after that, she planned to lay in her bed, eating cookie dough, catching up on Elementary, and snuggling with her cats Minion, Lucifer and Brimstone. *What? They're pretty names.*

It wasn't to be, however. With barely a 'what the fuck,' a mighty push from behind promptly had her toppling into a freshly dug grave. She face-planted onto something squidgy, and with a yelp that was hardly befitting of a tigress, she realized she had landed on a dead body. A fairly fresh dead body, and one that had just been divested of his arms.

"Gross!" she snarled as her tiger snapped her jaws.

Even worse, someone must have witnessed her less than elegant belly flop into the grave, as footsteps neared. Unless it was the one who pushed her – *in which case she was all for round two* – she just wanted them to go away.

Isis twisted around, mindful of where she was putting her hands. A light shone directly into her eyes and she growled.

"Ma'am, are you okay?" The deep, chocolate voice made her pause and had her tiger purring like a kitten. "Here, take my hand?"

And, for the first time in her thirty-year-long, man-eating life, Isis simpered and even swooned a little as she reached for the strong, masculine hand.

To be continued…

The author is an obsessive reader of cozy mysteries and supernatural stories – in particular she loves supernatural cozy mysteries, and has watched every single episode of Psych at least twenty times. She spends far too much time reading or watching TV and firmly believes that you can never have too many books, handbags or brooches. When she isn't writing supernatural stories she is at her day job, daydreaming about writing supernatural stories.

www.elizabethannprice.com

Printed in Great Britain
by Amazon